SEASONS OF SUMMER NOVELLA SERIES

The Complete Set

MELISSA BALDWIN

This is a work of fiction. Names, characters, places, and incidents either are the product of the author's imagination or are used fictitiously, and any resemblance to actual persons, living or dead, business establishments, events, or locales is entirely coincidental.

Copyright © 2017 Melissa Baldwin
All rights reserved.

ISBN: 0692945474
ISBN13: 978-0692945476

Formatted by Karan & Co. Author Solutions

Also by Melissa Baldwin

Event to Remember Series

Book 1 - An Event to Remember

Book 2 - Wedding Haters

Book 3 - Not Quite Sheer Happiness

Broadway Series

Book 1 - See You Soon Broadway

Book 2 - See You Later Broadway

From Gemma Halliday Publishing

Friends ForNever

Find Melissa's books at:

http://www.authormelissabaldwin.com/

Fall Into Magic

A Novella

Melissa Baldwin

About Fall Into Magic

After a devastating breakup in the middle of her summer vacation, Summer Peters knows she needs something to distract her. What better than the arrival of fall, Halloween, and a new client? Though she assumes that Alexander Williams will be a hands-off client, she is surprised to find him very down-to-earth. She's immediately drawn to him, much to the dismay of his overprotective assistant. When it becomes obvious that he feels the same, she begins to wonder if their meeting was meant to be.

Just when she thinks she could be ready to move on with her life, her ex-boyfriend Jake returns for a second chance. She's in for even more of a surprise when she learns her nosy, meddling neighbor is actually a psychic pushing to reveal details of her future.

Summer doesn't know which way to turn as she feels like she's being pulled in different directions. Between Alexander, his assistant, and her ex-boyfriend, she fears she may not be ready to move on after all. She considers turning to her neighbor for advice but the fear of knowing exactly what the future holds is more frightening than not knowing.

This is a work of fiction. Names, characters, places, and incidents either are the product of the author's imagination or are used fictitiously, and any resemblance to actual persons, living or dead, business establishments, events, or locales is entirely coincidental.

Copyright © 2016 Melissa Baldwin

All rights reserved.

ISBN: 0692785299
ISBN 13: 978-0692785294

Formatted by Karan & Co. Author Solutions

I dedicate this book to my miracle baby girl who shares my love of all things fall and Halloween.

Chapter One

I look out over the crashing waves as I enjoy my last few hours of vacation. Why do these hours always go by so quickly? I'm trying to soak up every last second, even though this summer coming to an end is somewhat bittersweet for me.

What should have been one of the best summers of my life definitely changed a few weeks ago when my boyfriend, Jake —insert: now ex-boyfriend—decided to end things. Who ends things in the middle of a fantastic vacation anyway? I could go into detail about his explanation, but I'd rather not relive those horrible fifteen minutes again. And to be honest, his explanation was rather vague. Let's just say "I'm not sure I'm ready to be in such a serious relationship" came into play. It was bad enough having to explain to my friends why Jake decided to head back to Connecticut early. My friend Angie's aunt has a place at Gurney's Inn and we've enjoyed summers here for several years. This is by far the worst one, at least for me.

Anyway, it took Jake all of fifteen minutes to wrap up an amazing eighteen months together. Following his quick breakup, I spent several hours doing the usual things women do after being dumped. I cried as I poured over photos and listened to sad love songs. And my friend Angie bought me three boxes of Little Debbie Swiss Cake Rolls, which I devoured over the following two days.

As devastating as it has been, there is light at the end of the tunnel and I'm trying my hardest to focus on that light. Fall is around the corner and that gives me something to concentrate on and look forward to. At least I still have my job, and first thing on Monday morning, I begin work with a new client, which will give me an opportunity to immerse myself into someone else's home (i.e. life). Thankfully, I'm one of those people who enjoys my career as an interior decorator. So, as sad as it is watching the summer roll away with the waves, I'm ready to begin the next new chapter in my life . . . I think.

"Are you thinking about Jake?" Angie asks as she sits down and crosses her legs on the lounge chair next to me. She rips open a package of Chocolate Twizzlers, holding it out to me. Typical Angie, she eats more junk food than anyone I've ever met but you would never know it. She's a marathon runner so that definitely helps to balance out her love of all things sweet and fattening. I take three pieces because—well, you know, when in Rome.

"No I'm not," I lie. "Well, not entirely."

She sighs as she looks out over the ocean. "Another summer comes to an end."

I nod. "That's actually what I was thinking about." I pause. "It's okay, though. I'm ready to get back. I have plenty of work to keep me busy."

She chews on a piece of Twizzlers. "Did Jake already pick up his stuff?"

I roll my eyes. "Yep. He texted to tell me that he left his key with nosy Mrs. Rothera, who lives downstairs. Now I'm going to have to give her an explanation, too, because you know how she lives for all the gossip."

"At least your dad will be happy," she adds. That is true; my dad never liked Jake, so this is sure to please him. He never told me why he didn't like him, though. He would just say that he had a feeling about him. Looking back, I really wish he would have told me why. He could have saved me several months of my life and definitely some tears. It's probably something silly like him being a Giants fan instead of a Jets fan. Football is a huge deal in my family being that my father has been a coach for years. I guess I should have known better from day one.

"Yes, he will," I agree. "But I'm not ready to admit he was right just yet. Still, I told Jake I would get the key from him later but he clearly wanted to be free of all ties to me."

"Oh well, it's his loss. He couldn't face you, what a loser," Angie shouts. Angie is so loud, being born and raised in Staten Island and coming from a big Italian family will do that to you. I do appreciate her loyalty, though—she's been my rock these past few weeks.

"Are you ready to get back?" I ask. She shrugs her shoulders. "I guess all good things come to an end."

I give her a sad smile. "Yes, they do."

∽

Home sweet home. As soon as I walk into my apartment I look around to see if Jake left anything—of course, he didn't. He really couldn't wait to get the hell out of here. We actually didn't live together but he was here all the time being that he has a roommate. Oh well, it's his loss just like Angie said. I need to make myself busy so I don't get sad again.

As much as I love traveling, I really hate this part—the unpacking and laundry is worse than a trip to the dentist. After I throw a load in the washer, I make myself a cup of peppermint tea and open my laptop. Time to get in work mode. I look over the proposal I put together for my new client, Alexander Williams. I haven't had the opportunity to meet Alexander yet, but I did do what every normal person in the world would—I stalked his social media. I admit I almost fell off my barstool when I first searched him out—a) he looks like Clark Kent from *Superman*, and b) his favorite movie is *Grease 2*, which also happens to be my favorite movie. Not that it's a big deal for him to like the movie, but it definitely caught my eye when he posted that he was watching *Grease 2* and always dreamed of being a T-Bird. I'm sure he only cares about watching Michelle Pfeiffer, and to give credit where credit is due, she was stunning in that movie. When I was younger, I wished I looked like Michelle Pfeiffer with her blonde locks and blue eyes. My mom would always get mad when I said this; she told me to embrace my brown eyes and thick reddish-brown hair. Don't get me wrong, I do love my hair and so does everyone else, but I think it's pretty normal to want what we can't have. I must get at least ten compliments a day on my hair . . . Jake always loved my hair. Crap, there I go again. How am I supposed to do this? Do I just pretend that I didn't spend all that time with him? Do I pretend that I wasn't in love with him? Ugh.

Anyway, back to my new client. All my communication has been done through his assistant Melanie. According to her, they heard Summer Interiors is the best in Connecticut. (I may or may not have danced around my office when she said this because business has been slow this year.) So from what I can tell, Alexander's story is that he just moved into a new home and he's in need of a decorator. However, I get the feeling there's more to the story than just that because, as I said, I did a little background checking. Disclaimer: I need to know what I'm walking into—you just never know what kind of crazy you might find, especially going into someone's home. I send one last reminder invite to both Melanie and Alexander, and I close my laptop. This job really couldn't have come at a better time with my relationship ending the way it did, and since Jake's so ready to move on, so am I.

∞

"Damn, you weren't kidding; he totally looks like Clark Kent," Angie says as she holds my phone close to her face and squints. "Jake who?" she says with a wink.

Yeah, right. There's no way that's happening. If only it was so easy to just forget him and move on to someone else. And even if I were to do that, it wouldn't be with a client.

"You need to get your eyes checked, Ang," I scold while

ignoring her comment about Jake. This is not the first time we've had this conversation about her squinting. I'm scared to get in a car with her.

"Summer, I told you I have perfect vision. Everyone in my family has perfect vision."

I roll my eyes as she continues talking. "And I told you there is no way in hell that I'm putting any foreign objects in my eyes. Contacts look like torture devices to me."

I giggle. For as open and loud as she is, she's also the biggest baby. I finally had to forbid her from checking WebMD anytime she had to sneeze.

"So, when is your meeting with Clark?" she asks as she takes a bite of her English muffin.

"His name is Alexander, and our meeting is at ten thirty," I say absently as I check my emails. Whew. Just making sure I didn't get a cancellation.

"Whatever," she says, waving her hand. "We need to discuss more important things—like our Halloween costumes."

I smile. I know this may seem silly to some people but Angie and I have dressed up every Halloween since we were in 11th grade. We almost missed one year because we had a huge fight, but she called me crying the night before, begging me to at least dress up for a party we were attending. She must have had a few drinks because she was rambling something about us missing our holiday together would curse all future Halloweens. I thought she was losing it but I'm not one to risk being cursed.

"I already told Brett that I had plans with you on Halloween," she says pointedly. "And he mentioned something about going to play poker. Who plays poker on Halloween, the best night of the year?" she shouts. I pretend to cover my ears just to make a point. Even though I don't need to being that everyone around us turns to stare.

Brett is Angie's boyfriend. At first, I thought he was weird and kind of scary. First of all, he's huge (Incredible Hulk huge) and he shaves his head. My first impression was that he was an MMA fighter but found out he teaches eighth grade history. I would have freaked out if I walked into a class in eighth grade and he was my teacher.

"It's totally cool if you want to hang with Brett that night," I say, even though the thought of being alone on my favorite night of the year is already starting to break my heart.

"Oh stop, seriously," she says, rolling her eyes. "I just told you he's making plans to play poker. Halloween is totally our night, and if you aren't bringing a man, then neither am I."

I give her a grateful smile. I was hoping she'd say that. I realize this will be the first holiday season in a few years that I've been single. Ugh. And let's face it, this is pretty much the worst time to be single, and not because of the whole gift thing. There's nothing better than curling up by a roaring fire with the person you love. And I don't even want to think about New Year's Eve. When I was eighteen, I spent New Year's Eve at a restaurant with my friend and her boyfriend. I acted like a total bitch the entire night because I was feeling sorry for myself. I definitely don't want a repeat of that, so I will do what it takes to avoid that at all costs.

I double-check the time and realize I better get going to my meeting.

"I'm out of here," I say, checking to make sure I have everything. "We will continue our conversation about Halloween later. We still have plenty of time."

"Not that much time," she insists. "The festivities will be here before we know it." She jumps up and gives me a hug. "Anyway, good luck in your meeting. I expect a full report on Clark."

"Alexander," I remind her. Of course, she's not listening to me. No surprise there.

I type the address that Melanie gave me into my GPS. Luckily, New Canaan isn't that far away. When I check my phone one last time before I get on the road, there's a text message from Alexander Williams. (What?)

Looking forward to meeting with you this morning.

I'm totally in shock because I haven't spoken to him once since Melanie contacted me. He hasn't responded to any of the emails I sent, so why now? I admit I was curious before, but now I'm completely intrigued by this man. His text has made me even more excited for what's next. Summer may be over but I'm ready for a fabulous fall and whatever comes my way.

Chapter Two

When I pull into the circular driveway, I'm in awe. I cruise really slow as I stare out the window at the pristine manicured lawn. The house is stunning but not a gaudy or oversized stunning. I can feel my excitement growing, and I can't wait to get inside and unleash my decorating magic.

Decorating magic... yuck. That's a phrase Jake came up with after I decorated his boss's Cape Cod cottage. According to him, my decorating skills were the talk of his office for months. I even got a few other jobs out of it, and he received all kinds of recognition because of me. I grip the steering wheel a little tighter as my frustration grows thinking about Jake.

I pull up close to the front door behind a sleek silver Audi. Taking a few cleansing breaths, I walk toward the door and ring the bell. I laugh because the doorbell tone sounds a lot like Guns N' Roses "Welcome to the Jungle." Should I be concerned?

A short, blonde girl with a round face meets me at the door. "Hi, Summer, I'm Melanie," she says as she holds out her hand. Wow, she's really short. I feel like a giant at my average 5'6" height. I guess I could have worn something other than these wedges.

"Great to finally meet you in person," I say cheerfully. It could be my imagination but it sounds like she groans.

"Follow me to Mr. Williams's office." She turns down the hallway to the right. Normally, I would be trying to figure out her strange behavior, but I'm too busy. Too busy looking at the bare walls, the circular wrought iron staircase, and the wooden beams in the kitchen. Wow. The possibilities will be endless with this place. Houses like this are exactly why I decided to be an interior decorator.

We walk into the office at the end of the long hallway and the first thing I notice is a wall of glass windows overlooking the beautiful garden. It reminds me a little of an English estate, except on a much smaller scale. The other walls in the office are bare except for a built-in bookshelf to the right when you walk in. Alexander is nowhere to be seen, and I'm starting to wonder if this guy even exists.

"Mr. Williams will be here shortly," she says in a cold, curt tone. "Can I get you a cup of tea or coffee?"

I smile and shake my head. "No, I'm fine, but thank you." There's no way in hell I'm taking a drink from this girl. Judging by the cold reception I've received, I would be afraid she would spit in it or maybe even poison it. Okay, so I know that's silly, but I can read people really well and this girl doesn't like me. Maybe she lured me into this house on purpose; I still haven't seen Mr. Williams. I'm really confused because she seemed fine the few times I spoke to her and her emails were always pleasant. I guess it's possible that she's just having a bad day.

I sit down on the edge of one of the big leather chairs to wait for Mr. Williams. The furniture is rustic and comfortable (and expensive). I look out the window over the sprawling yard. Wow, I would love to have a view like this.

"I apologize for keeping you waiting," a voice says from behind me. I stand up and turn around. Holy crap—Alexander Williams does exist and he looks just like his profile picture.

"Oh, um, no problem. I . . . just arrived," I stutter. I don't know why I'm feeling so nervous all of a sudden. He sits down at his desk, and I study his face for a few seconds. Immediately I notice his friendly smile and dark wavy hair, and he really does resemble Clark Kent. I take a breath and count to five.

"Your home is stunning," I say with a confident tone in my voice. "Of course, it's missing a few touches that will really bring out its charm. But, that's what I'm here for."

He nods as he takes a sip of his coffee (I'm sure Melanie didn't poison his drink). "It is a great house. I've only been here about three months. After my divorce, I started looking outside the city for something a little quieter. My mother grew up in Ridgefield, and I've always loved Connecticut. As soon as I saw it, I had a feeling this was the right place for me."

So, he's recently divorced? Very interesting. This is not the first new bachelor I've worked with. I wonder why he chose such a big house for just himself.

"So, you're from the city?" I ask.

He nods. "Originally from Westchester but moved to the city after college. My ex-wife and I lived in Tribeca."

I observe him as he mentions the ex-wife. No cringing, no profanity, and no name-calling—maybe they ended amicably. Good for them.

"I love Manhattan," I exclaim. "I actually thought about relocating there, but I just never made the move. I'm close enough to visit, so I guess that's the best of both worlds."

"I agree," he says, flashing me another warm smile. "I love it, too, but I just needed a change."

"Alexander," Melanie interrupts. "Your eight o'clock had to move to ten tomorrow." So she calls him Alexander, but when she spoke to me, she referred to him as Mr. Williams. I think I'm seeing the problem here. Melanie has a big time crush on her boss and she sees me as another woman who's getting ready to spend a lot of time in his home.

"Thanks, Melanie," he replies. "Can you get Ms. Peters something to drink?"

"No, I'm fine," I interrupt. "She already offered me something." I give Melanie a friendly wave, but she pretends not to notice. One thing is for sure—if Melanie is his right hand person, I need to get on her good side. I don't need any drama to get in the way of this job.

This time Melanie doesn't leave the office. She plants herself with her iPad to my right, barely looking at me. I remind myself not to take it personally. I'm here to do my job and that's it.

"Well, shall we get started?" I ask. All my stuttering and nervousness has disappeared and I'm ready to work my magic. Crap! I really need to come up with something else. Unfortunately, the cute phrase has been tainted by a bad breakup.

"Which rooms are you interested in decorating?" I ask, as I get ready to make some notes. I look around his office. "We could start in here," I say, standing up. "Honestly, I wouldn't change the paint color and this furniture is gorgeous. It really just needs some extra touches." I turn toward him and he's staring at me. Melanie notices it, too, and rolls her eyes. I'm definitely going to have to do some kissing up to get on her good side.

"That sounds great," he replies. "And as far as the rooms I want you to decorate, I say all of them."

Um . . . what?

"All . . . as in the whole house?" I ask, dumbfounded. I glance at Melanie, who looks as shocked as I feel. At least she's not shooting daggers at me with her eyes anymore.

"Are you up for the job or is that too much?" he asks, sounding a little worried.

That's a ridiculous question. Of course I'm up for it.

"Yes. Of course," I respond eagerly. "Melanie said you've checked my references and have seen some of my work.

He smiles. "I have. And you come very highly recommended."

I consider getting up and doing a little dance but that wouldn't be very professional. Instead, I reach out to shake his hand.

"Well, then, I guess we have a deal, Mr. Williams," I say as calmly as I can.

"We only have a deal if you call me Alexander."

I smile. "Okay, only if you call me Summer."

We laugh and Melanie forces a smile. Oh, wow, this is going to be fun.

∼

I'm in a great mood for the first time in weeks. My meeting at Alexander's went very well, and this is the perfect project to distract me from my recent relationship drama. We've decided to start with his office like I suggested, and I presented him with a list of possible ideas. He was very friendly and flirtatious, and I admit I had to stop myself from flirting back. Melanie sat there sulking most of the time but did offer up a few suggestions. I went out of my way to welcome those suggestions because chances are I will be spending more time with Melanie than Alexander. I try to count up the hours that I will be spending at his place. Considering he wants me to decorate the whole house, it looks like I will be around for a while.

Even though I work on location most of the time, I share an office space with my friend Gina. Gina is a telemarketer for three different companies and spends more time in the office than I do.

"Oh my gawsh. You look sooo tan," she says with her thick New Jersey accent. "Tell me all about your vacation."

I set my stuff down and pull my laptop out of my bag. Gina must read my blank expression.

"Oh no, what happened?"

"What makes you think something happened?" I reply sarcastically.

She folds her arms and sits back in her chair. "Oh puh-lease. I can tell when a man does something stupid to affect my friends. So spill."

And that's exactly what I do. I tell her all about Jake and his quick and easy breakup. She shakes her head angrily the whole time.

"Let me tell you something," she snaps. "That bastard is going to get his, you just wait. You know I'm more than happy to make a phone call if you want."

I throw my head back in laughter. Gina loves to offer her, um . . . family's assistance in situations like this. When I first met her, I thought she was exaggerating her family connections; little did I know, she was dead serious. Last year, I had a client who wouldn't pay me. I tried everything I could think of to collect, but they continued to ignore me. I would complain to Gina constantly about it, and finally, I was at my wit's end. She made one call to her Uncle Dominick and the next day I received the payment from my client.

"Thanks, Gina, but I think I just need to get over it and move on. Besides, no one can force Jake to want to be with me."

She unwraps a piece of gum and shoves it in her mouth. "Wanna bet?"

I let out a giggle.

"I'm kidding," she says. "But in case you change your mind, you know I got your back."

I give her a grateful smile. "I appreciate that."

I open my laptop and start to organize my notes for Alexander's house while I listen to Gina making her calls. She sounds like such a different person on the phone, her Jersey accent is barely noticeable.

"What are you working on so intently?" she asks a few minutes later. She's looking over my shoulder at my notes. I feel my excitement start to rise when I think about this new project.

I tell her all about Alexander's offer and about Melanie.

"I need to see this man," she insists. "Pull up his Facebook picture."

I type his name in the search box and turn the screen toward her. She raises her eyebrows.

"Oh, hell yeah," she yells. "I think he's just what you need to forget about Jake and that stupid decorating magic crap."

I start to laugh hysterically because I totally forgot about that. One afternoon Jake had come by the office and he was incessantly bragging to Gina about my decorating magic. He was really proud of that saying, and for some reason, she thought it was really stupid.

"I was just thinking about the magic thing this morning," I tell her. She doesn't say anything being that she's too busy nosing through Alexander's pictures.

"So, what do you think about this hottie?" she asks, pointing to the computer screen.

I shrug casually. "He's seems really nice," I say with a sheepish grin. "But he's recently divorced, so I'm not sure it would be a good idea considering it would be a rebound thing for both of us. That is assuming he would ever be interested in me."

She throws her arms up in frustration. "That's even more reason to give it a shot," she yells. "You both need a good distraction."

"Um . . . that's probably a bad idea," I say. "Especially because he's my client and this is huge for my career. That has to be my number one priority. Not to mention his assistant doesn't like me at all."

Gina gives me a curious look. "Why doesn't she like you?"

I shrug my shoulders. "I honestly have no idea. She seemed fine when I first spoke to her but not today. If looks could kill, I would be dead. I have a theory, though."

She raises her eyebrows. "What's your theory?"

I lean back in my chair. "I think she may have a little crush on her boss . . . or maybe she was just having a bad day?"

"Well, that would totally make sense; she's probably threatened by you. Just remember my offer still stands about the phone call. We can take care of both Jake and this Melanie chick." I laugh as I get up to give her a hug.

"Thanks. I promise I will let you know."

I get back to my work, and after Gina leaves for the day, I receive an email from Alexander.

Dear Summer,

It was great meeting you today. I'm looking forward to working with you and finally making my house a home. I will not be able to make it to the meeting on Friday after all, but Melanie will be there to assist you with anything you need. I look forward to seeing your ideas come to life.

Alexander

I make a face. I guess Melanie and I are going to have to figure out a way to coexist because it's clear she's not going anywhere and neither am I.

~

I guess I've been putting this off. Subconsciously, picking up Jake's key is the last reminder that things are over between us. I stopped by Mrs. Rothera's place when I got back from the beach trip, but she wasn't home. I still can't believe he left it with her just to avoid having to see me. Mrs. Rothera owns the building, and she fits the typical nosy neighbor profile perfectly. To be honest, she kind of makes me nervous, so I don't have much to do with her other than paying my rent and typical maintenance requests.

I knock loudly on her door. No answer. Just as I turn to leave, she opens the door.

"Hello, Summer," she says. My eyes immediately focus on her outfit. It looks like she's wearing some kind of costume. It's a colorful dress with beaded fringe and a matching headscarf.

She looks like a gypsy. Maybe she's preparing for Halloween, too. Angie would love it.

"I'm sorry if I'm catching you at a bad time," I say as I drag my eyes away from her headscarf.

"Not a bad time at all," she replies. "Just preparing for an event I'm attending this evening. Come on in."

She opens the door wide and ushers me in. She's attending an event dressed like that? I guess her idea of appropriate attire would differ from mine—depending on the type of event.

"I suppose you're here for this," she says, holding up my key. It's still on the key chain from our cruise to St. Thomas. Ugh. He didn't even keep the key chain.

I give her a weak smile. "Yes. Thank you." She cocks her head to the side and gives me a funny look.

"Why don't you come and sit down for a minute? Can I get you something to drink?"

"No thank you," I reply. "I just got off work, and I haven't even been home yet."

She looks at me with pity. "Dinner for one."

Ouch. That was a harsh reminder. As if it's her business anyway. There she goes again, sticking her nose in where it doesn't belong. I suck in a deep breath because I know I need to be nice to her considering she is my landlord.

"Yes," I say shortly.

"He will be back," she says under her breath. What did she say? Did she say he would be back? He . . . as in Jake?

"I'm sorry. What was that?" I ask.

"Your boyfriend. He will be back. I've seen it." She sits down at the table and that's when I notice the stuff covering her table. Cards, books, charts, and crystals . . . who is this woman?

She notices me staring at her table. "Have you ever had a reading?"

My eyes grow big. "A reading? Like from a fortune teller?"

She laughs loudly. "Not a fortune teller. A psychic reading."

I shake my head. The truth is, I've always been curious about psychics, but I'm too much of a chicken to ever go to one. I'm not sure I'm willing to open that door . . . or portal or whatever it's called.

"How about it?" she asks, pointing to the chair next to her. Hmmm . . . I may be curious about it but not curious enough to go to some amateur. I've lived in this building for over a year. How is it that I'm just finding this out about her now?

"You're a psychic?" I ask, trying to hide my skepticism.

She nods proudly. "Yes."

Okay, I guess she woke up one morning and said, "Hey, I think I will be a psychic today." This is really awkward, mainly because I don't believe her. Although, I keep my mouth shut because I definitely don't want to hurt her feelings. She certainly looks the part with her fancy new outfit, and I can see she has all the tools a psychic would have, but that doesn't mean she is one.

"You don't believe me," she says. Okay, so she figured that out, still doesn't prove anything. "That's okay. All in good time," she adds.

What does she mean by that? I feel like everything out of her mouth is some kind of hidden message.

"It's not that I don't believe you," I reply. "I just didn't know. I mean, you never said anything."

She fixes her headscarf and rearranges the things on her table. "It's not something I just announce to people. It has to be the appropriate time." She pauses. "Anyway, when you're ready, I will be here. But let me just give you one piece of advice." She closes her eyes.

I look around, waiting for something strange to happen. Maybe the chair will shake or she will start chanting . . . but nothing happens.

She opens her eyes and looks directly at me. "When he comes around, trust your instincts."

I wait for her to finish. But she doesn't say anything else.

"And . . ." I ask.

She shrugs. "That's all for now."

What does she mean *that's all for now*?

"Oh except, don't forget the pest control is on Friday," she says as she stands up.

Is this a joke? She goes from giving me some important information about my life to talking about the pest control? I don't move from where I'm standing, but she's obviously done as she gathers her things and starts filling a tote bag.

I thank her for the key, but I'm still confused as I walk up the stairs to my apartment. What just happened? Did she give me an important clue to my future? Is Jake going to try to reconcile? I'm wondering if I just had my first psychic reading.

Chapter Three

I pull the phone away from my ear because Angie is yelling. "Holy crap, can you turn your volume down?" I snap. "I'm going deaf over here."

"So what do you think? Those are fun costumes, right?" she says, toning down her voice but not addressing my demand.

"Honestly, it's been done," I reply. She suggested doing the whole *Grease* Pink Ladies theme again and I'm just not feeling it.

"Come on, we did that over ten years ago, people have forgotten by now." I know Angie is getting frustrated with me. I've shot down all of her costume ideas so far.

"How about a tootsie roll and gum ball machine?" she says sarcastically. "Or maybe *you* should come up with some ideas."

I feel bad. The truth is I've been distracted since my visit with Mrs. Rothera. After I left her place, I started recalling different interactions I've had with her. I always thought she was nosy, like she was watching us come and go or maybe listening through the air vents. The thought never crossed my mind that she had secret powers to see things happening.

"We'll think of something," I tell her. "We still have time," I say, glancing at my calendar.

"You keep saying that, and we don't have that much time, especially if we want to plan a party," she says innocently. Party? Who said anything about a party?

"No way. I don't think so," I tell her. "I'm about to start a huge project with work. The last thing I need to do is commit to planning a party."

I hear pots and pans banging around in the background. "Don't worry. I will do the planning, and it will be awesome. We just have to find a place to have it."

Hah! I know what she means by that; in other words, I have to find a place to have it.

"I don't know . . ." I trail off.

"Come on, it will be fun, and what better way to celebrate your exciting new single life than a Halloween party. It would be the perfect place to meet someone."

Okay, on that note, it's time for me to end this call. I check the time. I have to meet Melanie in forty-five minutes. We've been communicating back and forth via email for the last few days, and it's like she's a different person than the one I met at Alexander's. I'm hoping that she's accepted the fact that I'm going to be around for a while, meaning while I'm decorating (not because of Alexander). Otherwise, this is going to be a long few months.

"Oh fine, plan the party but remember this is all you." I agree. "Oh, and no tootsie roll or gum ball machine costumes."

She snickers. "Deal."

How does Angie always talk me into this stuff? The last brilliant idea she had was starting an online travel planning company. I thought she was crazy, but I'm happy to say that Friendship Travel is still doing very well. Angie is now running it by herself. I became hands-off when business started picking up for Summer Interiors. Angie has always embraced her entrepreneurial spirit, even in high school when she made a killing with friendship bracelets and headbands. Maybe a Halloween party won't be so bad, if anything, it's something else to look forward to.

∼

I don't know what kind of game this girl is playing. I've been waiting outside Alexander's house for fifteen minutes and Melanie is nowhere to be found. After pounding on the door for the third time, she finally opens it.

"There you are," she says. "I just sent Alexander a message asking if he heard from you. I thought you were a no-show."

Is she kidding?

"Melanie, I've been here for fifteen minutes," I say emphatically. "I called and texted you, and I've been pounding on the door."

She gives me a doubtful look. "I didn't get anything." She pauses. "Oh well, you're here now."

She holds the door open for me. I could stand here and argue with her, but I know it's not worth it. I walk into the house and she closes the door behind me.

I follow her into the kitchen. She sits down at the table where her laptop is open. I set up right next to her, and she's watching me the whole time. It's a little awkward for a few moments, but rather than draw any attention to it, I get right to work. I need to try my best to let her know that I'm here to do my job, and I have no intention of stealing her crush away.

"Since we're starting with the office, this is what I came up with. This is exactly what I was talking to Alexander about," I say, turning my laptop toward her. She looks and nods her head. She's obviously impressed but I'm not expecting her to admit it.

"What do you think?" I ask, trying to make it sound like her opinion is very important. I hate kissing up to her, but I don't know what else to do.

"Nice," she replies. I think I notice a tiny trace of a smile. She quickly goes back to her computer.

"So, how long have you worked with Alexander?" I ask, trying to make conversation.

I should have known that a mention of their relationship (professional or not) would make her more willing to talk.

"We've worked together for three years," she says with a smile (a real smile this time). "I did my internship with his company and I was assigned to work with Alexander. Upon completion of the internship, I was offered a position with his company but I stayed with him. I can't beat the pay or the freedom."

I nod. "Freedom is a big deal. Being able to make your own schedule is awesome."

She's looking at something on her laptop and her expression changes. And just like that the wall comes down again. I don't know what changed all of a sudden.

"Is everything okay?" I ask her.

She gets up from the table. "Yep. Just great."

We work silently for the next hour. I walk around the house, taking some pictures and measurements. I'm busy making notes in one of the guest rooms when I hear a man's voice.

"Hi, Summer," Alexander says as he walks into the room, and for a few seconds, I feel my pulse speed up. This is a welcome surprise. Not only because he looks amazing in his suit, but I don't know how much more of Melanie's silence and cold shoulder I can take today.

"What are you doing here?"

He clasps his hands. "My appointments didn't last as long as I expected, so I was able to make it home earlier. I sent Melanie a message, didn't she tell you?"

So that explains her sudden change of attitude. I've gone out of my way to be nice to her, so I'm not sure what else I can do. When Alexander and I head back to the kitchen, Melanie is slumped over the table.

"Summer has a great eye. So far she's living up to her name," he announces. I sit back down at the table and Melanie doesn't acknowledge me. Alexander excuses himself to change his clothes, and rather than waste my time forcing a conversation, I don't say anything to Melanie.

When Alexander returns to the kitchen, my mouth drops open so I quickly cover my mouth with my hand. He's changed into a pair of sweatpants and a T-shirt that clings to his chest. I notice that Melanie is watching my reaction out of the corner of my eye, so I drag my attention away from Alexander and his toned physique.

Before I know it, five o'clock rolls around and I'm still working. We've gone through every room from ceiling to floor. Melanie left around four and it was very obvious she was hoping I would be leaving at the same time.

"You must be starving," Alexander says. "Would you like me to order something . . . or do you have to leave?"

Hmm . . . believe it or not, this is a difficult decision. I could stay here and have dinner in this beautiful kitchen or I could go home to my lonely, empty apartment. Not to mention possibly running into Mrs. Rothera and her new magical psychic powers. At the same time, staying here would go against my plan of staying focused on this job and not crossing over into a nonprofessional situation. Before I can respond, he's on the phone ordering food from a local Greek restaurant. I guess I'm staying for dinner.

∽

I shouldn't be having this much fun, but I am. First of all, Alexander ordered the most amazing Greek food. I feel like an absolute pig because I have devoured everything. I'm really enjoying hanging out with Alexander; he's nice and really down-to-earth. Come to think of it, he's nothing like I expected he would be when they first contacted me about this job. I guess I was expecting someone more hands-off and distant.

"Are you happy living in the suburbs? It's a big difference from city life," I say, taking another bite of my baklava. I have a feeling I will be frequenting It's All Greek quite often after this evening.

He nods. "I'm enjoying the quiet, that's for sure. But it does get a little lonely being that all my friends are still in the city."

We're interrupted by the sound of my phone buzzing. I've been ignoring my phone for most of the evening.

"Sorry. I should check my messages." When I look at it, I have three texts and one voice mail from Angie. I have no doubt she's in full Halloween-planning mode.

"Everything okay?" he asks. "I'm sorry if I've kept you for too long."

I shake my head. "Oh, it's totally fine. It's just my friend Angie; she's obsessing over Halloween. It's nothing unusual."

His eyes light up. "I don't blame her. Halloween is my favorite holiday." I stare at him intently. This guy is officially too good to be true—first *Grease 2* and now Halloween.

"I totally agree, but Angie just has more free time on her hands than I do and she seems to forget that a lot." I tell him all about our years of celebrating Halloween and about her idea to actually throw a party this year.

"She promised she'd plan the whole night and all I'd have to do is find a place to host it." I take a sip of my water.

Alexander gives a thoughtful look. "You can have it here if you want," he says nonchalantly. I'm so shocked by his offer that I spit my water out all over the table.

"Oh crap. I'm sorry," I say as I quickly wipe the table. "Alexander, I appreciate your offer but that's a huge undertaking."

He holds up his hands. "No, it's really not. My ex and I hosted parties all the time in the city. And didn't I just tell you I was lonely? I would love to meet some new people, and I could invite some friends to come down from the city."

He's totally serious. I don't know what to say.

"There is one thing . . ." He hesitates. "Do you think we could have a few of the rooms decorated by then? At least downstairs."

I open my calendar. "I think so. I will have to get items ordered ASAP, but I think it's do-able."

He smiles excitedly. "That's great. I think a party is exactly what I need."

"Me, too. We could do some amazing fall and Halloween décor. I mean, if you want. Although Angie should be taking care of decorations," I add.

He nods as he picks up his phone. "Sounds good. Now I just have to come up with a good costume."

For some reason, Jake pops into my head right at that moment. Why does this happen at the worst time? My mind wanders back to last Halloween. Jake was such a pain about dressing up for an event we were all attending. Of course, Angie and I had our plan and Jake just wanted to wear a shirt that said, "This Is My Costume."

"Maybe I can get a few friends to dress up as the T-Birds from *Grease*," he says, snapping me out of my Jake daydream.

I try to hide my enthusiasm when he mentions *Grease*.

"You like *Grease*?" I ask, trying to act surprised. It's not like I'm going to admit that I already knew that because I stalked him online.

He hangs his head. "Yeah . . . are you going to take my man card?"

I start to laugh. "I'm not sure."

"And to be fair, I like *Grease 2* more. It's my favorite movie of all time," he says.

I pretend to be shocked.

"Let me guess . . . Michelle Pfeiffer?" I say as I roll my eyes.

He snorts. "Of course."

I knew it.

"You want to hear something funny," I say, folding my napkin in my hand for the hundredth time. "Angie just mentioned us wearing Pink Ladies costumes. We did it like ten years ago and I told her it was played out."

He leans back in shock. "I can't believe you just said that. The movie is a classic. It will never be played out. Maybe you should consider it. We would probably look great together." He stops talking suddenly, and I shift around in my seat. I know he didn't mean to say that the way it came out.

My phone rings again just in time to startle me. Sure enough, it's Angie again.

"I probably should answer."

He nods quickly. "Absolutely. And give her the good news." He gets up from the table and starts to clean up the dishes.

I try to contain my excitement as I watch Alexander walk around his kitchen. I have a feeling this Halloween is going to be one of the best yet.

Chapter Four

The next morning, I wake up extra early and lie in my bed for a few minutes. I think back over the events of yesterday. Professionally speaking, it was a great day with the exception of Melanie and her dirty looks. I got a lot accomplished at the house, and I have a good plan in place to get the rooms downstairs decorated before the party. On a personal level, I made a new friend, and that's always a bonus. The nice thing is that I didn't feel any pressure. Spending time with Alexander was like hanging with a good friend.

Angie was ecstatic when I told her about Alexander offering his house for the Halloween Bash, and of course she wanted to speak to him. I started laughing hysterically when he pulled the phone a few inches from his ear and I could still hear every word. I also cringed when she invited him to join us for lunch next week. She says it was to discuss the party, but I've been friends with her long enough to know that the curiosity is killing her and she wants to meet him in person. Not that I blame her, because regardless of him looking like Clark Kent (which he does), he's really funny. He agreed to join us for lunch after he checked his schedule (the schedule Melanie keeps for him).

Speaking of Melanie, he did make a strange comment about her. I can't remember how she came up, but I mentioned how dedicated she is to her job and his response was "almost too dedicated." I didn't want to pry, but it doesn't take a genius to know what he meant by that remark. Regardless, she still works with him after three years so he obviously doesn't mind her dedication. He would be a complete moron not to see how she feels about him, or he could just be a typical man.

Thankfully, after my eventful day yesterday, I will be running errands today so I won't be seeing Melanie or Alexander. I think I will let him break the news to her about his offer to host our Halloween party. It will probably be better if I'm far away from that conversation.

~

I'm about to walk out the door when Angie shows up at my door. She's wearing a tank top that says, "Yoga and Gangster Rap." Somehow she always finds these cute and quirky things.

"Nice shirt. What are you doing here?" I ask, folding my arms. I really have to get to work, so I don't have time to chat (or listen).

She walks past me and into my apartment. "Can't I pay my best friend a visit?"

I look at my watch. "At nine o'clock in the morning? You know you could have called me."

She completely ignores me and walks into the kitchen and opens my refrigerator. I don't mind because we do this all the time. I'm just waiting patiently for her to ask me about last night.

"So," she says.

I start to laugh. "So. Really, that's all you have to say? Seriously, just ask me."

The corner of her mouth curls up. "Okay, tell me HOW you persuaded your new client to host our Halloween party. I'm impressed, by the way."

She pours herself a glass of orange juice and takes a sip. I lean against the counter. "I didn't persuade him. He was telling me about moving out of the city and how it's been lonely. You started texting me about the party and I told him. He offered to have the party there. That's it."

She looks at me in awe. "You're good."

"Ang, I'm telling you the truth. I didn't do anything. Can we discuss this later? I really need to get to work."

She puts her glass in the sink. "Fine. But when are we going to talk about the plans?"

I hold up my hand. "Uh-uh . . . I did my part. I found a location. You said you would do everything else."

There is no way I'm letting her rope me into doing any party planning. Especially because now I have to get Alexander's house ready.

"I know, and I will take care of the party details. But, we still need to talk about our costumes."

The mention of costumes reminds me of Alexander and the Pink Ladies/T-Bird theme. I'm trying not to overreact to what he said, but I did enjoy hanging out with him and I have no doubt that he's usually the life of the party.

On our way out, we meet Mrs. Rothera in the hallway. I haven't seen her since her whole "I'm a psychic" reveal.

"Hello, ladies."

"Hi, Mrs. Rothera," we say politely.

"Summer, have you thought any more about coming to see me for the reading?" she asks. Wow, she's not wasting any time. I wish she wouldn't have said anything in front of Angie.

"You're welcome to come as well," she says, pointing at Angie.

"What are you reading?" Angie asks.

Ugh. I don't want to talk about this.

"I do psychic readings," Mrs. Rothera says proudly.

Angie looks back and forth between Mrs. Rothera and me. She's probably wondering why I didn't tell her sooner. This is exactly the kind of information that Angie loves.

"You do," she says excitedly. "Oh my gosh, you have to come to our Halloween party."

My mouth drops open. She can't be serious. Actually, I know Angie and she's totally serious. They start talking and I feel like I'm dreaming.

"I really have to go," I interrupt. "I will let you two work this out." They stop talking long enough to say good-bye and Mrs. Rothera reminds me to stop by to visit her.

When I get in my car, I think about everything that's happened over the last few days (and weeks). Maybe Mrs. Rothera can give me some insight into Alexander. And what about Jake? The last time I spoke to her she mentioned him coming back. I don't know what I would do if Jake came back or if I could get past the pain he caused me. Hmmm . . . maybe I don't want to know if he's coming back.

∽

I haven't spoken to Alexander (other than a few texts) since I left his place last week. Not that it's any of my business, but I know he's been working some really long hours. At least, that's what Melanie has told me. I have no doubt that she knows about the Halloween party because the tone of her emails has gotten worse. Emotion is usually harder to read in emails and texts but definitely not in hers. On a good note, I'm making great progress with the house. I was able to order quite a bit of the furniture, lighting, and wall décor. And, of course, Melanie has been right behind me to double-check and make sure every detail is perfect. I'm sure the girl is praying that I will mess something up.

Today is the day that Alexander is joining Angie and me for lunch. Normally I would be worried but for some reason I'm not. I've already made Angie promise that she wouldn't tell any embarrassing stories about me, and I've got so much dirt on her that I know she will keep her word.

As far as the Halloween party, her planning is in full swing, and much to my dismay, she has invited Mrs. Rothera to come, not as a guest but as a psychic. I know it's not a big deal but something about this whole thing makes me nervous.

Maybe it's the possibility of hearing something I'm not going to like.

When I arrive at the café, Angie is already there and she's talking loudly on her phone. She waves at me as soon as I sit down.

"YES," she shouts. "That's right, about a hundred people. Perfect."

One hundred people for what? There's no way she could be talking about the party . . . right?

I don't give her a chance to say hi before asking her about the guest list.

"You weren't talking about the party, were you?" I demand.

She gives me a blank look. "Um, yeah. Why?"

Holy crap.

"One hundred people," I shout. "We can't invite that many to Alexander's house."

She looks at me as if I've lost my mind.

"Of course we can."

I place my face in my hands. Maybe he won't care, but I'm embarrassed. She hasn't even met him yet and she's ready to invite the whole tri-state area to his house.

"Summer, relax. I'll ask him when he gets here," she says calmly. "I promised you I would handle everything and I will. You just sit there and look pretty."

I giggle despite being completely annoyed with her. "Very

funny. Remember, we are just friends. And speaking of friends, have you spoken to Mrs. Rothera?"

Before she has a chance to respond, Alexander shows up.

"Is this seat taken?" he asks playfully.

Angie raises her eyebrows, and I can read her expression. I can tell that she's already impressed with him. And I don't blame her a bit. He looks very dashing today with his glasses and tailored shirt. His tie is loosened, and for some reason, I think that is so sexy.

"Hi, Alexander," I say cheerfully. "This is my friend Angie."

"Oh, stop the formality," Angie exclaims. "We're old friends." She stands up and holds her arms out to give him a hug. And of course, being the nice guy he is, he hugs her back.

Formality or not, he's still my client but I know she doesn't care about that.

"Great to finally meet you in person, Angie," he says with a big grin on his face. He turns toward me and rubs my shoulder. "And it's good to see you, Summer."

I try not to overreact to his hand on my shoulder. Especially since Angie is already doing that as she's watching our interaction very closely. I give her a look that clearly says, "Keep your mouth shut and we will talk about it later."

"Okay, so let's get down to business," Angie says, following my lead. "Here are our plans so far."

For the next hour, we talk about the party, or rather, Angie and Alexander talk about it. I mostly listen and give a few suggestions. I have to admit it sounds like it's going to be a blast.

"Wait a second," Alexander interrupts, looking at Angie's notes. "You hired a fortune teller?" He starts laughing after Angie tells him about Mrs. Rothera.

"She's actually a psychic," I tell him. "At least she is now." I explain to them about how I just thought she was really nosy and that I just found out about her little secret.

"Well, I'm interested to hear what she has to say about my future," he says, giving me an innocent look.

Luckily, Angie chimes in at just the right time to break up what could have been a very awkward moment. She wants Mrs. Rothera to have a good spot so the guests can visit her if they want to. I begin to daydream as we continue to discuss the party. I can't believe I'm letting this happen. I never thought I would be interested in a client. I know it could be a total rebound thing or that he's just a really great guy. Either way, this is very unprofessional. Not only that, there's still so much I don't know about him, like how long was he married? Why did he get divorced? These are important questions. Of course, I'm totally jumping to conclusions here—just because I have a crush on him doesn't mean he has one on me.

"Jake?"

My daydream is interrupted when I hear Angie say Jake's name. My heart sinks. What the . . . ?

I turn around to see Jake standing behind me. He looks right at me and immediately a rush of different emotions comes over me.

"Hi, Angie. Hi, Summer," he says awkwardly.

"Hello, Jake," I reply. It came out colder than I intended, but after the way he hauled butt out of my life, I guess I'm entitled to that reaction. We're all quiet for a few seconds until I remember that Alexander is sitting with us. He's watching our interaction carefully.

"Alexander, this is Jake."

Alexander, being the nice guy he is, gets up to shake his hand.

"Alexander just moved to Connecticut from the city," I say. "He's hired me to decorate his house."

"And she's doing a great job already," he says proudly. I can feel myself start to blush.

Jake gives a sheepish grin. "I have no doubt. I've always said Summer has decorating magic."

I cringe as memories begin flooding back. Angie is watching the whole scene. I know she's holding back from going off on Jake.

"We're in the middle of planning a big Halloween party," Angie interrupts. She obviously noticed my discomfort. "Alexander was nice enough to offer to host the party at his new home."

Alexander shrugs his shoulders. "I'm happy to. It's a great way to meet people in a new town. You should come, Jake."

Angie and I look at each other in horror. I know it's not Alexander's fault, being that he doesn't know our history, but the thought of Jake crashing this party makes me nauseous.

"Um . . . maybe," Jake replies as looks at his watch. "I'm sorry, but I have to get to a meeting. It was nice seeing you two and great meeting you, Alex."

"Alexander," he corrects him.

"Uh . . . yeah, sorry. Good-bye."

Jake practically runs away. I rub my temples vigorously because that pretty much sucked. I knew I was bound to run into Jake at some point but I never imagined it would be that torturous. Alexander is eyeing me curiously.

"Okay, so do one of you want to tell me what that was about?" he asks. "I'm really sorry if I overstepped by inviting him. I figured you all were friends."

Yeah, friends, I think to myself.

"It's okay," I assure him. "We're not exactly friends . . . Jake is my ex-boyfriend."

Poor Alexander cringes.

"Oh man, I'm sorry," he exclaims. "And I just invited him to the party."

"Don't worry about it," Angie interrupts. "He won't show his face at this party, and if he does, he won't be there for long."

I nod in agreement. "No, he won't. But don't feel bad, it's fine . . . and I'm fine."

I really am fine . . . I think. In my defense, it was the first time I've seen him since he left the beach. It was bound to bring up some emotion. If anything, I think it was better having Angie and Alexander with me so I didn't have to face him on my own.

Shortly after we finish lunch, Angie leaves to run some errands. Alexander and I walk out together.

"So, I'm not trying to pry into your life and you don't have to tell me anything. I'm just curious about what happened with you and that Jake guy."

I stare at the sidewalk before making eye contact with him.

"We broke up over the summer," I say as nonchalantly as I can. He chews on his bottom lip as I continue. "Or rather, he broke up with me over the summer . . . at the beach . . . while we were on vacation. No explanation, just that he wasn't ready for anything serious—even though we had been serious for quite some time."

I hate to make it seem like I'm still bothered by this, but I would be lying if I acted like I wasn't.

He lets out a slow whistle. "Oh . . . that's harsh."

"Sorry to unload like that," I tell him. "I usually don't share my personal life with clients, but since you asked."

He nervously shifts from one foot to another. I get the feeling he wants to say something.

"Is everything okay?" I ask him.

He nods slowly. "Yeah. I just wanted to tell you that I think of you as a friend." He pauses. "I mean, other than you just decorating my house, so don't feel bad about giving me the scoop. And I'm the one who asked. I could sense something was off, and then I open my big mouth and invite him to the party." He shakes his head.

I put my hand on his arm. "It's okay. And I appreciate you saying that we're friends. I feel the same way." We're standing, facing each other in the middle of the sidewalk. Just then his phone starts to ring and he quickly grabs it.

"Excuse me for one second," he says as he answers.

"Yes, Melanie," he answers. I turn my face away from him and scowl. That Melanie sure has impeccable timing.

"Okay, I will call him now," he insists.

When he hangs up, he's scrolling through his phone. "I hate to cut this short but I need to take care of something."

"I understand. I actually have to run by your house and check on a delivery," I say. He holds out his hand to shake mine. Well, nothing says just friends like shaking hands.

Chapter Five

I'm exhausted. I've been working long hours at Alexander's for the last few days. I've only seen him for a few minutes as he's been in the city working a lot, which is probably for the best, but I admit I've missed him being around. He's definitely more fun than Melanie.

Unfortunately, Melanie has been around and she has been civil for the most part, with the exception of a snide comment about the Halloween party. She said something about all the "strangers" who were going to be in the house and how Alexander is too nice and that sometimes people take advantage of him. I wanted so badly to put her in her place, but I bit my tongue—again.

When I get home, I'm starving. I'm heating one of those gross Lean Cuisine meals (because I'm too tired to prepare anything else) when there's a knock at my door. I open it to find Mrs. Rothera with a saucepan in her hands.

"Hi," I say, forcing a smile. I really don't want to get into any conversations about my life tonight.

"I hope I'm not bothering you. I made this vegetable soup, and I thought you might be hungry. I have plenty."

Wow. Either she heard me complaining about the frozen meal or she *is* psychic.

"That's very kind of you," I say. I know I can't avoid this woman forever, so I decide to invite her in. "Would you like to come in?" She actually looks surprised but accepts my invite.

When she comes in, she sits down on my couch and I offer her something to drink. Even though I'm not into this psychic thing, I'm curious about what she said about Jake.

After I hand her a glass of water, I ask her the burning question. "I've been wanting to ask you about what you said about Jake. And please don't take this the wrong way, but I'm not really interested in a reading, at least not right now."

She gives me a tight-lipped simile. I hope that didn't come across the wrong way. I'm not trying to piss her off.

"Would any of this have to do with the new man you're spending time with?"

What? How does she know this stuff?

"Well . . . not exactly. You mentioned that Jake would be back, and I wanted to know if you could explain."

She looks around my apartment but doesn't respond for a few seconds. "You don't believe me, do you?"

Now she's staring at me but it feels more like she's staring through me. I don't want to make her feel bad because, honestly, I don't know what I think. She has mentioned things that she wouldn't know unless she has some kind of other sense. Things she couldn't possibly know about.

I hear my phone buzzing from the kitchen. I'm getting a text message, but I decide to ignore it.

"Honestly, I don't know," I reply as I lower my head. "I admit you've known certain things..."

She gets up from the chair and sits down on the couch next to me. "To answer your question. Yes, Jake will be back. And in regards to the new man, you should know that there is another woman involved."

What other woman? My phone starts to buzz again.

"You should answer that, and I will let you be," she says as she gets up to leave.

I want to ask her more questions but that's not really fair considering I basically said that I don't believe she has magical powers. "Thank you for the soup," I call as I go to grab my phone.

I almost drop my phone when I see the text. It's from Jake.

I was wondering if we could talk. Let me know.

My legs feel weak, almost like I may pass out. Okay, now I'm freaking out. Did Mrs. Rothera know Jake was texting me? The question is what do I do? Should I listen to what he has to say? The one thing I know is that I can't reply to him tonight. I'm completely exhausted and I need time to think—about everything.

Maybe I do have decorating magic? Alexander's office looks fantastic, if I do say so myself. I stand back and look around proudly. I'm not usually one to toot my own horn but I did a great job with this room. Alexander already had a gorgeous mahogany desk, so I just had to work around that. I found two chaise lounges and they matched perfectly. Then I added some wall décor, an area rug, and some amazing artwork with different views of the New York City skyline. I hope being in here gives him a sense of "home."

I happily wander back into the kitchen and sit down at the table. I've been trying to avoid my phone (mainly the text messages). It's been a few days and I still haven't responded to Jake's text. I know I need to say something, even if I just tell that I'm not ready yet. I hear the front door open; it's probably Melanie because she doesn't like me being at Alexander's house alone for too long. Maybe she thinks I'm going to prance around pretending to be the lady of the house. Not that the thought hasn't crossed my mind, but only because I love it here and not because of Alexander (well, not entirely).

"Hey. I thought you would be gone by already," Alexander says, dropping a bunch of bags on the floor. He looks really tired.

"Oh, I'm almost done," I say worriedly.

"No. I didn't mean it like that," he insists. "You're just working so late, but I'm glad you're still here."

We smile warmly at each other, and I hope that I'm not

starting to blush. I'm not going to lie; I really enjoy it when he's home.

"I just finished hanging everything in your office," I say without taking my eyes off him. "Would you like to see it?"

He loosens his tie. *Why is it so hot when men do that?*

"Of course," he exclaims. "Let's see if you live up to your reputation."

I lead the way. I feel like I should do a drum roll or say ta-da, or something.

Alexander walks in and looks around. He turns toward me and nods. "Wow, this is very impressive. I may never want to leave now."

"Thanks," I say proudly.

He leans against the front of his desk and rubs his temples. I don't know why but I get the feeling something is bothering him.

"Alexander, is everything okay?"

He drops his hands. "Yeah, it was just a hectic day at the office. That combined with seeing my ex-wife, I'm worn out."

My curiosity is piqued at the mention of his ex.

"Oh," I reply as I grit my teeth.

He sighs as he sits down on one of the new chaise lounges. "Yeah. Helena can be a handful, to say the least."

My mind starts to wander back to what Mrs. Rothera said

about another woman. Maybe she was referring to his ex-wife. I sit down on the edge of one of the chairs.

"If you don't mind me asking, how long were you two married?" I figure now is the best time to ask him. And since he brought her up, it doesn't sound like I'm being nosy. Besides, he asked me about Jake, so I shouldn't feel weird asking about his ex-wife.

He undoes his top two buttons. *First the tie and now the buttons . . . Whew.*

"We were married for four years," he replies. "It was kind of a whirlwind romance. She's originally from Sweden, and she was here working for a modeling agency. We met at a party in the city, and from that night on, we were inseparable."

A Swedish model—I think I've changed my mind about wanting to know more about her.

"The last year and half were rough," he continues. "I guess the intensity between us finally wore off."

I give him a sympathetic look even though I really don't want to hear anymore. I can only imagine what kind of intensity the two of them had.

"When did you divorce?" I ask. I know he's been in the house a few months, but he never mentioned how long he's been divorced.

"Our divorce was final in May, on our fourth anniversary actually."

I scrunch my face. "Oh wow."

"Anyway, we're still friends so it's fine. She stopped by my office today, and as I said, she can be a lot to deal with." I know I shouldn't have this feeling but the thought of Helena the Swedish model spending time with Alexander makes me really jealous.

"And . . . she heard about the Halloween party," he adds. "Unfortunately, we still have a lot of the same friends." Crap. I bite my bottom lip, but there is nothing I can say. This may be our party, but it's Alexander's house.

"I told her about you," he says softly.

I give him a curious look. "You did? What exactly did you tell her?"

He sits up and runs his fingers through his hair. "I told her about you decorating the house." He laughs nervously. "And . . ."

I swallow loudly. "And . . . what?"

He leans his head against the back of the couch. "And I told her that I like spending time with you." My pulse picks up again. He's now looking at me, obviously waiting for me to say something. I have so much going through my mind right now.

"I like spending time with you, too," I reply. The corners of his lips curl into a smile. The next thing I know he's leaning over me and he's kissing me. I start to run my fingers through his hair. I realize how much I've wanted this to happen. At the same time, I feel like we shouldn't be doing this.

All of a sudden, I hear Melanie's voice. "Alexander. Did you get . . . Oh my gosh!" Alexander jumps off the chair and I sit up straight.

She's standing in the doorway with the look of shock on her face. "I'm so sorry," she says quickly and rushes out of the room. I close my eyes and put my face in my hands. This is bad. What was I thinking?

"Hey," he says, tapping me on the shoulder. "Don't worry about her." I nod my head, but I feel horrible. Not only have I broken my own rule of not getting involved with a client, now Melanie will hate me more than she already does.

"You should probably go talk to her," I say as I stand up. "I need to get going anyway."

I start to walk out of the office, but he catches my elbow. "Summer, please don't go yet. I meant what I said."

I smile. "I know, but you need to check on her. We can talk later."

I pack up my laptop and my things, which are strewn all over the table. I'm not sure where Melanie ran off to. As I walk to my car, I almost feel like I'm doing the walk of shame after being caught making out. When I'm safely in my car, I run my fingers across my lips. Wow. I smile to myself. Other than Melanie walking in on us, it couldn't have been any more perfect. One thing is for sure, I also meant what I said. I really enjoy spending time with him, too.

Chapter Six

"Do you like any of these costumes?" Angie asks for the hundredth time. "What do you think, Gina?"

It's Saturday morning and the three of us are having brunch. I'm hardly paying attention being that I'm still in a bit of a daze since my intense encounter with Alexander. He texted me after I left and told me he talked to Melanie and everything was fine. And then he said he was looking forward to continuing our conversation. Conversation? I guess that's one way to describe it.

"I think you should do your own thing," Gina says. "Forget this one over here."

She's pointing at me.

I roll my eyes. Gina dresses the same every Halloween and her costume is always some kind of sexy animal. Meaning lingerie with some kind of animal theme. Last year, she was the sexy tiger.

"I told you they were all fine. You can choose."

She glares at me. "What's your deal? You seem really distracted. Do I need to call Mrs. Rothera here to help?"

I snort. "No way. I have enough going on without being told what my future holds." I pause. "Jake texted me. He wants to talk."

Both of their mouths drop open, and then they both start yelling at exactly the same time. "What? When did this happen?" Angie asks.

"Just let me make one call," Gina exclaims. "One call and this will be taken care of."

I ignore Gina's mention of the phone call. "He texted last week sometime. I haven't responded yet because something else happened since then."

They glance at each other. I guess I made it sound worse than it really is. "Nothing bad," I assure them.

"Well, are you going to tell us?" Angie asks.

I tell them about Alexander and that amazing kiss. And then how the moment was ruined when Melanie interrupted us.

"Not that assistant again," Gina says, sounding exasperated. "Please tell me you aren't letting her get to you."

"Why are you upset?" Angie asks. "You made out with Clark Kent. He's freaking hot."

I laugh. "Yes. He's attractive, but I guess I'm confused. What do you think Jake wants?"

She rolls her eyes. "Who cares what he wants. He probably

noticed the intense attraction between you and Alexander that day we saw him at lunch. I'm sure he's jealous."

"Forget about him. He abandoned you when you were on a vacation with him," Gina exclaims. "He ended things, so now he has to live with his stupid mistake. Serves him right."

"I agree," Angie says as they toast their glasses.

Could that be it? Is he jealous? He only saw us for a few minutes. I don't think we acted like there was anything going on between us.

"I doubt he's jealous," I say. "We were just having lunch when we saw him. It's not like we were on a date."

Angie folds her arms. "Don't underestimate him. Guys can be just as jealous and catty as women. The question is, would you really give him another chance if he asked?"

Both Angie and Gina are looking at me, waiting for my answer. But I don't have an answer because I don't know. I was so hurt when he ended things, but there is a part of me that still has feelings for him. You just don't stop loving a person because they hurt you.

"Let's decide on our costumes," I say, changing the subject.

Thankfully, that is the perfect distraction. I know I won't be able to avoid Jake forever, but making him wait is nothing compared to what he put me through this summer.

"Let's go with the Disney Villains—Cruella de Vil and Evil Queen," I say finally.

Angie claps. "Finally."

Both Angie and Gina leave after brunch. The café is right near a small park, so I decide to take a walk since I have the day off. There has always been something magical about this time of year. I notice the leaves changing, the smells, even people seem to act differently. I sit down on a bench and take it all in for a few minutes. I know I need to call Jake, and even though he's the one who wanted this breakup, I'm really nervous to talk to him. I'm assuming he's finally ready to give me the real explanation, so I plan on being honest with him and tell him how much he hurt me. I don't know what's going to happen with Alexander but maybe that's okay. Maybe I can just enjoy being single and my friends and my job. I take my phone out of my bag and scroll through my messages until I find Jake's. I finally send him my reply:

Okay. I will meet you. When?

A few seconds later, my phone rings. Jake is calling me.

I take a few deep breaths.

"Hello."

"Hi, Summer. I just wanted to thank you for agreeing to meet me."

Ugh. This is almost as awkward as seeing him in person, but somehow I muster up a huge dose of courage.

"That's fine. I will be home this afternoon if you want to stop by." I'm not planning on putting a lot of effort into this, so I will make him come to me.

"That sounds good. How about this evening? I can bring something from Antonio's."

My heart sinks. What's he trying to do, twist the knife even further? Antonio's was one of our favorite takeout spots.

"Um . . . don't worry about it. Just come by anytime," I reply.

After I hang up, I'm practically shaking. It's done. Jake and I are meeting tonight. *It's going to be okay*, I tell myself. I need to get this closure in order to move on with my life. I enjoy the park for a few minutes, and then I head home. I hope this isn't a mistake.

∼

There's a knock at my door, and I close my eyes and take a few breaths. I've spent most of the afternoon trying to mentally prepare myself to talk to Jake. Except when I answer the door it's not Jake, it's Mrs. Rothera.

"Hi," I say, trying to hide my surprise. She looks very concerned.

"I'm sorry to bother you. I was just making sure you were okay."

I have an uneasy feeling. What does she mean by that?

"I'm fine."

She still doesn't look convinced, and now she's starting to scare me. I guess I should just tell her about Jake coming over.

"Okay, fine. Jake sent me a message last week about wanting to talk. He should be here any minute."

I bite my lip and wait for her chime in. I'm sure she has

something to say, and I kind of want to know what it is, but she doesn't say a word.

"Okay, I give in—am I making a mistake?" I plead as I grab ahold of her arms.

She stares into my eyes. "Well, that all depends on what you want to come out of this meeting."

That's not the answer I was expecting from her. I turn around, leaving her in the doorway.

"I want closure," I say as I fall down on the couch. "I want to know why he ended things so abruptly with no warning." I cover my eyes with my arm. "We were on vacation, enjoying our time together, and he just left."

She closes the door and joins me in the living room. "You will get your answer. As long as you ask for the right reason."

What is she saying? Why is she talking in code? Just then, there's another knock at the door.

Mrs. Rothera looks at me and puts her hand on my arm. "Sometimes things aren't what they seem."

There she goes again. I want to ask her what she means, but Jake knocks a second time. I go to the door to answer it.

"Hey," he says with a nervous smile. When he sees Mrs. Rothera, his smile fades.

"I was just leaving. Have a good night." She hurries out the door.

My heart is beating so fast. I look at Jake who shoves his hands in his pockets as he rocks back and forth on his heels.

"Thanks for letting me come over," he says as he walks in and looks around the room. I wonder if he's thinking about all the time we spent here together. I hope he is, and I hope the guilt starts eating away at him. I still live here and I'm reminded of it every day.

"It's fine," I reply. I'm waiting for him to start talking because this was his idea.

"Why was Mrs. Rothera here?" he asks.

I walk past him and sit down on the couch. "She wanted to check in on me. We've kind of become . . . friends." I guess that's what you could call us . . . or something like that.

Jake walks over and sits across from me. "There's something strange about her." He pauses. "When I dropped the key off to her, she kept asking me if I thought about what I was doing. I didn't give her any information about what had happened but it was like she already knew."

Hah. This still doesn't prove anything. He was giving her his key and it doesn't take a genius to figure out that we had broken up.

"I'm sure it wasn't too hard for her to figure out," I say coldly. "Giving her your key when you could have left it with me. That's kind of obvious."

He hangs his head. "I know. I just couldn't face you. I didn't know what else to do and it just seemed like the easiest thing."

I fold my arms defensively. "Easy? So you just wanted the easy way out after almost two years together."

I surprise myself with the way I just blurted that out, but I may as well get to the point.

He frowns. "I definitely deserve that . . . which is why I'm here." He pauses. "After seeing you and Angie the other day, I haven't been able to stop thinking about everything that happened."

Hmm . . . maybe Angie was right and seeing Alexander influenced his decision.

I purse my lips. "Okay."

"I freaked out," he exclaims. "I mean, come on—we were on vacation together. I just wasn't ready to get engaged."

Engaged? What the hell is he talking about?

"All those girls talking about rings and weddings just got to me. Especially when they said that we were going to be first to get married."

I jump up from the couch. "What are you talking about?"

He gives me a blank stare. "Angie, Lauren, and Shelby were sitting out on the deck planning our wedding before we were even engaged," he exclaims.

I don't believe this. He broke up with me because he overheard a conversation. This has to be a joke. I consider throwing him out, but then I remember what Mrs. Rothera said about things not being what they seem.

I rub my forehead. "So you threw away our relationship based on a conversation you overheard, is that what you're telling me? You didn't even think of discussing it with me. You just up and left."

He stares at the floor. "I guess," he whispers. "When I got back, I felt so bad that I came here to get my stuff. I gave Mrs. Rothera the key, and I just threw myself into work. I realized pretty quickly that I made a huge mistake, but I assumed it was too late."

I don't look at him as he gives me his explanation. "It wasn't until I saw you that day at lunch that I realized I had to see you again, at least to tell you how sorry I am."

I can feel the tears coming but I hold them back. I finally look at him.

"Well, you've seen me," I snap. "You can leave now."

His face falls. "I'll leave, but can I just ask one thing?"

I glare at him. "What?"

"Would you consider just taking some time to think about everything? I'm not going to ask you to give me another chance, yet. But, if there's a chance you still love me . . ."

I get up and walk to the door. I pull it open, waiting for him to walk out. "Good night, Jake."

He frowns but he doesn't try to argue.

"I still love you," he says before he walks out.

I shut the door behind him and fall to the ground. The tears that I was holding in finally make their way down my face. So much for a fresh new start. I feel like I'm back on the beach the night he left me in tears.

Chapter Seven

When I arrive at the house, Melanie's car is parked out front. I haven't seen her since she walked in on Alexander and me kissing. I already gave myself a pep talk to keep my cool and be as professional as possible. Not to mention I'm really tired. I didn't get much sleep after seeing Jake last night and I'm really not in the mood for Melanie's attitude.

I quietly walk into the house, which is completely ridiculous because there is no way I can avoid her.

"Good morning, Summer," she calls warmly. I stop in my tracks. That's Melanie's voice but she sounds different, almost happy. I follow her voice into the living room.

She's sitting on the couch surrounded by stacks of papers. She looks up when I walk in. "How are you?" she says cheerfully. Admittedly, I don't know what to say.

"Hi. I'm fine," I say slowly. She's humming softly to herself. I feel really stupid just lingering in the doorway. "Um—the electrician should be here soon to switch out the lighting fixtures in the kitchen. Can you let me know when they arrive? I'll be in the office."

She nods. "Okay."

I walk toward Alexander's office. Maybe the little talk Alexander had with her did some good. Regardless, I'll take it. I don't have the energy to put forth a ton of effort with her today. I sit down at the desk and pull out my planner. I'm trying to work but I can't concentrate. And it's not just because of what happened with Jake last night. Melanie's behavior has completely thrown me off guard.

"Are you ready for the party?" I look up to see her standing in the doorway. I hate to be so negative but I don't trust this woman.

"We're getting there," I reply. I scroll through my emails in order to make it look like I'm busy (which I'm not). My efforts fail because she comes in and sits down across the desk from me. I look up from my screen to see her staring at me. I hate feeling like I'm being watched.

"Did you need something?" I ask her politely as I lean back in the chair.

She gives me a smug smile. "No. I just wanted to tell you not to worry about me walking in the other night." I shift around uncomfortably in my seat. I guess it's good that she's putting it out there so it's not the elephant in the room.

"Oh. Well, thanks." That sounded really stupid, but I don't know what else to say. Mostly because I'm not worried about what she thinks other than I prefer to not have to work in a hostile environment. She's still looking at me, and I'm growing more and more uncomfortable.

"Melanie, I don't want things to be awkward between us. I know you've worked with Alexander a long time."

"Yes, I have," she interrupts. "And that's why I'm telling you not to worry about it. This isn't the first time this has happened."

Okay. What is that supposed to mean?

"This isn't the first time what has happened?" I ask. I can feel my blood pressure creeping up.

She gives a fake laugh. "Come on. Let's be honest, Alexander has a lot going for him. Do you really think you're the first woman to come around here and mesmerize him?"

I raise my eyebrows. This girl has issues, either she's trying to antagonize me or she's trying to make herself feel better. Either way, I need to keep my cool.

"I don't think I mesmerize him," I say flatly. "We enjoy each other's company and we have a lot in common." I try to focus my attention back on my computer screen. I can see out of the corner of my eye that her smile has faded to a glare.

"Think what you want, but as soon as you finish this job, you will be gone—just like the rest of them."

Hmmm . . . the rest of them? I know what she's trying to do and I'm not going to let her get to me.

"I'm going to do what I was hired to do. And if I make a new friend in the process that's great."

She rolls her eyes. "Anyway, I'll let you get back to work." She practically dances out of the office.

I clench my fists. *Don't let her get you upset*, I think to myself. I know she's trying to convince herself that there's nothing between Alexander and me. And maybe there isn't other than a physical attraction. Either way, this is my career.

I somehow make it through the rest of the day without any more run-ins with Melanie. Luckily, I'm busy with the electrician and doing different tasks around the house. And she's busy with whatever it is that she does for Alexander all day. It's not until right before I leave that she speaks to me again.

"Alexander gave me a list of a few things to do for the party, including inviting some of his friends. He said I needed to contact your friend Angie."

I smile. This is actually a good thing. I would love to see her try to interact with Angie.

"Yep. Angie is the one planning this party. I don't really have anything to do with it."

She glances at her phone. "Angie may be doing the planning, but being that the party is here, I will be handling things for Alexander *of course*."

I want to remind her that as his assistant she works for him just like me, that she's not his girlfriend or his wife. And I really want to tell her that the way she falls all over him is pathetic. However, I bite my tongue (I seem to be doing this a lot).

I scroll through my phone and forward her Angie's contact information. "I just sent you her info. Give her a call."

I leave for the day before I say anything that could get me fired. I'm just going to ignore her comment about Alexander and the other women. Or at least I'm going to try to.

∼

I'm really trying to ignore everything Melanie said but it's proving to be really hard. She's totally succeeding in getting under my skin, which is exactly what she wanted. Over the next week, whenever Alexander is around so is Melanie. It could be just me but I notice that he's very careful around her. It's almost as if he's trying to spare her feelings so he's been keeping his distance.

We are one week out from the party and I'm busy hanging garland on the banister when Alexander joins me on the stairs.

"Everything looks great," he says. "Are you excited for the party?"

I nod. "Yeah. How about you?"

He nods. I can tell he's about to say something else.

"Summer . . ." He hesitates. "I owe you an apology."

I give him a curious look. "For what?"

He scratches his neck. "Because I've been so out of it lately. I don't want you to get the wrong idea."

I lay the garland down and sit down on the step below him.

"The wrong idea? What do you mean?"

I don't like the sound of this. Maybe Melanie got to him after all.

"I don't want you to think that me being distracted has anything to do with you. Things at work haven't been great."

I give him a sympathetic look. "I'm sorry to hear that."

He takes a deep breath. "I did want to ask you something, though. I was wondering if you were going to the party with anyone?"

I smile. "Going with anyone—as in a date? No. I just figured Angie would put me to work when I got here."

He laughs. "Probably."

I bite my lip, waiting for him to say something else. I'm not sure if he's going to ask me to be his date or not. Or maybe he's checking to see if I'm going with someone else.

"I was going to ask if you want to go together, but I just realized that sounds pretty stupid considering it's at my house and we were both going to be here anyway."

I start to giggle. "I'm sorry for laughing," I say. He starts laughing, too. "But, to answer your question, I would love to go to your party with you. We can just meet here," I say, trying to keep a straight face.

He doesn't say anything. Instead, he leans down and kisses me. And it's just like I remembered. It's a good thing I'm sitting down because my legs feel weak. When we pull away, I look around to see if Melanie is watching from anywhere. I think it's finally time to address the situation with her.

"I actually wanted to talk to you about something," I say as I look around again. "In private, if possible."

He gives me a concerned look but follows me up the stairs into one of the guest rooms. He sits down on the bench at the end of the bed.

"What's wrong?" he asks immediately.

I sigh. "I just wanted to talk to you about Melanie."

His smile quickly fades. "I told you I spoke to her. Everything is fine."

I sigh. "Actually, I don't think it is."

Not a second later, there is a knock on the door, which is ajar. Sure enough, it's Melanie. I roll my eyes.

"I'm so sorry to interrupt," she says innocently. "Edward has been calling you nonstop. He just called my phone looking for you."

Alexander groans. "Of course he is. Summer, can we continue this later?"

"Yes, definitely."

He leaves to go call Edward back (I have no idea who Edward is). I automatically think of Edward Cullen from *Twilight* when I hear that name.

Melanie is lingering in the doorway. I walk toward the door when she stands in front of me.

"Is everything all right?"

I give her a fake smile. "Everything is great. Just making plans for the party."

She glares at me as I nonchalantly walk past her. I go back to hanging the garland, and she silently walks past me down the stairs. I think it's safe to assume that we've officially drawn a line in the sand, and if there is any possibility of a future with Alexander, I need to address this with him.

Chapter Eight

I officially hate my costume. I told Angie that I didn't care which villain I was so she took the Cruella de Vil costume. I'm dressed as the Evil Queen from *Snow White* and I'm sweating like a pig. Although this costume could look good on some people, I'm not one of those people. So much for looking cute and sexy on the first holiday I'm single. I guess, technically, I'm Alexander's date for the evening, but I'm still very single.

Unfortunately, I still haven't had a chance to talk to him about Melanie. Every time I saw him this week Melanie was right there (shocker). Speaking of this, the house looks amazing. I'm almost finished decorating the entire downstairs with the exception of a guest room and bathroom, and Angie and I spent the whole day yesterday setting up for the party.

I stand in front of the full-length mirror looking at this hideous costume. I guess I can't blame Jake for wanting to wear a T-shirt last year because that actually sounds awesome right now.

I hear a knocking at my door, and I make a face in the mirror. I really don't want to answer the door looking like this, much less go out in public. When I answer the door, I find Mrs. Rothera dressed in her psychic costume . . . or is it a uniform? Maybe psychics have to wear a uniform, too.

"That's a very nice costume," she says kindly.

I frown. "Thanks for being nice but you can admit it's awful."

She smiles. "I'm on my way to meet your friend Angie. I just wanted to check on you."

Why does she keep checking on me? I'm starting to get a complex that something is always going wrong.

"Everything is great. It's Halloween," I insist.

She nods slowly. "All Hallows' Eve—the most mysterious night of the year. A lot can happen tonight." I stop fidgeting with my costume. "Is that your way of telling me to expect something to happen tonight?"

She looks around my apartment. I wonder if she's looking for something. "Let's just say I have a strong feeling that tonight is going to be very eventful," she says softly.

Crap. Nothing like freaking me out before the evening even starts. "Eventful as in good or eventful as in bad?" I ask.

She gives me a weak smile. "I'm not exactly sure. Everything is kind of blurry."

Blurry? This is just great, Angie hired a psychic who can't see anything.

"Why is it blurry? Are you saying you can't see anything?"

She places her hand on my arm. "I didn't say that. I see a lot of things, but for some reason, this isn't clear." She's waving her hand around me. "I need to go get set up. I'm glad everything is okay here." She walks toward the door and I follow her.

Well, it was okay before she came and made me worry. Figures. She drops a hint like that and then has to leave. "I guess I will see you later," I say.

She nods. "Yes."

After she leaves, I'm really nervous. I wish I knew what to expect tonight. I run through every possible scenario in my head. Maybe it has something to do with me and Alexander or maybe me and Melanie. What if something happens to Alexander's house? Angie did say that she was expecting a hundred people. I suddenly feel sick to my stomach. I'm not sure if it's nerves or that I'm overheated under this disgusting polyester dress and headpiece. I try to calm myself down, so I take off my costume and hang it in the garment bag. I will just change when I get over there so I don't have to drive in the stupid thing. I load up my car and make my way to Alexander's. I guess it wouldn't be Halloween without some excitement.

~

"Why aren't you dressed?" Angie yells as soon as she sees me. Of course she looks great in her costume. I really should have paid more attention to the costume selection. I was too distracted with that stupid Jake.

"Relax," I say, holding up the garment bag. "I was about to pass out in the thing, so I figured I would change here." Angie scowls and walks off in a huff. I can't believe she's mad at me about this, although, maybe that's what Mrs. Rothera was referring to. Maybe this is part of the eventful evening she couldn't see.

In order to put off changing into my costume, I decide to wander around and check on the party; after all, I am supposed to be helping. The house looks fantastic, and I'm not just talking about my decorating. The fall/Halloween décor makes it look and feel so festive. In the kitchen, there are trays of catered food everywhere and it all smells divine. I recognize Angie's cousin, Vinny (a bartender) and her boyfriend Brett setting up a full bar in the corner of Alexander's game room. Vinny is dressed as a prisoner and Brett is dressed (or sort of dressed) as a Chippendales dancer. My eyes grow wide and I quickly cover my mouth to hide my shock. He looks as scary as ever.

When I walk past the French doors that lead out to the lanai, I notice a tent set up with a sign that says, "Psychic Readings." I have to admit it does give a fun Halloween-like feel to the party despite the butterflies I feel in my stomach.

"Summer, I promise I'm not mad at you but please go get dressed before the guests start to arrive," Angie says, interrupting my thought. She has her hands in prayer position.

"Fine," I say, rolling my eyes. "By the way, have you seen Alexander?"

Her exasperated look turns into a wicked smile. "Oh yeah, and he looks good."

"Shhh," I shriek, pulling her outside on the lanai. "Don't forget a lot of his friends will be here, so please don't say anything to embarrass me." She looks shocked that I'd ever suggest such a thing. "Oh, come on, don't act like it's not a possibility. Anyway, do you know where he is?"

She shrugs. "I'm not sure, but he was asking about you," she says in a singsong voice. I can feel myself start to blush as she continues talking. "That doesn't matter now, you can chase after him later—go get changed," she says as she starts to drag me back into the house. Just then, Mrs. Rothera pops out of her tent, startling me.

"Oh, you scared me," I exclaim.

"Sorry," she says as she fixes her sign. Angie heads inside but not before giving me a stern look. She's acting like my mom.

I stand awkwardly with Mrs. Rothera. "I met your friend Alexander a little while ago. He's very handsome."

I'm not sure if she's telling me this to make conversation or if there is another reason. I've realized I've become extremely paranoid over everything she says.

"Yes," I agree. "Well, I suppose I need to get changed before Angie has a meltdown. Um, good luck tonight," I say. I don't know if that's the appropriate thing to say to a psychic. It's kind of like telling her not to screw up anyone's idea of his or her future. I walk inside and pick up my costume from the bench I dropped it on and head to the guest room to change. Alexander's office just happens to be on the way, and sure enough, he's sitting at his desk with his hair slicked back, wearing a black leather jacket. I should have known he would dress as a T-Bird. I sigh. I should have gone with Angie's first suggestion and worn a Pink Ladies costume.

"Nice costume," I say playfully. He looks up from his laptop and smiles. "Hi. And thank you." He pauses, eyeing me curiously. "And where is your costume? I thought Halloween was your day."

I hold up the garment bag. "It's in here and it's absolutely horrible. I look like a nun, and the headpiece is so tight around my face I feel like it cuts off my circulation."

He laughs. "I'm sure you look very cute."

I roll my eyes. "Don't hold your breath."

He stands up and walks around to the front of his desk to where I'm standing. He puts his arms around my waist and pulls me close to him. I admit I'm taken aback a little. I can smell the leather of his jacket.

"I think you're gorgeous," he says softly. "And I'm sure you look great even in a horrible nun costume."

He pulls me even closer and clasps his hands together behind my back.

"Well, it's actually the Evil Queen from *Snow White*," I whisper.

He doesn't say another word as he leans in and kisses me. This kiss is more intense than last week when we were sitting on the stairs. In between kisses, I drag my lips away from his. "The party will be starting soon."

"Mmmhmm," he mumbles.

I pull away again. "You have to promise me you won't avoid me like the plague when you see me in my costume."

He laughs. "I promise."

I sigh. "Okay, here I go. I'll see you out there," I say, giving him one more kiss. I pick up my costume from where I dropped it.

"Can't wait," he exclaims.

As soon as I turn the corner out of his office (and out of his sight), I jump up and down excitedly. If the last few minutes are any indication of what Mrs. Rothera was thinking would happen, then it's going to be an awesome evening.

Chapter Nine

"It doesn't look *that* bad," Gina says. She has to be the worst liar on the planet. And it's easy for her to say being that she's dressed in lingerie. She says she's dressed as a sexy cat but really it's just lingerie and a pair of cat ears.

"Thanks, but you're lying," I reply, taking a long sip of my wine. I'm going to need a lot of wine tonight to hide my embarrassment. I've been looking around for Alexander but I haven't been able to talk to him since our little make out session in his office.

The party is a huge success so far, and there is a line outside Mrs. Rothera's tent. I guess I'm the only one who's a chicken when it comes to knowing what my future holds.

"Where is he?" Gina asks, looking around. I know she's referring to Alexander.

"He's around here somewhere. I just, um . . . saw him in his office." I can feel myself blushing. Of course it could be that it's about one hundred degrees under this costume. "He may be hiding from me after having seen me in this."

All of a sudden I notice Angie rushing toward us, and she looks worried.

"What's wrong?" I ask.

She fans herself with her hands. "So, do you remember when we went to lunch with Alexander and we ran into Jake?"

My heart sinks. "Yeah."

She cringes. "And do you remember when Alexander invited Jake to come tonight?"

"Yeah. Don't tell me . . ."

She nods. "Yep, Jake's here. He actually showed his face here. I was so shocked to see him that I didn't even say anything. I just came to find you."

"Are you serious?" Gina chimes in. "I told you I should have made that call."

I can't even think straight. "She was right," I say.

Gina and Angie look confused. "Mrs. Rothera. She told me tonight was going to be eventful. Now my ex-boyfriend and my . . . um, and Alexander are both here."

Just then, Jake walks into the kitchen and looks right at me. He's actually wearing a costume; he never wanted to dress up while we were together. I'm not going to lie—my heart rate speeds up when I see him. I know I shouldn't be surprised. I was in love with Jake and those feelings don't just go away overnight, even after he explained why he broke up with me.

"Who do you think you are showing up here?" Gina shouts across the room. The other guests who are milling around turn to look at her.

"Gina, stop," Angie demands.

Jake calmly walks toward us. "Not that it's any of your business, Gina, but I was invited." I'm completely silent.

"Yeah, well, Alexander didn't know who you were when he invited you," Angie says, raising her voice.

"Okay, guys, I will handle this," I interrupt before a brawl breaks out and before Gina makes a phone call. "Jake, let's go outside and talk," I say, walking toward the front door. He follows me outside.

"Look, Summer, I know this might have been a mistake, but I needed to see you," he pleads. I stand with my arms tightly folded over my chest. Again, I'm wishing I wasn't wearing this stupid costume.

"I wish you wouldn't have come," I say softly. "I met someone else Jake and I really like him."

His face falls. "So, you're saying you don't have any feelings for me anymore?"

I bite my bottom lip. What am I supposed to say? Of course I have feelings for you but you broke my heart.

"I don't know," I say calmly. "But, I do know that I like spending time with Alexander."

He nods. "Okay, I understand but just think about it, okay? I know I messed up but I'm not ready to give us up yet." He leans over and kisses me gently on the cheek. I close my eyes as the familiar scent of his cologne floods back and so do the memories.

"You were very ready to give us up this summer," I snap.

He hangs his head. "I explained that to you already."

I look away. "Just go, Jake."

He doesn't argue, and without another word, he walks away leaving me standing in the middle of Alexander's pristine manicured lawn. I touch the tips of my fingers to my cheek where he kissed me. I want to cry because I'm so confused. I meant what I said about Alexander, I really like him—a lot. I guess this proves that I should have gone with my gut and never gotten involved with him. I don't know if I'm ready yet.

Suddenly, a light bulb goes on in my head and I know what I need to do. I head back into the house and make my way toward Mrs. Rothera's tent. As I walk through the living room, Melanie jumps in front of me. She's dressed as Wonder Woman. "Having fun, Summer? Nice costume by the way." She gives me a wicked smile.

I groan. "Thanks. And, yes, I'm having a good time, but if you'll excuse me, I have to do something."

She ignores me. "It's a great party, kudos to your friend Angie. Too bad you've been too preoccupied to enjoy it."

I feel sick to my stomach. "I don't know what you're talking about."

She cocks her head to the side. "Oh, sure you do." Crap! She must have seen me talking to Jake. Was she watching me the entire time?

"I don't have to explain anything to you because it's none of your business," I say as I start to walk away. She grabs my elbow. I look down at her hand and yank my elbow away from her grasp.

"That's where you're wrong. It is my job to look out for Alexander's best interest, and it's very clear that you're playing him."

We're standing in the middle of the room ready to face off when I notice Alexander and Angie watching us. My eyes meet Alexander's and I can tell he's not happy. I decide to be the better person and not respond to Melanie's accusation. Angie quickly walks toward us and asks to speak to me in private.

"What has gotten in to you tonight?" she demands. "First you disappear with Jake and now you're arguing with Alexander's assistant. Did Jake leave or do I need to have him escorted out?"

I don't want to explain anything to Angie. I want to talk to Mrs. Rothera and try to figure out what's going on in my head.

"He's gone," I say softly.

She gets a big smile on her face. "Good for you. I was hoping you would tell him to get lost. I still can't believe he showed up."

I look down and remember I'm still in this horrible costume. Maybe I should just change, because I'm not enjoying this party at all.

"Ang, I need to take care of something," I say, ignoring her comments about Jake.

Thankfully she doesn't question me. I rush out to Mrs. Rothera's tent, and she emerges from her tent as soon as I approach.

"I'm ready to talk," I say boldly. She nods and holds the side of the tent open. It almost seems as if she knew I was coming. When I sit down on the stool inside, I look around. I notice a few books and crystals on the table. She sits down across from me.

"I just wanted to say I'm sorry," I say immediately. "I shouldn't have been so cold toward you. I was just surprised about all of this," I say, waving my arms.

She shrugs. "I know. It can be overwhelming, and I was pressuring you to get a reading because I wanted to help you. After you returned from your vacation, I could feel the pain you were going through. Your aura is strong and you usually give off a very positive vibe. But when you came home, you were dark and distant . . . that is until you became involved with this man." She points toward the house. I know she's talking about Alexander.

She closes her eyes and takes a few deep breaths before she starts talking. "You're confused and you want to know if you should give Jake another chance. You still have feelings for him."

I let out a frustrated sigh. "Yep."

"You shouldn't feel guilty about this," she says as she reaches over and takes my hands in hers.

I do feel guilty—guilty and confused.

"Yes, I still have feelings for Jake, but I'm also very drawn to Alexander," I whine. She leans in and looks me directly in my eyes. Of course it feels like she's looking through me again.

"There was a reason that you were meant to come here," she says firmly. "Both you and Alexander were searching for something. He was searching for a fresh start and you were searching for a distraction."

I think about the timing of everything. I received the message from Melanie right after Jake ended things. Were Alexander and I meant to find each other at just the right time? Then I remember what she told me the last time we talked about him.

"The last time we talked about this you mentioned there was another woman involved. Is that something I should be concerned about?"

I remember what Alexander told me about seeing his ex-wife, a.k.a. the hot Swedish model. Every time I think about her I cringe. I can only imagine what her Halloween costume looks like.

"There is another woman, but the connection you and Alexander have is strong, almost magical," she says firmly. "You should go talk to him now."

All of a sudden it hits that I haven't seen him all night other than in his office. After my altercation with Melanie, I rushed out to see Mrs. Rothera. He looked very upset and I ran off.

"Melanie!" I scream. "It's her; she's the other woman."

I jump up from the stool and rush out of the tent, running into a line of people waiting for their own time with the Halloween psychic. I tear through the house, passing Gina who's doing shots. *Seriously? Are we at a frat party?*

I rush from room to room searching for Alexander. I don't see him, so I make my way to his office. The door is closed but I barge in. Sure enough, he's standing at the window looking out over the lawn. He looks at me and then turns back toward the window. It's obvious that I'm too late. Melanie already got to him.

"Alexander. I'm so sorry," I apologize.

He turns around and walks toward me.

"Summer, you don't have anything to apologize for. I'm happy for you."

What? I open my mouth to say something, but he continues talking. "I should have never pursued you, especially after you told me about your recent breakup. I tried to keep my distance as much as possible. I even stayed in the city when I knew you would be here because I knew if I were here I would want to spend time with you and get to know you better. Honestly, I didn't intend to have you decorate my whole house until . . . well, until I met you. I was drawn to you."

My mouth is hanging open as I listen to him unload is feelings. "I guess I only have myself to blame. I did invite your ex-boyfriend to come tonight."

Something comes over me and I'm not sure what it is. Maybe it's the memory of when Jake left me at the beach or maybe it's the feeling I have when I'm here. I think about the many days I didn't want to go home to my lonely apartment that's full of memories of the past.

"Jake and I are not back together," I blurt out. He looks confused, so I explain. "I'm not going to lie and tell you that I don't still care about him, it's probably too soon for that. But, I really like being here and being with you. I want to get to know you better, if that's something you still want."

He sits down on one of the chaise lounges, so I do the same.

"I'm confused. Melanie said you were outside with Jake and things were . . . intense. And then I saw you and her arguing before you ran off."

I look down at the ground. "I know—I've wanted to talk to you about Melanie but we haven't had much of a chance to be alone, and when we are together, we . . ."

The corner of his mouth curls up. I'm sure he's thinking the same thing as me.

"Melanie hates me, and she doesn't want me anywhere near you," I tell him. "She's counting down the days for this job to be finished. I know how important she is to you so I would never ask you to choose."

He sighs. "She's very protective of me. I know there may be deeper feelings there, but I've told her there would never be anything more between her and me."

Alexander and I sit quietly. I look down at my hideous costume and remember that I'm supposed to be enjoying a Halloween party right now. This entire night has been a nightmare, and I'm sure Angie is really mad at me.

"I should check in with Angie. I will let you think," I say, breaking our silence. I stand up and make my way toward the door.

"Wait," he exclaims. I turn around and Alexander walks toward me. He takes my face in his hands and kisses me. I wrap my arms tightly around his neck, and his hands move from my face to around my waist.

When he stops kissing me, he touches his forehead to mine. "The first day we met, right here in this office, I knew you were meant to come into my life. The time I spend with you is ... it's like magic." *Wow. That's what Mrs. Rothera just said.*

"I want to see where this can go, more than anything, but I don't want to rush you. We could continue to take things slow," he continues.

I run my hands down his arms. "I would really like that."

He smiles. "There is one thing, though—tonight doesn't count as our first date."

I laugh. "Please no. It has been very eventful, though, but I guess it wouldn't be Halloween without some craziness."

I know I still need to address the issue of Melanie and her hatred of me.

"What about Melanie?" I ask. "I really made the effort to get along with her in the beginning. I finally just gave up."

He scratches his head. "I will sit down and have a talk with her. She's my assistant, and she does an excellent job. However, she needs to stay out of my personal life."

I feel a sense of relief come over me. Without saying a word,

Alexander takes my hand in his and leads me back to the party. Of course, Angie gives me a dirty look as soon as she sees me. However, her dirty look fades when she notices Alexander's hand tightly holding on to mine. She raises her eyebrows but tries to hide her curiosity. Hopefully she will recognize my happiness and forgive me for ditching her on our holiday.

Chapter Ten

What a night. Surprisingly, I enjoy the remainder of the party despite all the chaos that ensued earlier. I spend a good ten minutes talking to Gina, trying to convince her *not* to make any phone calls to her family members. She can't seem to get over Jake showing up. Of course I'd rather not talk about Jake because I've made my decision and I know I'm ready to move on with my life.

Angie finally breaks her silent treatment to me after I practically have to get on my hands and knees asking for forgiveness. According to her, I broke the cardinal rule of our holiday, which is paying more attention to a man than us celebrating together. She also made me take a bunch of pictures in our costumes. I'm planning on blocking all those photos from all of my social media sites.

Alexander happily introduced me to all of his friends. I even meet a few people who are interested in a new interior decorator. I never thought about it but having this party at his house is a great way to show my talents. I guess I owe Angie a big thank you for harassing me with all those calls that day I was here with Alexander. I wish I had a picture of Melanie's face when she saw Alexander and me hand in hand. At least she knows that her big plan backfired.

While Alexander is talking, I glance out toward Mrs. Rothera's tent and, sure enough, she's watching me intently. I excuse myself and make my way over to her.

She gives me a wave and a smug look. "Hi, looks like you're enjoying yourself."

She's acting like she's surprised but I know she isn't. "Now I am." I pause. "It's been quite an eventful night, just like you said it would be."

She gives me an innocent smile.

"Anyway, I just wanted to thank you for being so kind to me over the past few weeks, for constantly checking in on me, and for bringing me that yummy soup. It was much better than a Lean Cuisine meal. I really appreciate your friendship."

She laughs. "I'm glad I could help." She points to where Alexander is still standing. "I take it everything is working out."

I shrug my shoulders. "We're taking things slow. He knows I'm still getting over a broken heart."

She pats me on the shoulder. "Good."

A part of me wants to ask her what's going to happen with Alexander and me. But when I look over at him, I feel an overwhelming sense of excitement. Maybe it's better that I don't know what's going to happen. I look back at Mrs.

Rothera and suddenly she has a very concerned look on her face.

"What is it?" I ask worriedly.

She scrunches her face. "I just . . . if I can offer you one more piece of advice."

I nod quickly. "Of course."

"Be honest with him and *demand* the same in return."

I stare at her blankly. "Okay."

Alexander joins us, and she gives him a warm smile. "Are you ready for your turn?" she asks him.

He starts laughing. "No. I think I'm good." He takes my hand in his. "I don't need to know what my future holds. I'm very content with where I am right now."

I can feel my face get red again. This time I know it's not the costume.

The party rages on until the wee hours of the morning. Okay, so maybe it doesn't rage on, but it does go really late and everyone seems to be having an awesome time.

"Another Halloween under our belts," Angie says in between her yawns. "I guess tonight turned out okay after all. It certainly looks like it did for you anyway."

I hit her on her arm. "It was a great night. Your party was a huge success."

She raises her eyebrows. "Are you going to give me details of your night or do I need to ask Alexander?"

I giggle. "The only details you need to know are that Alexander and I are taking things slowly and that for the first time in a while I'm really happy."

She gives me a hug. "I'm happy for you." When she pulls away, she grabs my arms tightly. "Does that mean Jake is finally out of the picture?"

I nod. "Yeah. I'm ready to move on."

Angie starts clapping. "So, since this party was such a smashing success, let's talk about Christmas."

I hold my hands up. "Uh-uh, you're on your own for that one. I'll help you with decorations but that's it."

She giggles. "I was hoping you would say that. I'm sure I will be in need of some of your decorating magic."

Surprisingly, I don't cringe when she says that. Moving on from the past also means accepting it.

"That's a deal," I say happily.

When I arrive home, I look around my apartment. For some reason it doesn't seem as lonely as it did before. I think I've come a long way in a short amount of time. The only thing that has me curious is Mrs. Rothera's advice, but like I told her, I don't need to know what my future holds. For now, I'm going to enjoy my life and take things as they come. I have high hopes for my relationship with Alexander as long as the issue with Melanie gets under control. After all of tonight's drama was over, I made some good business contacts thanks to Alexander. I already have three potential new clients and I'm ready to use my decorating magic to the fullest. I've decided I shouldn't try to shy away from that phrase or my past. If there is anything I've learned this fall, it's that everything happens for a reason and people come into our lives for a reason. I'm ready for the next season of my life and whatever it may bring.

THE END

Winter Can Wait

A Novella

Melissa Baldwin

About Winter Can Wait

Following a fabulous fall, Summer Peters is not looking forward to the frigid winter.

Much to her dismay, she knows this winter is a time for many changes in her life, including moving on from the heartache of the past.

Her professional life is flourishing, especially after her company is hired to decorate a trendy New York City restaurant. Summer sees this as a fantastic opportunity to build her clientele. However, she doesn't anticipate the few surprises she encounters along the way, some of which could threaten her future.

Although her relationship with superman-lookalike Alexander Williams seems almost perfect, she finds it more and more difficult to compete for his time with his possessive personal assistant. To make matters worse, she doesn't expect the return of Helena, his supermodel ex-wife who many say is his soul mate.

On the big opening night of the restaurant, she's faced with making yet another difficult decision. She knows it's time to take her life in the right direction; although in order to do this, she may need to let go again.

Continue to follow Summer on her wild one-year journey in this second book of the Seasons of Summer Novella Series. Stay tuned for two more installments coming 2017.

This is a work of fiction. Names, characters, places, and incidents either are the product of the author's imagination or are used fictitiously, and any resemblance to actual persons, living or dead, business establishments, events, or locales is entirely coincidental.

Copyright © 2017 Melissa Baldwin

All rights reserved.

ISBN: 0692831495
ISBN 13: 978-0692831496

Formatted by Karan & Co. Author Solutions

I dedicate this book to my dad who rescued me on that awful Valentine's Day many years ago. I love and miss you!

Chapter One

As much as I love Connecticut, I despise the cold. Wasn't it just summertime yesterday? I wrap the large fleece blanket even more tightly around me while I look over the contract for my next project. Summer Interiors has been flourishing, thanks to my amazing boyfriend, Alexander. One of my latest projects is his friend Nick's new restaurant. I've never decorated a restaurant before and I'm really excited about it. It's coming along quite nicely, and we're on schedule for a Valentine's Day opening. I would think there would be no better night for a grand opening of a restaurant.

Nick is an interesting guy—very outspoken and charismatic—and this weekend we're having dinner with him and his girlfriend, Caroline. I'm looking forward to getting to know Alexander's friends better. I haven't had much interaction with them other than at the crazy Halloween party at Alexander's home. And let's just say that wasn't the ideal setting to make new friends.

Another job I'm working on is my landlord's apartment. This

definitely isn't as fun as the restaurant. Mrs. Rothera and I have an interesting, err . . . friendship. I guess you could say we're friends. Anyway, a few weeks ago she asked if I would be interested in helping her decorate her place. I reluctantly agreed, and I should have gone with my gut feeling. It turns out she's one of the most high maintenance clients I've ever worked with. Our building consists of four large apartments, and her place is directly below mine, so it's the exact same layout. It's a nice size, so that's not the issue—the issue is the way she questions every suggestion and move I make. Being a psychic, I think she views the world a little differently. Yep—a psychic. I lived here a year and never had any idea until she sprung this little detail on me a few months ago.

I gather my notes and some paint swatches and head downstairs to show her. When I approach her door, I hear strange music coming from her apartment. I press my ear to the door to get a better listen. All I can hear is the sound of tambourines and chanting. I roll my eyes—here we go.

I knock loudly on the door, and surprisingly, she answers right away. I wasn't sure she would be able to hear over that noise, but on the other hand, she probably could see me coming. She is a psychic after all.

"Come in. I was just finishing my meditation," she says softly.

I walk into the dark room. She has the blinds and curtains closed. Thankfully, she turns off the music and opens the curtains. The sunlight pours into the room—much better.

"I just wanted to drop off these swatches, and I made some notes for you to take a look at," I say as I lay everything out on the table.

"Ohhh. Very nice," she says excitedly. She takes her time looking through everything. In the meantime, I get a text from Alexander, which makes me smile to myself.

"A message from your sweetie?" she asks, giving me a curious look. "I'm assuming by the expression on your face that things are going well."

I blush. "Yes, they are. And I will finally have the opportunity to get to know his best friends a little better this weekend. It will be the first time we will hang out in a social situation. I've only met with Nick to discuss his restaurant."

Suddenly, her smile fades. "Well, don't be too disappointed after only one night with new people," she says vaguely.

What's that supposed to mean?

"Disappointed?" I repeat. "Why would I be disappointed? I'm looking forward to it."

She starts flipping through the paint swatches again. "It will just take some time."

I'm silent for a few seconds. "Mrs. Rothera, what exactly are you implying? Are you saying they're going to hate me or something?" I give a nervous laugh.

She puts the swatches down and folds her hands on the table. "Hate is such a strong word."

She always does this—she avoids the question and gives vague answers. What I'm getting from this is that Alexander's friends are not going to be receptive to me at first. And that's fine, because I can deal with that. It's not like they would come between us, right?

I need to make up an excuse to leave so she doesn't start giving me any more unsolicited advice.

"Okay—well, I'm going to leave these with you," I say, pointing to the samples I brought. "As soon as you make your decision, I will get everything ordered."

She nods. "I will look through them now." She pauses as she takes another peek through the stack. "Do you have any with purple? I'm thinking purple and gold would be nice, maybe a Moroccan theme? Lots of mosaics and we could hang lanterns everywhere."

I grit my teeth as I force a smile. *Here we go again.* Every other day she wants to use a different theme. The first style she wanted was Victorian, next she wanted Shabby Chic, and then those styles were too much so she decided on Minimalist. I guess that was too boring, so now she wants Moroccan.

"I'm not sure I have any of those colors in this batch. I can bring some next time I come."

She claps her hands together. "Wonderful. I promise this will be it. I have a feeling this will suit me best."

I smile. "It's no problem. I want you to be happy with what you choose."

I make some notes of her requests, and I can see that she's staring at me out of the corner of my eye. I have no doubt she's watching for my reaction or she's having some kind of vision. Probably both.

"I hope I didn't worry you by what I said about Alexander's friends," she says softly.

"No," I lie. She gives me a skeptical look.

"New relationships can be exciting but challenging in some aspects. Especially when blending two lives together with old friends and new friends."

I nod in agreement.

Of course I'm totally worried and nervous about spending time with Alexander's friends. I'm especially nervous because they used to be Alexander and Helena's friends. Helena is Alexander's ex-wife, she also happens to be a model from Sweden, and according to Alexander, she can be a lot to take. (Whatever that means.)

Their divorce was mutual and very amicable, so at least I won't have to deal with a crazy ex. And if Nick and Caroline had a good relationship with Helena, then I will for sure be known as the *new* girlfriend. You never know how that will be received.

Now that Mrs. Rothera has shared her latest piece of advice, I'm completely frazzled and I'm sure I will be thinking about it for the next two days. I definitely didn't sign up for having my own psychic. And now it appears that I do.

I've tried to tell her many times that I wasn't interested in any details of things to come, but she doesn't catch my drift. And what makes it even worse is that she's my landlord. Taking all of this into consideration, I think it may be time for me to find a new place to live.

∽

The more I think about it, I really hate the idea of moving

because it's so much work, even though it's probably the right thing to do. As much as I love my place, it's also a reminder of my past, and by past, I mean a past relationship.

My ex-boyfriend Jake and I were together for eighteen months until he freaked out while we were on vacation together. Shortly after that breakup, I was hired to decorate Alexander's home and we clicked right away. Jake tried to win me back, but I had already moved on (mostly).

My relationship with Alexander has been pretty great so far; of course, it's still new and exciting. We have had our share of things to overcome in a short amount of time, namely his overbearing assistant Melanie. I actually don't have any issue with her, but she certainly doesn't care for me, and to her credit, she doesn't try to fake it, which I can totally respect. She's worked with Alexander for a long time and I would never try to interfere with his business relationships. I'm pretty sure that Melanie did (or does) want their relationship to be more than just business, but that's just a feeling I have. Alexander insists she's just "overprotective" and cautious. He is sure it has nothing to do with romantic feelings on her part, but I disagree. For one thing, Alexander is quite a catch—he's very successful, incredibly good-looking (he could be identical twins with Clark Kent from *Superman*), and very attentive. What woman wouldn't want to find someone with these qualities? I'm actually surprised he wasn't scooped up between May, when his divorce was final, and when we met in September.

When I first met Melanie, I went out of my way to befriend her, but she wanted nothing to do with it so I no longer waste my time. I guess you could say that we are learning to coexist with one another, and some days are better than others.

When I arrive to meet my best friend, Angie, for lunch, I'm preoccupied with both the possibility of moving and my upcoming night out with Alexander's friends.

"What's wrong with you?" Angie yells as soon as she sees me. I pretend to cover my ears and she rolls her eyes.

She's not actually yelling at me, she just speaks so loudly that it sounds like she's yelling.

"Seriously, I don't talk that loud," she exclaims, making every effort to lower her voice.

I laugh. "Okay, did you forget how long we've known each other?"

She waves her hand. "Whatever. Now tell me what's bothering you. And don't ever go to Vegas with that poker face."

I tell her about my conversation with Mrs. Rothera.

She shakes her head. "You need to stop stressing about this. Why don't you just embrace her trying to help you?"

Her reaction doesn't surprise me. She actually hired Mrs. Rothera to do psychic readings at our Halloween party. She's all about knowing what's going to happen in her future.

I take a sip of my water. "It's not just that. I'm nervous about what she said because I know she's right. It doesn't take a psychic to know that it may be difficult getting to know Alexander's friends who also happen to be Helena's friends."

She makes a face. "Come on. I'm sure they know that the

divorce was a mutual decision. There's no reason for them not to like you. Maybe you won't be besties right off the bat, but I doubt they're going to hate you."

I give her a grateful smile. "I know I'm probably overreacting, and considering Nick already hired me as their decorator, I shouldn't be so concerned."

"Exactly," she exclaims. "On that note, how are things with my friend Alexander?"

She likes to take credit for Alexander and me getting together, which isn't exactly the case considering things were already heating up while I was decorating his house. However, it was her Halloween party that pushed us to take that step forward.

I can feel myself start to blush. "Things are good other than we haven't had much time together lately," I reply. "He's been working some long hours in the city, and I've been busy with my new clients. That's even more reason for things to go well this weekend."

She waves her hand at me. "Stop."

I decide to change the subject before Angie continues to yell at me for making a big deal out nothing.

"So, I'm thinking of looking for a new place to live."

She gives me a confused look. "Really? Why?"

I shrug my shoulders. "Mostly because Mrs. Rothera is constantly in my business, but besides that, it's probably time to move on. The whole place still reminds me of Jake. I made a decision months ago to move on from the past, and I think

I've done really well so far. Finding a new place to live will make that decision complete."

She gets a wicked grin on her face.

"What?" I ask. I know her well enough to know that the wheels are turning in her brain.

"I was thinking you could probably move into Alexander's house. There's plenty of space and you did decorate the entire house. You could make it more of a roommate situation."

I knew she had some crazy plan in her mind.

I shake my head. "No way. We've only been seeing each other a few months. I'm not going to kill our relationship by making that mistake so soon."

Angie has a familiar gleam in her eyes. "Don't even think about it," I demand.

She gives me an innocent look. "I have no idea what you're referring to."

I know she's already planning out some way to casually suggest something to Alexander about me staying at his house.

"You know exactly what I'm referring to, and if you do it, I will never forgive you." I fold my arms tightly to my chest trying to show her that I mean business.

She rolls her eyes. "That's a bit dramatic, don't you think? I'm sure Alexander would love having you stay with him. I've seen the kind of chemistry you two have . . ." she trails off. I have no doubt where her mind is.

Truthfully, it's not that I would mind living with Alexander. I fell in love with his house (read: *his house*) the first time I went over there. And of course I feel extremely comfortable there being that I know it like the back of my hand. However, I definitely know that neither of us is ready for this kind of commitment, at least the commitment of living together.

"Very funny," I say with a laugh. "What about you? Why haven't you moved in with Brett yet, since you seem to think living together is such a great idea?"

She throws her head back in laughter. "I said it was a good idea for you. I'm not the one looking for a new place to live."

I knew she would say that. Angie is always coming up with brilliant ideas and somehow I always get caught up in them.

Chapter Two

"They are going to love you," Gina says, smacking her gum. I'm spending most of my day in the office, which rarely happens. I share a small office space with my friend Gina. It's Friday and I'm getting more and more nervous as the time gets closer. You would think I was meeting Alexander's family for the first time.

"I don't understand why you are so worried. Didn't you already meet them?"

I nod my head quickly. "Yes, but very briefly. Nick and I were discussing his restaurant. I only said hello to Caroline. She's actually the one I'm more worried about. You know how women can be."

Gina gives me a look. "I certainly do," she says emphatically. "But, so what if they don't like you? It's not like Alexander is going to stop seeing you or anything."

I shrug. "I know. But they're his best friends. I just want to make a good impression."

Gina nods nonchalantly. She's obviously already lost interest in our conversation. Maybe I am making a bigger deal out of this than I need to. It wouldn't be the first time.

I start searching some new décor ideas for Mrs. Rothera's new Moroccan-themed apartment. I've been taking my time being that she will probably change her mind again anyway.

I actually stayed up late last night looking up places to live online. Alexander has been so busy this week with work, so he has no idea about my sudden plans to move. And I know for a fact that Angie hasn't said anything to him because I threatened her. Let's just say we all have secrets and I have a great memory. I know she thinks she's helping and it's the thought that counts, but I really don't want Alexander to think it was my idea that we should move in together.

"Hey, Gina?" I call, looking up from my laptop. She turns around to face me.

"Can you let me know if you hear about anyone selling or renting out places?"

She gives me a curious look. "Who needs a place to live?"

I smile innocently. "Me. I'm thinking of moving out of my apartment."

Her eyes grow wide. "Why? You've been in your place forever. It's the perfect setup and Mrs. Rothera seems like the perfect landlord."

Ugh. I wish my friends would stop making me question my decision.

"She's fine, but I just think it's the right time. And so many memories were with Jake that I feel like I need to start fresh."

She frowns. "Has he been coming around? Don't you dare let him try to worm his way back into your life again."

I shake my head. "Oh, he hasn't been around at all. I just feel like it's a good time. Starting a new year, so why not have a fresh start?"

Gina was not a fan of Jake at all. After he broke things off and started coming around again, she wanted to call her uncle to "scare" him. I don't know her uncle personally, but apparently, he's a powerful man who has ways of getting people to do what they're supposed to do.

My phone rings, startling me. I get excited as soon as I see that Alexander's calling.

"Hi, stranger," I answer.

He laughs. "I know. It sure does feel that way. How are you?"

"Good. Just working on Mrs. Rothera's apartment. She changed her mind again . . ." I trail off.

He starts to laugh. "Why does that not surprise me?"

"Anyway, I'm really looking forward to tomorrow night. Are we still planning on driving into the city?" I ask, changing the subject.

"That's the plan. How does Delmonico's sound to you?" he asks. "As you can imagine, Nick is pretty picky when it comes to restaurants."

"I'm fine with anything," I exclaim. "I can meet you at your house to save you a trip."

That's my way of keeping him away from Mrs. Rothera. I feel bad thinking like that, but she's always asking him tons of questions, and although he's always polite, I know it's frustrating. I also don't want her making any comments about how complicated new friendships can be.

"Sounds great. I have an afternoon meeting with a client, so in case I'm not home when you arrive, I'm sure Melanie will be."

I'm so glad we're on the phone and he can't see me roll my eyes. Melanie actually works from his home a lot. He splits his time working between Connecticut and the city but she usually stays here.

I've gotten used to the fact that she's there all the time, but should we ever become more serious, that's something that may have to change for the sake of my sanity.

"Okay," I hesitate. "By the way, I have some news. I think I'm going to find a new place to live."

He's quiet for a few seconds. "What happened?"

I give him a watered-down version of my reasons for moving. I don't say anything about Mrs. Rothera's comments about Nick and Caroline, but I do mention Jake and being ready to move on from my past.

"I totally get it. I'll get in touch with my realtor; he will be able to find you something. He did a great job with my house."

This is why I adore Alexander. He always has a solution and he didn't try to talk me out of it.

We hang up a few minutes later but not before he tells me how much he's missed me and he can't wait to see me tomorrow night. I may or may not have jumped up and down and danced around the room. Gina makes gagging noises from her desk.

This weekend is going to be great. I just can't let what Mrs. Rothera said stress me out.

∼

Right before heading home, I'm surprised to get an email from my former client Brad Cooper. I decorated his summer cottage in Cape Cod and I still think it's one of my best projects to date. Apparently, he's bought his son and daughter-in-law a home and he's in need of a decorator. This is excellent news for Summer Interiors, but there is one thing that makes this awkward for me on a personal level: Brad Cooper is Jake's boss. Of course, just because I do business with Mr. Cooper doesn't mean I have to have any interaction with Jake, however it is a little weird. I send Mr. Cooper a response letting him know that I'm very interested and request a meeting.

It's amazing what a difference a little time makes. When I first started Summer Interiors, I thought it would never survive, but within two years, I'm finally busy enough to call it a success (at least a success in my mind). Mr. Cooper was one of my first clients and I really do owe him for taking a chance on me. I guess I owe Jake, too; he was very supportive of my work.

And now, thanks to Alexander, I have practically tripled my

business. He says my work sold itself, but I'm sure the fact that I'm his girlfriend helped to "encourage" his friends to hire me. Thanks to him (or my work on his house), I have two official new clients, one being Nick's restaurant, the other being his friends Chantel and Levi's apartment in SoHo. Now, if only I could finish Mrs. Rothera's apartment so I can focus on these bigger projects. When I get home, I stop by her apartment to drop off the latest ideas I found with the Moroccan theme.

"Hi. What a nice surprise," she says when she opens the door.

"I just wanted to drop these off to you," I say, holding up a few catalogs and pictures.

"Hi, Summer," a voice calls from inside the apartment.

I recognize the voice right away; it's Melanie, Alexander's assistant. What the hell is Melanie doing here in my building? When I peek inside, I can see the lights are dimmed.

I give Mrs. Rothera a dumbfounded look. Obviously she can read my expression, or maybe she can read my mind? I really don't know how this whole thing works.

"Melanie is here for her reading," she says, obviously responding to my facial expression. "We met at the Halloween party."

Melanie comes to the door with a big smile on her face. Of course she has her best behavior on here. She rarely shows her bitch side when other people are around.

"Hey, Melanie," I say, trying my best to not show how I really feel. "I'm sorry to interrupt. I will leave you to your work. Let me know what you think of those ideas."

I turn to walk away when Mrs. Rothera stops me. "We haven't started yet. Would you like to come in?"

I put a big fake smile on my face. If I don't stay for a minute I'm sure Melanie will run back to Alexander and make it seem like I'm the bad guy.

"For a few minutes. I have a lot of work ahead of me tonight. Fun Friday night for me," I say, trying to make friendly conversation.

When I sit down, I can feel all eyes on me for some reason.

"Melanie was just telling me you're looking for a realtor," Mrs. Rothera says. I can tell that she's pretending to be nice but I'm sure she's upset.

I'm completely frozen. How the hell . . . oh, I know exactly what happened. Alexander probably had Melanie contact his realtor for me and she must have blabbed it to Mrs. Rothera. Crap. There's no way I can talk my way out of this one. I glance at Melanie who has an innocent smile on her face, but I know better. Underneath that sweet exterior is a master manipulator. I have no doubt her mind came up with a similar idea to Angie's, except she doesn't want me moving in to Alexander's.

"I am," I reply. "I've been toying with the idea of buying a house, but nothing is set in stone."

Okay, so maybe that was a tiny lie. While I would love to purchase my own house, I'm not sure if I'm ready for that yet. But, I can't just come out and tell her that I want to move out to distance myself from her.

"I was wondering why you were in need of a realtor," Melanie exclaims. "Alexander asked me to get in touch with him for you. I know he would love to help you find a place of *your* own if that's what you're looking for. Although, it seems like you have a great setup right here."

She's so transparent. She would probably have a meltdown if Alexander asked me to move in with him. I wonder if Mrs. Rothera can see through her act?

"I know, he's such a sweetheart," I reply with a big cheesy smile. "He offered to help me even though I told him it wasn't for sure just yet."

She nods. Mrs. Rothera hasn't said much, so I'm not sure what's going through her head.

"Anyway, I'll leave you to your meeting," I say, practically leaping off the chair. "Have a great night."

I hurry toward the door before either one of them says anything else. I know this conversation isn't over but I will leave it for now. If anything, I guess I should be grateful to Melanie for breaking the ice at the possibility. Even though she had ulterior motives, it will probably make it easier in the long run.

Chapter Three

*D*id I mention how much I love Alexander's house? It's exactly how I imagine my dream house would be. As soon as I pull into the circular driveway I get this strange feeling, almost as if I'm home. Ugh! Angie is getting in my head. This is crazy.

Sure enough when I arrive in the afternoon, Melanie is still there. Alexander arrives about two minutes after me, so Melanie and I pretend to be happily chatting even though we barely said a word to each other before he walked in the door. After he excuses himself to get ready, I decide to be the better person (again) and make conversation with her.

"How did your reading go last night?" I ask, taking off my coat. I rub my hands together, trying to get my hands warm. I figure I should try to sound as sincere as possible. Honestly, I really don't care but I am curious.

She gives me a skeptical look. "It went well. She's such a great lady."

I nod. "She sure is."

Melanie finally looks up from her laptop. "I could tell she was really disappointed at the possibility of you moving out without telling her."

I grit my teeth. This woman is so infuriating, "I had no intention of moving out without telling her. I just barely started thinking about it, which is why I haven't had a chance to discuss it with her yet."

Of course you had to open your big mouth, I think to myself. I take a deep breath. I refuse to let her get me all frazzled right before my evening with Alexander.

"Anyway, it really doesn't matter right now being that it's in the early stages."

She completely ignores me as she packs up her computer. I really want to ask her why she's here on a Saturday, but I already know the answer. She's a star employee, and in order to be that, she is 100% dedicated to her job and immersing herself completely into Alexander's life.

"Is everything okay here?"

We both turn to see Alexander standing in the doorway.

"Just fine," Melanie says cheerfully. "I'm done for the day. I have your calendar set for next week and all your travel arrangements are booked for next month."

Travel arrangements? Where's he going?

"Thanks," he says. "Have a great rest of your weekend."

As soon as she leaves Alexander gives me a skeptical look. "Are you going to tell me what that was about?"

I certainly am going to tell him. Hopefully he sees what an awful person she can be.

I purse my lips together. "Melanie told Mrs. Rothera that I was looking for a realtor and now she's upset with me."

He looks confused. "What? When did she do that?"

I let out a sigh. "She was at her apartment last night. I guess she's seeing her now for all her psychic needs," I say sarcastically. "When I stopped by to drop off some décor ideas, she asked me about it."

He rubs his face. "I'm so sorry. I asked her to get in touch with my realtor for you. I had no idea she would do something like that."

Of course he didn't. This just proves he doesn't know what she's capable of.

"Where are you traveling to?" I ask, thinking back to the travel arrangements Melanie mentioned. I admit it does bother me a little that she knows more about Alexander's life than I do.

He rolls his eyes. "Dallas, San Diego, San Francisco, and Vancouver. I just decided to do them all in one shot. Less back and forth for me."

I nod my head silently. He walks over to me and pulls me into his arms.

"How about we don't talk about work anymore? I just want to enjoy being with you tonight."

I smile. "That would make me very happy."

I promised myself I wouldn't let Melanie ruin my evening and I meant that.

~

I love Manhattan. I really don't take advantage of living so close but I really should. When we arrive at Delmonico's, Nick and Caroline are already there. Alexander gives them both a kiss on the cheek and turns to me.

"You both remember Summer. She's agreed to be my date again tonight," he says as he takes my coat from me.

"Of course," Nick says, leaning in to kiss me on the cheek and Caroline follows his lead.

"Your dress is to die for," she says as she holds up my arms. She gives me a warm smile.

Okay, so far so good. It's possible that even psychics can be wrong, right?

"Look at you two," Nick says, raising his eyebrows. "I can see things are moving along rather nicely."

Alexander starts laughing. "Shocking, isn't it? I'm expecting her to get sick of me and kick me to the curb any day now. She's a saint to put up with my crap."

I nod playfully. "That I am."

Of course I'm totally kidding. Alexander is a pretty amazing guy, and so far I haven't seen anything that would make me want to kick him to the curb (other than his choice in personal assistants). Granted, it took Jake eighteen months to turn out to be a complete ass, so who knows.

I lean in to kiss him on the cheek and he gives me a wink. After a bit more playful banter, Nick orders a bottle of champagne to celebrate.

"So, Summer, tell me all about you," Caroline asks, while Nick and Alexander chat with each other.

She seems extremely nice, almost too nice. I guess Mrs. Rothera got in my head. I'm not usually this negative.

"I'm afraid I'm incredibly boring," I say. "I grew up here in Connecticut. I started Summer Interiors about two years ago. No pets, never been married."

Crap! I wish I didn't mention the whole marriage thing.

She grins. "You're too modest. From what I hear, your company is doing very well. The restaurant looks amazing and Xander's house looks fantastic."

Xander? I didn't know he had a nickname.

"Well, thank you," I say sincerely. "I didn't know anyone called him Xander."

"No one calls me that," Alexander interrupts. He obviously overheard that part of our conversation.

Caroline shakes her head. "It was a nickname Helena gave him. He never really liked it."

And there it is. I was wondering if she was going to come up in conversation tonight.

"I hate it," he exclaims.

Nick and Caroline start to laugh.

"There's a great story behind it," Nick says, taking a sip of his drink. "The four of us were on vacation in Aruba and somehow the subject of nicknames came up. Alexander over here insisted that he never had a nickname, even in his childhood. At that point we decided he needed one, so Helena started calling him Xander. It started as a joke but it stuck after that."

I'm half listening to Nick's story because I'm too busy obsessing over the fact that they've all been on vacation together. I'm trying not to overreact, but it's becoming very clear just how close they all were (or are). I know that Alexander had a life before me, complete with a wife of four years.

"And you both promised to never call me that, remember?" he replies.

They both nod, trying to hide their smiles.

"That was one of the best trips we've ever been on," Caroline adds. "I love Aruba. Remember the casino? We always had the best time together."

I'm quickly feeling like the fifth wheel here, behind the three of them and their memories with Helena. Alexander must see my discomfort because he takes my hand and kisses it.

I give him a grateful smile.

"Have you been to Aruba?" Caroline asks me.

I shake my head. "Oh, I wish."

The conversation shifts to vacation destinations, which is fine with me. Anything is better than more trips down memory lane with the happy foursome. The rest of our dinner is uneventful. Before dessert, Caroline and I excuse ourselves to visit the restroom because . . . well, I'm not sure why but we do. I think it's the law or something.

I'm washing my hands while she reapplies her lipstick.

"Summer, I want to apologize for earlier," she says sincerely. "I hope I didn't make you uncomfortable by bringing up Helena."

I open my clutch to find my makeup.

"Not at all," I lie. "Honestly, I was worried how you were going to feel about me. You know as the 'new' girlfriend. I know you were very close with Helena and Alexander."

She has a very somber look on her face. "We still are, even if they aren't together. Helena is also seeing someone else. As difficult as this is for all of us, we want them both to be happy."

Okay, I'm not sure how to take that. Who is this difficult for? I take out my gloss and slowly apply it on my lips.

Caroline leans up against the counter and faces me. "Helena is my best friend. I tried to talk to her about making the marriage work, but they came to the mutual decision to end things. I think they will regret it someday. I've never in my life seen two people more connected than those two; their chemistry is so overwhelming that other people can feel it."

I stare straight ahead in the mirror. How am I supposed to respond to this?

"Please don't take any offense to this. I'm not trying to upset you," she pleads. "You're an absolute doll, but I truly believe Alexander and Helena are soul mates who will find their way back to one another. I promise this has nothing to do with you."

Mrs. Rothera was right again.

A few minutes later, we return to our table. I stay pretty quiet through dessert other than discussing the opening of the restaurant. Alexander keeps giving me looks and asking me if I'm okay. We go out for drinks after dinner where we finally have a few minutes alone.

"Are you going to tell me why you seem so distracted?" he asks, wrapping his arms around me. "I can tell so don't try to pretend."

I shrug my shoulders. "It's not a big deal."

He frowns.

"Okay, one more toast," Nick exclaims, interrupting us. He holds up his drink and we all follow his lead.

"Cheers to new friends and partnerships." He puts his arms around both Alexander and me, pulling us into him along with Caroline. We stand in a small huddle for a few seconds. When we separate, Alexander reaches for my hand again. I know he's trying to reassure me, but unfortunately, it's not working. There's no way I can compete with possible soul mates. It's my own fault for letting myself get in so deep this soon. I knew better.

Chapter Four

The ride back to Connecticut is quiet, at least for me. Alexander is chatting about anything and everything. He really is trying hard and I'm probably just being a pain in the ass. In my defense, the whole day has been a bit frustrating. It all started with Melanie telling me about his upcoming travel plans. Believe it or not, I'm definitely not an obnoxiously clingy and controlling girlfriend. I just can't help but feel like I come last, as in I'm the last to know about anything that's happening in his life.

Nick and Caroline were fine at dinner, but of course I keep thinking about what Caroline said to me on our little trip to the ladies' room. I don't blame her for wanting to see her best friends get back together. And just because she believes Alexander and Helena are soul mates doesn't mean they are.

"Babe?" Alexander calls, snapping me out of my daydream. He keeps shooting me worried glances.

"You ready to tell me what's bothering you?" he asks. I want to tell him because I believe that honesty is always best, but I also don't want to be the cause of a rift with his best friends.

"I don't know if I should." I hesitate. He reaches over and puts his hand on my leg. "Please tell me. I hate seeing you worry; whatever it is, we will get through it."

I let out a loud sigh. "When Caroline and I were in the bathroom we were talking..."

"Did she do something to upset you?" he interrupts.

I put my hand on his hand. "No... I mean, not exactly. She was very nice, both of them were. I just know that you and Helena have a very strong bond with them. From the way it sounds, the four of you were pretty inseparable."

He shakes his head. "I'm sorry. I don't really have anything to say except yes, we have a history with each other, but I promise you that's in the past. Helena is in a new relationship and I'm with you. We have wished each other well and are both moving on with our lives."

We pull into the driveway and Alexander turns toward me.

"Caroline told me that Helena was seeing someone," I say, looking straight ahead. "She also said that she believed you two were soul mates and that no two people have ever had a more powerful connection. She believes that someday you will find your way back to each other."

I turn my whole body to look at him. "And if that's what is meant to be, I would never stand in your way. I would want you to do whatever is going to make you happy."

He turns off the car but doesn't say anything. I don't know how to take his silence.

"I should probably head home," I say as I open the door and get out of the car into the cold air. Ugh. I really hate the cold.

As I fumble inside my bag for my keys, Alexander joins me and pulls me toward him. "Will you come inside with me?" he whispers. "Just for a few minutes so we can talk."

He engulfs me in his arms and I immediately forget about leaving. "Okay."

∼

Alexander sure is making it really difficult for me to want to go home. Especially giving me a cozy velour blanket and a cup of peppermint hot chocolate. If he turns on *Grease 2*, I may never leave. (That's our favorite movie.)

"I promise I'm not trying to overcompensate here." He pauses. "I know you don't like the cold. And selfishly, I don't want you to leave yet."

I give him a grateful smile. "I appreciate all of this but you don't have to." He's always very attentive so this is not unusual behavior.

When he sits down next to me on the couch, I push my cold feet under his leg.

"I want to give you a little background so you can understand where Caroline is coming from," he says as he puts one leg under the other. "She was in our wedding, and we did take most of our vacations with Nick and her even before we were married. She made every effort to try to keep Helena and me together, but honestly, it was over. We had such a whirlwind, intense courtship but eventually that wears off. Even though Helena and I were ready to move on, I suppose our friends weren't."

I'd rather not hear about how intense they were in the beginning of their courtship again. When Alexander first told me about Helena, that's all he kept referring to. It's kind of hard to try to live up to a relationship that's described in that manner.

He leans in and puts his forehead to mine. "I need you to believe that I want to be with you and only you."

I chew on my lower lip. "Mrs. Rothera predicted it would be a rough night. She told me not to be disappointed if tonight didn't go well. I asked her if they were going to hate me."

He leans his head back on the couch. "They definitely didn't hate you. You need to stop listening to everything she says because it really stresses you out." He pauses. "It may be a good idea that you're moving after all."

As soon as he mentions the move, I think about Melanie. He must read my mind. "And about Melanie, I'm going to have a talk with her about her conversation with Mrs. Rothera. She should not have disclosed that information."

Yes! Finally.

"Things aren't better with her. I'm really trying, though," I tell him.

He nods slowly. "I know you are, that's why I plan to talk to her again."

I snort. "You know she really loves to get under my skin. She couldn't wait to brag that she knew all about your travel plans and I didn't."

He frowns.

"Ugh. I'm sorry," I say, putting my face in my hands. "I sound like an annoying, jealous girlfriend."

He rubs my back. "No, you don't. I should have told you about my trip. Honestly, I just didn't think about it because when I'm with you I don't want to talk about work."

I smile. "Me neither."

I crawl into his lap and start to kiss his neck. I'm not going to waste any more of our evening worrying about other people. I need to put them out of my mind and enjoy our time together.

When I pull away, he clasps his hands around my waist. "Want to come with me?"

I raise my eyebrows. "On your business trip?"

He smiles. "Yeah. Have you ever been to any of those cities?"

Oh my gosh! He's just asked me to join him on a trip. I'm trying to hide my excitement. I can only imagine what Melanie would think of this, and if I was to accept, her head may explode.

"I would love to, but I don't think I can leave with so many projects coming up."

He gives me a thoughtful look. "How about joining me on the weekend?"

As much as I would love to travel with him, it's not necessary. Just the fact that he asked me makes me happy.

I take his face in my hands. "I don't want to interrupt your work trip, but I love that you invited me."

He runs his hands up and down my arms. "I just want you to know how important you are to me. I know it doesn't always seem that way."

I shake my head. "That's not true. I'm sorry for overreacting. I just know how important Nick and Caroline are to you also."

He runs his fingers through my hair. "Yes, we've been friends for a long time. But, both Helena and I made the choice to end our marriage. We've both moved on with our lives and our friends need to accept that."

Chapter Five

Why do Mondays have to be so hard? My weekend turned out to be pretty good after all. Alexander assured me not to worry about what Caroline said and that she would come around eventually. So, of course I'm not completely surprised when I receive an email from Caroline inviting me to lunch. I'm sure her sudden invitation is only because Alexander said something to her, but I send her a response accepting the invitation anyway. I'm not sure I want to go but I know I need to make every effort to build a relationship with Alexander's best friends.

I'm drinking a cup of coffee, reading emails when Angie randomly shows up to my apartment like she does at least once a week. I immediately show her the invitation from Caroline.

"You really want to hang out with her after what she said to you?" Angie yells as she's scrolling through her phone. "She made her agenda very clear when she told you she wants

Alexander to get back with his wife. She might be up to something."

I cringe. I probably shouldn't have said anything to her because I knew she would make a big deal out of it, but I needed to tell someone.

"I want to have a relationship with Alexander's friends. Caroline wasn't intentionally being mean; she was just explaining her feelings. Maybe she's trying to make up for it with this. And for Alexander's sake I need to meet her halfway, even if she has another agenda."

Angie rolls her eyes. "I guess. Just remember what Mrs. Rothera said about this situation needing time. It seems like this Caroline girl got over things awfully quick."

I'm not surprised by Angie's warnings. She's all about Mrs. Rothera and the advice she gives.

"I'm not sure she *is* over it. Like I said, I think she only sent this because Alexander asked her to make me feel comfortable. I think this is a bit overboard, but at least she's making an effort."

Angie gets a wicked smile on her face. "Well, then maybe I should join you?"

I give her a confused look. "Join me where? You mean at lunch?"

She shrugs her shoulders. "Yeah, why not? She's one of Alexander's best friends and I'm your best friend. I think it's a great idea." She leans back in her chair proudly. You would think she just came up with the cleverest plan ever.

"Maybe next time," I reply. "I mean . . . if there is a next time."

The truth is, I would love Angie to come with us because she always knows exactly what to say. However, this is the time I need to get to know Caroline and give her a chance to get to know me without any distractions, and Angie is a definite distraction.

"I appreciate it, Ang, but I think I got this," I say finally.

Thankfully, she doesn't argue.

"What are you doing today?" she asks, taking a sip of her coffee. "How about we go house hunting. Unless, you're secretly hoping that Alexander will ask you to move in? I'm betting he will before too long."

I roll my eyes. Here we go again.

"Seriously, what do you think I'm doing? It's Monday morning and I have a business to run." I pause. "And no, I'm not secretly hoping Alexander asks me to move in with him."

She waves her hand at me. "First of all, the beauty of having your own business is that you can make your own schedule. Just look at me."

I start to laugh. I guess you could call Angie an entrepreneur of sorts. She's been involved in many different ventures including Friendship Travel, an online travel planning company we started together.

Come to think of it, I don't know when she actually works or *if* she does.

"What's so funny?" she asks defensively.

I try to hide my smile. "Nothing. Don't get defensive. I really wish I could house hunt today, but I really can't. Let's plan it for another day."

After what seems like forever, I finally convince Angie to leave so I can get to work. I send Alexander a text letting him know about my lunch plans with Caroline. Hopefully he appreciates me taking one for the team here, because that's exactly what it is. I'm convinced Caroline has no interest in having lunch with me, and other than me making an effort for Alexander, I'm not too thrilled with it either.

∽

My conversation with Brad Cooper, aka Jake's boss, goes really well. Thankfully, Jake doesn't come up in our conversation and I'm praying it stays that way throughout the project. I set up a meeting to tour his son's new home and (hopefully) sign a contract.

I keep reminding myself that I built a professional relationship with Mr. Cooper that was separate from Jake, but should he ever come up, I will be honest and let him know that Jake left me in tears on a beach in the Hamptons. I'm kidding, if he asks I will do the politically correct thing and site irreconcilable differences.

Anyway, the day has finally come. Today is my lunch with Caroline. Last night she sent me a very nice message letting me know she was looking forward to it, to which I responded the same.

The fact that I'm decorating Nick's restaurant is the perfect icebreaker for our lunch. I admit I've been spending a lot of time reviewing the plans just in case we run out of things to talk about. I'd rather talk about the restaurant than have to hear about all the amazing trips, life experiences, and unforgettable moments the fabulous foursome (Caroline, Nick, Alexander, and Helena) have shared. I'm usually not a jealous person, but it sure does feel like I have a lot to measure up to.

I take my time getting ready, carefully selecting my outfit and accessories. I finally decide on a navy shift dress, which looks terrific against my auburn hair, and tan suede over-the-knee boots. I will probably freeze but sometimes we have to make sacrifices. It's not that I'm trying to *impress* her, but I want to make it clear that I'm confident in myself and in my relationship with Alexander. No matter what, I'm not going to let the past interfere with our future.

We made plans to meet at the restaurant since I have to be there for a delivery anyway. I'm sure Caroline has selected a perfectly pretentious location for us to dine at. Ugh. I don't know why I'm being so negative. I'm trying not to take everything she said so personal.

I arrive just in time for my delivery, and I'm busy looking through boxes, making sure everything is accounted for when I hear a voice.

"Hello."

When I look up from the box I'm buried in, I see a stunning tall blonde woman standing next to me. When I stand up, she's still towering over me. I glance down to see she's wearing three-inch-heel boots. However, even without the boots, she would still have several inches on me.

"I'm looking for Caroline," the tall woman says. She has a strong accent, it almost sounds like . . .

"I'm here, I'm here," Caroline calls, she practically jumps down the four steps that lead into the restaurant.

She rushes over to the tall woman and they give each other air kisses on both cheeks. She turns to me and gives me the same air kisses on both cheeks.

"Summer, I'm so happy you could join us today," she says excitedly.

Us? Who is she referring to?

I give her a confused look, and she smacks her forehead with her palm.

"Please forgive me for my rudeness. Summer, this is Helena; Helena, this is Summer."

I feel like I've suddenly been thrown into an alternate universe. I figured at some point my path would cross with Helena considering she and Alexander still have the same friends. However, I didn't expect a complete blindside on a lunch date.

"Summer! We finally meet," Helena exclaims, pulling me into a tight embrace. I stand with my arms tightly at my sides, not knowing what to do next. When she finally pulls away after what seems like hours, she grabs my hands.

"I was just telling Xander that we must meet. It has taken far too long."

I have to say something. What was I just thinking . . . something about taking one for the team?

"Well . . . it's great to finally meet you, too," I reply awkwardly.

I study Helena and she's as stunning in person as she is in pictures. (I may or may not have looked her up on one or two occasions.) Her eyes are such an impressive shade of blue that I don't think I've ever seen that color. And her teeth are so perfectly white; they might as well be glowing under a black light.

"Shall we head out, ladies?" Caroline asks, breaking up our long-awaited introduction. "This is going to be so much fun."

～

I walk along the Manhattan street in a complete daze that I barely notice the cold wind hitting my face. Caroline and Helena are a few steps ahead of me, chatting a mile a minute, and I'm still trying to figure out what just happened. It's becoming clear that Caroline planned it this way for whatever reason. She wanted me to join her and Helena today and I'm not quite sure why. Thinking back to our conversation from the night we met and her feelings about Alexander and Helena reuniting, what would she hope to accomplish today?

When we reach the café, I absently sit down in the chair between the two of them.

"Summer, I've heard very good things about your work," Helena says with a huge smile. "I'm so happy that Caroline set up this meeting because I'm desperately in need of a decorator, and they say you're the best."

Is this really happening? Is she saying she wants to hire me? I stare at her in disbelief, trying to come up with something to say. She must notice my discomfort.

"Now I know you may be concerned because I was married to Xander. But I assure you there is nothing to worry about. I'm quite happy in a new relationship and Xander is happy with you."

I glance at Caroline who's busy on her phone. I don't know if she's purposely ignoring this conversation or not. Although, it is somewhat reassuring hearing Helena say the same thing that Alexander has been saying all along.

"I appreciate that Helena," I say sincerely. "I know that you and Alexander have been able to remain *friends* and I think that's great." I give Caroline a side-glance.

Helena flashes me a gorgeous smile. I can't get over how stunning she is, and I feel completely inadequate sitting next to her.

"Yes. We will always have an amazing connection, nothing will ever change that," she says emphatically.

I nod in agreement even though inside I want to die. "So what are your thoughts for your apartment?" I ask, taking my iPad out of my bag.

Caroline has put her phone down and has suddenly become interested in our conversation.

For the next hour, Helena describes her Tribeca apartment and all the changes she wants to make. After listening to her specific requests, I realize Mrs. Rothera may have competition for the title of most high maintenance client. Of course, Helena's not an official client yet, but we shall see. Before I make any decisions, I need to talk to Alexander.

Chapter Six

It's such a joy to be able to come to Alexander's house and Melanie be nowhere in sight. Following my lunch with Caroline and Helena, I texted Alexander and let him know I had a lot to tell him. I want to talk to him in person about Helena's request for me to decorate her apartment. Who knows how he's going to react to it. I'm still not sure how I feel about it.

After talking to Helena, it definitely seems like she has moved on as well. And neither she nor Alexander can control how Caroline feels about the situation. Regardless, I'm still not sure that working with her is the right decision. On another note, both she and Caroline were very pleasant, so maybe it's the beginning of a friendship I was hoping for, with Caroline anyway.

I decide to go directly to Alexander's house instead of going home. I arrive before him so I curl up on the couch under a heavy blanket with my laptop. I've always felt very at home in his house even before I started decorating it. In the beginning,

Melanie would insist on being here, which is understandable considering I was a stranger. But Alexander never seemed to mind and always had an open-door policy. I realized later that her issues with me were because of her feelings for Alexander, not necessarily because she didn't like me. Although, now it's definitely both; in fact, I think her dislike for me grows by the day.

"Hello?" Alexander calls. My heart does a little flip like it always does when he's around.

"Living room," I call.

He's loosening his tie with one hand as he walks in. For some reason, I think that's one of sexiest things men do.

"Hi. You look gorgeous," he says, leaning down to kiss me.

I smile. "Thank you."

I watch him intently as he pulls his tie off.

"I can't wait to hear all about your day, just give me five minutes." He turns around before leaving the room. "How about I order in some dinner from It's All Greek?"

I nod excitedly, he knows me so well. It's All Greek is my favorite restaurant.

He heads upstairs to change and I take a deep breath. Sometimes I don't know how I get mixed up in this stuff. When I began working with Alexander, I made a promise to myself that I would never get romantically involved with a client—and here I am. To complicate the situation more, his personal assistant despises me because she has feelings for him. And now his ex-wife wants to hire me to decorate her home. My life is quickly becoming potential talk show material.

While Alexander's upstairs, my phone rings. It's Mrs. Rothera and she's probably checking up on me because I've been going out of my way to avoid her, well not her exactly, just the topics of her apartment, me moving out, and basically my entire life.

"Hello," I answer, trying to sound rushed. I figure if I give her the impression that I'm extremely busy she might skip the interrogation.

"Oh, you answered. I figured I would need to leave a message because you're quite the busy woman these days."

Hmmm . . . I've often wondered if she knows I purposely avoid her. I mean, she's supposed to be a psychic, right?

"I *have* been busy," I reply defensively. "I was in the city all day today. And I'm getting ready to have dinner with Alexander."

I don't know why I felt the need to give her the play-by-play as if she's my mother.

"That sounds nice," she says. "I wanted to tell you that I think I've finally made a few selections from the sample ideas you left me. When will you be free to discuss them?"

I'm not going to hold my breath. She's told me the same thing on three different occasions. I even delayed another project because she thought she needed to have the décor changed before winter solstice. I guess it would be bad luck until next winter solstice or something like that. Okay, so I totally made up the bad luck part, but she did act like it was urgent and then changed her mind at the last minute.

I check my calendar and give her a few different options.

"How did your dinner with friends go?" she asks, changing the subject. I hesitate before giving her the short and easy answer.

"It went just fine," I tell her.

"Oh really. Well, good then," she says, sounding surprised.

Why does she seem so surprised? She must have been really expecting our meeting to be miserable. I have to remind myself that I don't owe her an explanation. So instead, I confirm our meeting to discuss her choices and end the call.

I must be deep in thought when Alexander finally comes downstairs.

"Why do you have that look on your face?" he asks.

I furrow my brow. "What look?"

He gives me a half smile. "You may not know this, but your facial expressions give away your feelings. Like right now, you're feeling a mix of confusion and frustration."

Crap. Am I really that obvious? It is kind of sweet that he pays so much attention to my feelings, though.

He sits down and faces me. "Was Caroline nice today? Be honest with me."

I chew on my lip nervously. "Yes, she really was." I pause. "Actually, someone else joined us at lunch."

He looks confused. "Did Nick go?"

I shake my head. "No, not Nick. But someone else you know pretty well." I hesitate. "Helena joined us."

Alexander stares at me as if I have three heads.

"What? Why would Helena go with you?"

I force a smile. "She was perfectly nice. It was just unexpected, as you can imagine."

He's still giving me a blank stare. He finally pulls me in toward his body. "Summer, I'm so sorry."

A few seconds later, I reluctantly pull away. "I'm okay. It started a little awkward but ended fine."

He shakes his head. "The point is that was wrong of them to put you in that position. Despite the fact that Helena and I are friends, she's still my ex. I'm sure that wasn't easy for you."

I drop my head. "There is one more thing."

Alexander looks like he's going to be sick.

"Oh, it's nothing horrible," I say, trying to reassure him. "She just asked me to redecorate her apartment."

He expression changes. "Our apartment? I mean, our *old* apartment—she still lives there."

Oh, I didn't even think about that when she mentioned her place in Tribeca.

"She didn't say anything about that. She just asked me, and I told her I would think about it. I wanted to talk you first."

One thing I have noticed about Alexander is that he very rarely lets things bother him, and if he is bothered, he does an amazing job at covering it up. It's very obvious he's bothered right now.

"Are you okay?" I ask.

He grits his teeth. "I'm not sure what Caroline's intentions were by blindsiding you today, but I will find out."

I put my arm around his shoulders as I try to calm him down. I appreciate that he's willing to defend me to some of the most important people in his life, but at the same time, I can't help but feel guilty about this. I just hate the feeling that I'm coming between his relationships.

"I don't want to be the cause of issues with your friends," I say, looking down at my hands.

"Hey. Don't do that," he demands. "*You* haven't done anything wrong. Just let me handle this, okay? And of course I would never expect you to work with Helena. That's insane."

I appreciate his support in this, but I can't help but wonder if there is more going on here. He's never made it a secret that he and Helena are still friends, and I know they've seen each other at events in the city. However, he does seem very cautious about this. I know he's trying to spare my feelings, but I also feel that if I don't take the job I'm drawing a line in the sand. That's something I don't want to do, ex-wife or not.

"Can I ask you something?" I say.

He grins. "Of course."

I can't believe I'm going to say this.

"Would it bother you if I did take the job?"

He looks so confused, and I don't blame him one bit because I'm also confused.

"What?"

I hold up my hand. "Hear me out," I exclaim. "Here's the deal, Nick and Caroline are your best friends. Helena and you are still friends. If I don't take the job, it would appear that I'm separating myself from a huge part of your life. When you and I got together, both of us had a past or, for lack of a better word, baggage. We decided we wanted to be with one another and with that comes our pasts. I'm willing to do this to prove that I'm secure in what we have."

He shakes his head. "I understand what you're saying but you don't have to prove anything to anyone, especially me. And you certainly don't have to work for my ex-wife."

I smile. "How about I think about it and let you know what I decide?" I stop. "Unless you really don't want me to."

He shakes his head. "It's not that. I just don't want you to feel like you're being forced into an extremely awkward situation."

I wrap my arms around his neck and give him a long, slow kiss. "I'm ready to talk about something else," I whisper.

He pulls me close to him again and whispers in my ear, "I have a few ideas."

Right at that moment, the doorbell rings interrupting our close moment. Alexander groans.

"Don't move," he demands, leaping off the couch to answer the door. He's back a few minutes later and sits down next to me.

"Now, where were we?" he flirts.

I couldn't be happier to change the subject.

~

"I'm sorry, Ang," I yell into the phone. She's reprimanding me because I canceled plans on her again.

I'm walking through Whole Foods trying to get some groceries so I won't have to eat white rice and lime-flavored tortilla chips for dinner again tonight.

"Don't apologize to me," she says. "You're the one who wants to move and you're the one who keeps putting off house hunting."

She's absolutely right. I've been so busy that moving has fallen to the bottom of my to-do list.

"I'm going to look this weekend," I demand. "I'm not sure how much longer I'm going to be able to fend off Mrs. Rothera. I'm sure she's caught on to my busy schedule and all my attempts to avoid her."

Angie and I make plans again to house hunt this weekend. After we hang up, I continue my shopping. My dad always used to tell me to never go into a grocery store when I'm hungry. *He's a wise man*, I think to myself. I look down in my cart and roll my eyes. I definitely don't need five different kinds of granola.

"Summer?" a voice says from behind me.

My heart sinks. I turn around and see Jake standing next to me. Even though we live in the same town, we very rarely run into each other. I suppose it was bound to happen at some point.

"Hello, Jake," I say politely.

He gives me a warm smile. "Summer, wow—you look great. I'm assuming life is treating you well?"

I nod my head. "Yes. It's wonderful." I hesitate. "How about you?"

He nods slowly. "Really good. I've actually just bought a new home."

Wow. Good for him. He had been living in a bachelor pad with a roommate when he wasn't visiting me. It sounds like he's finally making decisions that benefit his future.

"I'm very happy for you," I say. "I wish you the best in everything."

I start to walk away when Jake taps me on the shoulder.

"Brad told me you're working on another project for him. He wouldn't stop raving about you."

Well, I suppose that answers my question about Mr. Cooper knowing about our breakup.

"Did you tell him that we were no longer together?" I ask. I would like to know what Jake said so I'm prepared should he ask me about it.

He nods. "Yes." He pauses. "And don't worry, I told him it was my fault."

I pretend to be looking at something on the shelf in order to escape the awkwardness.

"Okay," I say nonchalantly. What am I supposed to say to that? Maybe I should say something like "good" or "it was your fault"?

"Summer, I hope there comes a time when we can be friends again," he says cautiously. "My actions this past summer have forever affected my life and relationships. I have a lot of regrets and I know it's too late for us, you made that clear on Halloween." My mind wanders back to when Jake crashed the Halloween party at Alexander's. In all fairness, Alexander invited him. (It's a long story.)

Crap. I hate when this type of stuff happens. Jake was an important part of my life, and when he broke up with me, it turned my world completely upside down. Now we're stuck in one of those awkward public moments in the middle of Whole Foods.

"I don't know," I tell him. "I really do wish you well, but I'm not sure we can be friends, at least not yet."

He looks down at the ground. "I understand."

As I'm standing here with him, I realize that I will always care about him even though I've moved on.

"You make sure that Alexander guy takes good care of you," he demands. He turns to walk away but stops and turns around again. "Summer, if you ever need anything, I will be here for you."

After he finally leaves, I walk aimlessly through the store. Talking to Jake makes me think about Alexander and Helena's situation. They were together and married for longer than Jake and I were together. They've been able to move on and remain friends. Maybe after I have a little more time to heal, Jake and I will get to that point, or something like that.

On a positive note, at least Brad Cooper knows we're no longer together. Now that he knows I'm hopeful the subject won't come up again because I really don't want to talk about it anymore.

Chapter Seven

Another good thing about moving is that I won't have to live on the second floor anymore. It takes me a few trips to bring my groceries in. I try to bring them all on one trip but things started falling out of bags, so I decided to give up my dream of being superwoman today.

After my two exhausting trips up the stairs, I'm unpacking the bags when I hear six knocks on my front door. I know that's Mrs. Rothera; she says she knocks six times because that's her lucky number. She must have heard me huffing and puffing while I climbed the stairs.

I take my time answering the door, and sure enough, she's patiently waiting when I open it.

"She's alive," she yells as if she was announcing it to the world. "I wish you would have asked me to help you carry your bags."

I shrug my shoulders. "It's okay. I'm just putting away my groceries, if you give me about a half hour I will be happy to look at your selections for the apartment and hopefully we can knock it all out."

She gives me a curious look. "Trying to be done with me, are ya?" She starts laughing hysterically, but I have no doubt she believes it.

"No," I say defensively.

"Have you had any luck finding a house?" she asks, changing the subject. I know she's watching me for my reaction. At least I can give her an honest answer, and the truth is, I've had no time to house hunt.

"I haven't even started looking," I tell her. "And about that, I promise you I was not keeping that from you. I just didn't get the opportunity to talk to you, and of course Melanie got to you first."

She nods her head. "Yes, I know that." She gives me a thoughtful look. "There's obviously a lot of tension between you and Melanie."

I laugh loudly. "You could say that. That woman hates me."

I would go into detail about Melanie but I'm not sure I want to give Mrs. Rothera any information. With Melanie coming to see her for readings, I have no doubt they're building a close bond. I wish I could ask her what she has to say about Alexander, although there's probably some kind of patient/psychic confidentiality agreement. I've never heard of such a thing but you never know.

"She doesn't hate you," she says flatly.

Hah. I find that hard to believe. I'm guessing Mrs. Rothera

now feels the need to protect her because she's coming to see her professionally.

"Hmmm . . . well, I'm not so sure about that. Things have been awkward since the first day I started working for Alexander."

She nods slowly. I get the impression she wants to say something else.

"Is there something you want to say?" I ask.

She tightens her lips.

"Do you want me to?" she asks with a gleam in her eye.

Aha. I know what she's trying to do by turning this back on me. It may be some form of manipulation or maybe even mind control. At the same time, I am curious to know more about Melanie.

"Why not," I say sarcastically.

She gives me a smug look. I guess she thinks I'm taking a step toward coming to her for help.

"Of course I'm not able to go into much detail, but I can tell you that Melanie feels threatened by you. I'm sure you already knew this, though. She feels that after Alexander's marriage ended she finally had her time with him and then you came along."

I roll my eyes. "What do you mean by her time? She works for him."

She nods. "Yes. I reminded her of that and also let her know that there would be no future for her and Alexander."

Aha. I admit there is a tiny sense of satisfaction in hearing that.

"Oh, I'm sure that didn't go over too well," I exclaim.

She shakes her head. "No. It didn't, but if it makes you feel any better, she doesn't dislike you as much as Alexander's ex-wife."

"Helena."

She gives me a shocked look. "Have you met her?"

I hesitate. "Yes."

It could be my imagination but she looks very uncomfortable all of a sudden.

"Surprisingly, she's not as bad as I thought she'd be," I tell her. "What does Melanie say about her?"

Again, I'm not sure about the confidentiality rules, but I'm especially interested now being that she doesn't hate me as much. Whatever that means.

"She didn't say too much. Only that Alexander's wife tried to get her fired on multiple occasions and that she's a conniving evil woman."

Well, this is interesting. I have no doubt that Helena wanted Melanie gone, especially if she was anything like she is now with Alexander and me. I'm not even Alexander's wife and I'm already irritated by her presence. And as far as Helena being conniving and evil . . . well . . . the jury is still out on that.

"I can understand why Helena would do that. Melanie is way

too involved in Alexander's life. It's completely over-the-top, even for an assistant."

Mrs. Rothera is quiet for a few seconds. "Is it really? I mean, if Alexander doesn't mind, then why should it be a problem? It sounds to me like he's perfectly content with her, um . . . involvement in his life."

I snort. "Well, not completely." I pause. "He certainly wasn't happy when she took it upon herself to tell you about me looking for a realtor."

She gives me a half smile. "Yes, I would agree that Melanie did that on purpose."

We're both suddenly quiet until Mrs. Rothera speaks up again.

"Does it bother you that Alexander has kept her around?" she asks. "Even when his wife tried to get rid of her, she stayed."

I would be lying if I said her constant presence doesn't get to me sometimes.

"I care about Alexander, but I'm in no place to force him to do anything," I tell her. "Melanie has worked for him for a long time and I respect that. And not only that, you just told me that she would never have a future with Alexander. I would say that's more than enough reassurance for me."

She shrugs her shoulders. "Yes, I did. But . . ."

"But nothing," I interrupt her. "Can we please change the subject? How about you show me what you've chosen for your apartment?"

She tightens her lips again. "Yes, we can. There is just one more thing." She pauses. "Not everything is how it seems. Just be careful."

I'm about to ask her what she means when she begins talking about her apartment. Unfortunately, I'm only half listening. It hits me that if things continue to progress with Alexander I may have to put up with Melanie for a long time. I wonder if we will ever be rid of her. Obviously, Helena never was.

Hmmm . . . not everything is how it seems? I refuse to let this worry me. I will just have to keep my guard up—as usual.

~

"The lighting fixtures have arrived and the electrician is on his way. I will be here most of the afternoon." I give Nick a rundown of my list for today. The restaurant is coming along really nicely despite a few tiny issues, and we're on right on schedule for the Valentine's Day opening.

Caroline sent me an email with a few small yet very important changes that "absolutely needed" to be done. (Her words not mine.) Those small, important changes she was referring to were the accent pillows for the couches in the waiting area. I honestly think she was purposely looking for something she didn't like and that was all she could find. There have been no more lunch invitations since the last one. Not that I was expecting one. Thankfully, I've been extremely busy for the past week so I haven't had much time to obsess over Mrs. Rothera's latest warning. Don't get me wrong, I have thought about it, but at least it hasn't consumed me . . . yet. I didn't tell Alexander about it because he would remind me not to let her get in my head.

I'm sitting at a corner booth with my laptop in front of me when I get an email from Helena. Thankfully, she's only reached out to me once since our impromptu lunch because I still haven't made a decision. Alexander said he was fine with whatever I decided so unfortunately that leaves me to make the decision on my own. All of a sudden, a random thought pops in my head. Maybe I should ask Melanie about Helena . . . or should I ask Helena about Melanie? Seriously. Why are there so many women in Alexander's life?

I look over Helena's requests. Hmmm . . . maybe I should at least look at the apartment. For professional reasons of course . . . and maybe I'm a tiny bit curious to see where Alexander used to live. I send Helena a message letting her know I want to see the space.

I think I use my time very wisely. While "working" at the restaurant, I order a few items for the Cooper project and I catch up on emails. I also got a message last night from Chantel and Levi that they want to wait until the spring to begin their apartment, which makes me somewhat relieved. The contract is signed so I know they aren't going anywhere. I really need to focus on finishing Mrs. Rothera's apartment, and more importantly, I have to search for a new place to live.

A few hours later, Helena sends me a message inviting me over for tea later this week. (Tea?) I could be walking into a trap but here goes nothing. After I accept her invitation, I remind myself that it's for business. Sometimes we do things for our careers that we may not like. Now I just have to figure out how to tell Alexander that I will be joining his ex-wife for tea.

Chapter Eight

After a long day in the city I just want to sit in front of a warm fire under a blanket. Have I mentioned how much I hate the cold? I honestly don't know how I've made it this long in the north. I think at some point I may need to move to Florida. I would even be willing to put up with those super-hot summers.

Melanie is still at Alexander's when I arrive. They're discussing his upcoming travel when I walk in.

"Hey, babe," he says, jumping up from the table to embrace me. I see Melanie scowl. "How was your day?"

"It was really good," I say after he gives me a big hug. "Just freezing."

He laughs. "There's a surprise."

I watch how Melanie's demeanor completely changes when I enter the room. Truthfully, if looks could kill, I would have been dead a long time ago.

"Nick says the restaurant is almost finished and they're still shooting for Valentine's Day?"

I nod. "Yes, that's the plan. And Valentine's Day is around the corner." *Hint!*

Alexander's phone starts ringing and he excuses himself to take the call, leaving Melanie and me alone. She doesn't look up from her phone and I start to make myself busy as well. It occurs to me that this may be my chance to ask her about Helena. I'm not sure what she will tell me, but I have nothing to lose.

"Um . . . can I ask you something, Melanie?"

She gives me a side-glance, barely looking up from her phone.

"It's about Helena."

And that's all it takes for her to give me her undivided attention.

"What about her?" she asks curiously.

I decide to go all in because I'm sure she will find out about it eventually anyway.

"Well, she's asked me to decorate her apartment." I hesitate. "I don't know her very well, so I guess I'm asking for your advice."

Ugh. I have to practically spit those words out. Who would have thought I would have to turn to Melanie for advice?

"My advice would be to stay the hell away from her," she demands. "Helena Williams is awful, one of the most selfish, conniving people I've ever met. The best decision Alexander ever made was to get divorced."

My mouth hangs open, probably because Melanie is actually talking to me like a normal person. Of course, I can't help but remember what Mrs. Rothera said about her hating Helena much more than she hated me.

"I thought their decision to divorce was mutual?"

She nods. "It was, however, I'm sure Helena Williams will come around again. As soon as she gets tired of her new toy of course. And by new toy, I mean the new man."

"You mean come around to Alexander?"

She rolls her eyes. "Yep. She will want him back, you just watch."

"So sorry about that," Alexander says, interrupting our conversation.

He looks back and forth between Melanie and me.

"Everything okay?" he asks with a worried look on his face.

I look at Melanie.

"Of course," she says nonchalantly. "I was just about to take off for the day."

I try to process what she said about Helena. I need to remember that she may hate Helena but she definitely doesn't like me either. I know she doesn't want me to be with Alexander. It's very possible that she could be trying to get in my head to scare me away from him and his big, bad ex-wife. I have no doubt that she and Helena have a rocky past but that doesn't mean that Helena wants to reconcile with Alexander.

"What was that all about?" he asks after Melanie leaves.

I know he's skeptical and I can't blame him. He's walked in on some heated moments before.

I wave my hand. "Nothing actually. We were just talking."

He raises his eyebrows. "I could see that. Are you going to tell me what you were talking about?"

I cringe because I don't really want to tell him, but on the other hand, I don't want to keep anything from him either.

"We were actually talking about Helena," I say finally.

He makes a face. "Oh no. I can only imagine what she had to say."

I force a smile. "Well, I'd say it's pretty obvious that Melanie isn't a fan of Helena's."

He snorts. "That's an understatement. Those two despised each other. It was a very stressful time for me because I was always stuck in the middle."

I nod. Listening to him makes me feel guilty because my issues with Melanie probably bring up a lot of the same memories for him.

"Of course I sided with my wife and that made work difficult at times," he continues. "And there were times Helena was in the wrong and I told her she was. But, I loved her and was going to stand by her regardless."

I don't say anything. I can understand where Helena was

coming from because I have now been on the receiving end of Melanie's wrath and her, um . . . feelings about Alexander's personal life.

"I probably shouldn't tell you this, but Melanie seems to think that Helena will want to reconcile with you at some point."

He stares at me for a second and then starts laughing.

"She has said that since we separated and it's absolutely ridiculous. Helena and I are much better as friends and there will never be anything more."

I feel a sense of relief after hearing that. One of the reasons I told him was to see what kind of reaction he would have at the possibility. Watching his expression was exactly what I wanted to see.

"Would you think bad of me if I told you I was relieved to hear that?" I ask.

He smiles. "Not at all."

I wrap my arms around his neck and kiss him. Our kissing becomes more intense by the second.

A few minutes later, we are wrapped around each other and I've finally warmed up from my excursion in the frigid cold.

I pull away. "There's something else I have to tell you."

He closes his eyes as he leans his head against the back of the chair.

"It's really not that big of a deal," I say, trying to assure him.

"Okay."

"Helena invited me over for tea and to see the apartment. I said I would go." I cringe as I wait for his response.

He takes a deep breath. "So, does that mean you are taking the job?"

I shrug my shoulders. "I don't know yet. I know it's an awkward situation, but at the same time, I probably shouldn't turn away clients. I need to take advantage of all the exposure I can get."

He nods his head slowly. "I understand. You know I will support you any way I can."

I give him a grateful smile.

"On another note, have you had any luck in your search for a new place?" he asks, pushing a piece of my hair behind my ear.

I groan. "No. Your realtor sent me over a bunch of options, but I haven't had any time to look."

He gives me a big smile. "Well, let's take a look now."

Without saying a word, I jump off the couch to fetch my laptop. As we look through the options, he shoots down every single one I suggest.

"What was wrong with this one?" I ask, pointing at an adorable little Cape Cod floor plan.

He shrugs his shoulders. "It's too far away. All of those are all too far away."

I raise my eyebrows. "You want me nearby."

"Yes," he whispers. My mind wanders back to what Angie was

saying about me moving into Alexander's house. Which is a crazy idea, right?

"I think everything around here is much too big, not to mention out of my price range."

He gives me a thoughtful look. "Steve will find you something, don't worry."

We enjoy the rest of the evening together with no more mention of Melanie or Helena. I'm not going to lie when I say that for a second I thought he was going to ask me to stay with him. It's a good thing Angie hasn't been in his ear yet, because if he was to ask, I don't know if I would be able to say no.

∼

I have no idea what to wear for "tea." I know in Europe tea is another meal, but of course I want to look the part. And this isn't just a normal invitation. This is an invitation to have tea with my boyfriend's ex-wife in his former apartment. Wow. The more I think about it the more I realize how insane this sounds.

"I would wear four- or five-inch heels," Gina says, smacking her gum. "That will show her that she better not mess with you."

I start to laugh. "That might work normally but don't forget that Helena is a gorgeous Swedish model who is easily over six feet tall. She would still tower over me."

Gina nonchalantly flips through a *People* magazine.

"Maybe I should come along as your assistant?" she adds.

I shake my head. I can only imagine how that would go. She would probably start asking a million questions and maybe threaten a phone call to someone who has the ability to make people disappear.

"I appreciate that, but I think I can handle myself."

Both Angie and Gina have offered to come along with me. I guess they don't think I can handle Helena on my own. I was able to handle Helena and Caroline's best friends forever tag team. If I can handle that, then I can handle anything.

Thankfully after talking to Alexander, I feel better about everything. I'm confident in my career and even more confident in making our relationship work. I refuse to let anything else stand in our way.

Chapter Nine

When I arrive at Helena's building an older gentleman is there to greet me. I'm not surprised she lives in a building with a doorman. I can totally see this nice doorman carrying in her shopping bags from her daily trips to Saks, Bergdorf's, and Louis Vuitton. (Of course, I'm totally jealous.)

"Good morning, madame. And who are you coming to visit today?" he asks, holding the door open for me. He might as well have rolled out a red carpet.

"Good morning. I'm here to see Helena Williams."

He nods. "Ah, yes. Elevators straight back. You have a lovely day."

My heart begins to beat faster as I embark on what feels like the longest elevator ride ever. When I step off the elevator and walk toward the apartment, I hear shouting. I stop dead in my tracks and look around. Sure enough, the shouting is coming from Helena's apartment.

I double-check my messages to make sure I'm in the right place. I hesitate as I try to decide if I should leave or knock on the door.

Before I can do anything, the door flies open and a very attractive man rushes past me. He either pretends not to see me or he's purposely ignoring me. It sounds like he's mumbling something in French. I stand still, wishing I could find somewhere to hide. There's a potted plant in the corner but I would look ridiculous trying to hide behind it. A few seconds later, Helena appears in the open doorway. Her eyes grow wide as soon as she sees me.

"Summer. Please come in," she says, holding the door open.

I slowly walk into her gorgeous apartment, and as soon as I'm inside, I notice that her apartment really doesn't need a decorator, which makes me wonder why I'm here.

"I apologize for that . . ." she trails off, and then the tears begin to fall down her cheeks.

Before I know what's happening, she's crying hysterically on my shoulder. This has to be the strangest thing I've ever experienced. I pat her on the back trying to comfort her, which for me is miserable considering I'm not a very nurturing person. I can't help but wonder how I got here, sitting in my boyfriend's old apartment comforting his ex-wife who has had what appears to be a huge argument with her new boyfriend. Angie's right—how does this stuff always happen to me?

When Helena finally manages to calm herself, she pulls away and blows her nose loudly into a Kleenex. I have to admit she looks like hell. Well, hell by her standards—which means she still looks stunning. There's another reason to hate her.

"Thank you for being such a wonderful friend," she wails. *Friend?* "Jacques and I have had a terrible falling out, and I'm afraid things may be over for us."

She begins telling me a long story about how she and Jacques were planning a trip to Bora Bora and something about a disagreement over excursions. To be honest, she lost me halfway through her story.

"I'm sure you two will work things out," I reply. She immediately shakes her head.

"I don't think so," she says, dabbing the corners of her eyes. "Although we've had an exhilarating time together, some things aren't always meant to be."

I shift around awkwardly on the edge of the couch. I still don't know why I'm here.

"Oh dear," she says, practically jumping off the couch. "We were supposed to have a lovely tea together and I've been carrying on unmercifully."

She runs off and I can hear her banging around in the kitchen. I begin to wander around when something catches my eye on the shelf behind the gorgeous white baby grand piano. I walk over to get a better look, which is when I notice three photographs. The first photo is of her and Alexander on a beach, the next one is them standing under the Eiffel Tower at Christmas time, and the last one is their wedding photo. I'm not so naïve that I don't think there's a reason these pictures are still on display. I know they're still friends, but to have pictures of their life together still lining her shelf?

"Here we are," Helena says, startling me.

I spin around and she's eyeing me curiously.

"I was just looking around, you know to get a feel of the space," I tell her. "Do you have any ideas of what you would like to change because, to be honest, your apartment is already gorgeous?"

She smiles smugly. "Just a few things here and there. Colors, and maybe some accent pieces."

I take out my iPad and make some notes.

"So, is that a yes?"

What's that old saying? Keep your friends close and your enemies closer? And for some reason I have a strong feeling that I need to keep Helena close.

"Yes," I say, giving her my most sincere smile. "I will draw up a contract later today and send it over to you."

She claps and throws her arms around me. When she pulls away, she holds out her hand and gives me a sly smile. "I think this is going to be a great partnership."

I take her hand and we shake. In other words . . . game on.

By the time I get home I'm so tired, both emotionally and physically. I'm convinced that my body does not work right in cold weather. The whole way home my brain is replaying everything that's happened recently, including the first conversation I had with Caroline, my conversation with

Melanie, and Helena and her apparent breakup with the hot French guy Jacques. I still can't get those photos out of my mind. I think it's safe to say that the writing is on the wall, maybe Melanie was right.

I'm not home more than fifteen minutes when there's a knock at the door. I groan loudly. I have only one guess at who is waiting for me at the door. I could pretend not to be home, but I have no doubt that Mrs. Rothera already knows I'm here. As soon as I open the door, I notice a look of concern on her face. That's never good.

"Is everything okay?" she asks.

I let out a huge sigh, and without saying a word, I open the door wide to let her come in, because honestly, I'm too tired to fight her anymore.

She closes the door behind her and follows me to the living room where I (overdramatically) fall down on the couch.

"Do I even need to tell you about my day? Or do you already know?" I say, without looking up.

She laughs. "Summer, I think you're confused. I don't know the details about your day, but I can sense that something is very off."

I sit up and look at her. "Just shoot me straight here. Do you think I'm wasting my time with Alexander?"

She purses her lips but doesn't respond for a few seconds.

"I can't answer that if you don't tell me what has you so upset," she says flatly.

I rub the outside corners of my eyes. "I'm just so confused.

Melanie told me that Helena would eventually want to get back together with Alexander. Considering my history with Melanie, I'm not sure I completely trust her. Today I was at Helena's apartment and she still has photos up from their marriage. Maybe I'm making a big deal out of nothing. I know they've remained friends."

"Do you believe Melanie is telling you the truth?" she asks me, picking up a copy of *Vogue Living* magazine.

I stare at the floor. "Yes and no."

She looks up from the magazine and stares at me, although it actually seems like she's staring *through* me.

"I think she thinks there's always a possibility they could reconcile but right now I'm her biggest obstacle."

One corner of her mouth curls up into a half smile. "Well, it seems like you've come up with an answer on your own."

I let out a huge sigh. It's obvious she has no intention of helping me through yet another crisis and that's what I've wanted all along. I can't have it both ways.

∽

"This is why you need me to come to any meeting that involves these women," Angie shouts. "Why didn't you ask her about the pictures? I certainly would have."

Hah. I know she would have and she would have made a huge scene and there would go all of my potential clients in Manhattan.

"Yeah, right," I exclaim. "And if I had drilled her with

questions about the pictures, then I would have looked like the insecure girlfriend. No thanks."

After a few days, I finally decided to tell Angie about my *tea* with Helena. I continued to avoid the subject until I knew she wasn't going to give up. At first, she thought the whole dramatic breakup with Jacques was funny, until I told her about the pictures.

"Well, just because her new relationship is over doesn't mean she's crawling back to Alexander," I say, trying to convince myself as well.

"Mmhmm," she mumbles.

I roll my eyes.

"Anyway, the main reason I'm calling is to confirm that you and Brett are coming to the restaurant opening on Valentine's. I have you down on my guest list."

I can't believe Valentine's Day is in less than two weeks, with all the drama of my life it totally snuck up on me. Alexander hasn't mentioned it in a while, which isn't a big deal being that we already had plans to go to the opening. At the same time, it is the holiday of *love* and I'm starting to wonder if he has anything special planned in addition to that.

"Are you kidding me?" Angie exclaims. "Of course we will be there. I'm especially excited to meet all your new friends."

I'm expecting a sinister cackle from her at any second. The idea of Angie hanging out with them makes me a little anxious. I can see it now, her meeting Caroline for the first time and warning her to be nice to me or else she will have Gina make a phone call.

"I'm assuming Helena will be there," she adds with way too much excitement in her voice.

"I'm sure she will," I reply. "And you will be on your best behavior. This is a big night for me. I don't want to see you being removed by security."

She starts to laugh, and I really wish I were only kidding.

"I take offense to such a suggestion, but I promise I will be on my best behavior, unless of course I need to step in for any reason."

I knew there would be some kind of stipulation in there.

"You will not have to step in," I assure her. "Let's just have a fun evening."

After I hang up, I smile in spite of the feeling of dread that's crept up on me. I know Angie means well; her heart is in the right place. I'm just not sure where her brain is sometimes.

Chapter Ten

What's the point of Valentine's Day really? I've personally never been a fan of the day, maybe that's because I've had some pretty bad ones, and I mean some doozies. There was that year that my car died in the middle of the parkway during rush hour. I barely made it off an exit and called my dad crying. Thankfully, he came to pick me up. I guess you could say he was my Valentine that year.

Of course, last year I was with Jake and he did make it a nice day with the usual roses, dinner, and a gift. That was of course before he turned out to be a complete ass.

This will be my first Valentine's Day with Alexander, and I can't imagine he does it small. We had barely been together a few months at Christmas and he gave me a gorgeous while gold cuff bracelet as well as a stocking full of my favorite candy and a gift card to Nordstrom.

We've barely seen each other in the last several days because of work and I've been at the restaurant almost every day making sure the finishing touches are perfect for the opening. I never told him about the photos in Helena's apartment; in fact, I was very vague about the entire visit. I didn't even mention the whole Jacques-Helena breakup fiasco. As Angie says, they probably made up later that day anyway when he came crawling back with something like diamond earrings or a pair of Louboutins.

Speaking of Helena, I sent her a contract and have not heard back from her yet since she told me she would look it over. I can honestly say that I'm not in any kind of rush to start working with her. And maybe she wasn't expecting me to say yes so she's trying to figure a way out of it. One can only hope.

Oh well, I'm not going to think about that because tonight I'm looking forward to spending the evening with Alexander. I have to admit the only good thing about not seeing him is not seeing Melanie.

"I've missed you," he says, taking my face in his hands and kissing me.

When he finally pulls away (and when I catch my breath), I tell him I've missed him too.

"Are you ready for the big night?" he asks excitedly. "Nick says it's going to be a blast."

I grin. "Yes, as long as Angie's on her best behavior."

He cocks his head to the side. "And why wouldn't she be?"

I hesitate. "Do you really want to know?"

He furrows his brow. "I don't know, should I?"

Hmmm . . . how do I tell him that Angie might take it upon herself to be the protective best friend and give Caroline a warning?

"You know . . . with the whole Caroline-Helena situation."

He grimaces. "Oh."

"I told her she couldn't cause a scene on my big night, especially with all the potential clients that will be in attendance. Her causing a scene could blacklist me forever. Needless to say, I think it will be fine."

He grabs my hand. "It will be fine. Nick has been raving about the restaurant all over town so be prepared to be very busy."

I smile. "That's what I'm hoping for. Now if only I could finish Mrs. Rothera's apartment, and I'm still waiting on Helena to send the contract back."

He rolls his eyes. "Yeah, you may be waiting on that for a while. She's too busy using retail therapy to recover from her breakup."

I give him a curious look. I guess he heard about the breakup after all, and Angie was obviously wrong about them getting back together.

"So, they did break up?" I ask. "How did you hear?"

He twists my hair between his fingers. "I saw her and Caroline in the city. She claims she's devastated, but the last I heard she's already on the search for someone to fill Jacques's shoes."

I have an uneasy feeling about this. I wonder if I will ever get used to them running into each other. Even though they both say things are over, the fact that she still has the pictures up says something.

"Anyway, we are not talking about them tonight," he demands. "I haven't seen you in days and I want to enjoy every second with you."

I force myself to put every distraction out of my mind for the rest of the night, and we do enjoy every second together.

~

I don't believe it, Mrs. Rothera actually chose all her décor and didn't change her mind (at least not yet). I spend most of the morning going over last-minute details before placing an order for her new magnificent Moroccan motif. That's what she's calling her new apartment.

"I'm so excited," she says, clasping her hands together. "I never knew choosing new décor would be such a difficult decision but now that I have, I can't wait. There are just so many possibilities. It almost makes me feel like a new woman."

I laugh. "Yes, I guess that's why I love my job so much. It's like having a fresh start.

The possibilities are endless."

I start to gather up all the samples, magazines, and color swatches. It's actually been a nice meeting. No mention of my life or hints about how things may or may not go in my future.

"Do you have any exciting plans for Valentine's Day?" she asks.

I smile. "Yes, I'm attending the opening of the restaurant I decorated."

She gives me a curious look. "Oh. Melanie mentioned attending an opening, too."

I force a smile. I already knew Melanie was going to be there. I'm pretty sure anyone with any kind of connection to their circle of friends will be there. I'm actually kind of curious to see if her and Helena have any interaction at all. And it will be nice not to be the one to take the brunt of Melanie's hostility for a change.

"It sounds like it's going to be quite the event," she says knowingly. I'm waiting for her to add a hint or some sort of advice but she doesn't say anything else. I guess she's finally figured out that I'd rather not hear it.

"Hopefully not too eventful, if you know what I mean," I reply.

She gets a wistful look on her face and I can tell by her expression that she knows exactly what I mean, and I think it's safe to say that I probably won't get my wish. I guess it's better to be cautiously optimistic, and for once, I actually feel like I'm prepared for anything.

∼

I should have known that if anything were to go wrong with the opening it would have something to do with Caroline. Of course the one issue she's brought up throughout the whole process is still incredibly wrong according to her. Those damn accent pillows are going to be the death of me.

Luckily, Alexander had a car pick us up and we're going to the restaurant early because I've already received five phone calls from her.

"Don't take it personally," Alexander says, laughing. "She will never admit it but she's really nervous about tonight. I doubt it has anything to do with you."

Yeah right, I think to myself.

I let out a frustrated sigh.

"Hey. Everything is going to be perfect," he says, squeezing my hand. "And don't forget that even though we're going to be with hundreds of other people, it's still Valentine's Day."

I sigh. "I know."

I actually don't mind the opening being today. I think it's been a good distraction from the forced stipulations that come with Valentine's.

When we arrive the restaurant, Nick is running around barking orders and Caroline is sitting in the lobby pouting.

"Snap out of it, kid," Alexander says, clapping his hands in front of her face. She swats his hand away.

"Whatever," she shouts. "Nicky is on my last nerve. You need to talk to him."

He wanders away laughing loudly and leaves me in the lobby with Caroline.

"I'm sorry the pillows didn't turn out right," I say, trying to sound sincere. I really could give two craps about the stupid pillows because the restaurant looks fantastic.

"It's fine," she mumbles. "I just wish Nicky would listen to some of my suggestions."

I bite my lower lip. I'm definitely not going to make a comment because I know better than to get involved in other people's relationship squabbles, especially on Valentine's Day.

"Hopefully, Alexander can talk some sense into him," she adds.

I pat her on the shoulder. "I'm sure he will."

I glance at the time. "I better do a quick spin around to make sure everything is in its place and take some photos before all the guests arrive. And don't worry, I have a feeling this is going to be a huge success."

She gives me a half smile. "Fingers crossed."

I leave Caroline in the lobby to take some photos. I'm not trying to sound conceited but this place really does look fantastic, especially the chandeliers. I ordered several different sizes and it turned out amazing. I float around the room admiring my work.

"There she is," I hear Angie yell from the front door. "Summer, we're herreeee." I see her practically dragging Brett over to me.

"Hey, guys. Thanks for coming tonight."

They both give me a hug.

"Just point me in the direction of the drinks," Brett says, with a grin.

Angie rolls her eyes. Brett is very quiet and intimidating but he's a really nice guy.

After he wanders off to the bar, Angie turns to me with a wicked gleam in her eye.

"Okay, so which one is Helena?" she asks loudly.

I shush her. "I haven't seen her yet. Remember, you promised you wouldn't make a scene."

"Yeah, yeah," she says as she takes a glass of champagne off a tray that magically appears in front of us.

We start to scope out the room.

"That's Caroline, right?" she says, pointing toward the door where she and Nick are now greeting guests. "I think I remember her from Halloween."

"Yep."

"Summer?"

I turn to see Brad Cooper standing next to me.

"Mr. Cooper," I say, trying to hide my shock. "What a nice surprise."

He smiles warmly. "I've done business with Nick for years. I wouldn't miss the opening. I'm assuming this is another one of your projects."

I look around proudly. "Yes, it is."

"Ahem," Angie interrupts.

"Oh, I'm sorry. Brad Cooper, this is my friend Angie Luca."

"Charmed," Angie says politely.

"I decorated Mr. Cooper's home in Cape Cod last year, remember?" I tell her.

Angie's obviously not listening and her smile suddenly fades.

"What the hell is he doing here?" she snaps.

I spin around to see whom she's referring to, and sure enough, Jake is walking toward us.

"Are you following her?" she yells at him. "I seriously doubt anyone would invite you here."

"Angie," I exclaim. "Stop."

Her eyes grow wide. "Are you serious? He should..."

"Angie," I say calmly. "Mr. Cooper is Jake's boss."

Poor Brad Cooper is silently watching this whole scene transpire. It's obvious that he invited Jake as one of his guests and it's an unfortunate coincidence.

"Hi, Summer," Jake says awkwardly.

"Hello."

Angie's face is turning bright red. "If you will excuse me," she growls, and then hurries away leaving me with Jake and his boss.

I force a smile. "I apologize for that. I'm afraid she's a very overprotective best friend."

Jake smiles sheepishly. "You definitely don't need to apologize. She's right and Brad already knows all about our situation."

Brad Cooper nods in agreement. "Yes, please don't apologize. I'm sure this is awkward for everyone involved." He pauses. "I will leave you to talk. You did a great job here," he says, putting his hand on my shoulder.

After Brad leaves, Jake and I stand awkwardly.

"So you decorated this place?" he asks. "I can see you brought your decorating magic as usual."

Decorating magic is the way Jake used to describe my work. It annoyed me for a while after he broke up with me but it's not a big deal anymore.

"Thanks," I say proudly. And that's when I see it, Alexander and Helena standing together near the bar, they each have an arm around each other and they're laughing.

Wow. I admit I wondered what it would be like to see them interact with each other . . . and now I know. Caroline was right about one thing, their connection is very obvious.

"Summer." Jake's voice snaps me out of the trance I'm in as I watch *Xander* and Helena.

"What?" I say absently.

He eyes me curiously. "Are you all right? You look pale."

I glance back at the bar to where they're still standing together. Nick and Caroline have now joined them and the happy foursome is together again.

"Summer," he repeats.

I look back at Jake standing in front of me and I'm reminded of all the pain he caused me last summer. Without saying a word, I hurry toward the door, weaving in and out of the guests, with Jake at my heels.

Chapter Eleven

As soon as I'm out the door of the restaurant, the cold February air hits me.

"Summer, what's wrong?" Jake asks, grabbing my arm.

I exhale loudly and spin around to face him. "What do you want from me? You're the one who ended things, so why do keep showing up everywhere I am?"

My heart is beating so fast. I actually don't know who I am angry with more—Jake, Alexander, or myself. I got involved with Alexander despite having many reservations. I suppose I brought this on myself.

"I had no idea you would be here tonight," he says emphatically. "Brad invited a group of us from the office."

I put my face in my hands. "I know."

I feel like I want to cry, but I'm really not surprised by any of this, especially after seeing the way Alexander interacts with Helena.

I feel Jake's hand on my shoulder. "I know I ruined everything between us and I will never be able to change what happened. I accept that you've moved on, and I really wish you all the best."

Just then the image of Alexander and Helena flashes in my mind and my eyes fill with tears.

Jake looks horrified. "Summer, please don't cry."

He pulls me into a hug and tears roll down my cheek and onto his sweater. I'm so confused right now that I almost forget how cold it is and I don't pull away from Jake.

"Well, well, what's going on here?"

I close my eyes, praying that this isn't happening right now. When I do finally pull away from Jake, I see Melanie watching us. This doesn't surprise me since this is how my night seems to be going.

"Oh, don't stop on my account," she says with a wicked smile. I wipe the corners of my eyes with my fingers. I don't think it's possible for this night to get any worse. And then right at that moment the door opens and Alexander comes outside. Damn, I spoke to soon.

"Summer, where did you go?" he asks. His mouth hangs open as he looks at my tear-stained face and then at Jake.

"What happened? Why are you crying?"

I can't take this anymore. I need to take my frustrations out on someone and Melanie seems like the perfect option.

"Go ahead, Melanie," I yell. "I know you're dying to tell him that you saw me in Jake's arms."

Alexander frowns. "What the hell is going on?"

"Nothing's going on," Jake answers. "She was upset and I was just comforting her."

Melanie is silent and obviously trying to look innocent in front of Alexander. And she is innocent, because I'm the one who just announced I was in Jake's arms.

"Everyone just leave me alone," I scream, and I start walking away. I'm in such a daze that I have no idea where I'm going. And I have no coat on.

"Summer, wait," Alexander shouts, running after me. He stops in front of me, blocking me from going any further. "Please tell me what happened. I've been looking everywhere for you and a few people said they saw you run out."

I need to be honest and tell Alexander how I feel. The fact is I have no chance of competing with this great love story. Not to mention I don't think I will be as accepting of Melanie as Helena obviously was.

I sigh. "Alexander. what are we doing? We're fooling ourselves into thinking this is going to work out."

He gives me a look as if I just slapped him across the face.

"I don't . . . what are you talking about?"

Sure enough, the tears begin to fall again.

"I can't compete with her and I never will," I say, hanging my head. "I think Caroline was right. I saw you together and there is no mistaking that chemistry."

Alexander is frozen in shock. (He may actually be frozen, too, because I'm so freaking cold I can barely stand it.)

"I don't understand," he stutters. "I didn't do anything..."

"You didn't have to," I interrupt. "I saw your arm around her; it's obvious. And I don't know if you knew this but she still has pictures up in the apartment from your life together, including your wedding picture." I start to shiver.

He shakes his head. "First of all, let's get you out of the cold. We can discuss this inside."

"There's nothing to discuss." I pause. "But I would like to get out of the cold."

I dab around my eyes as we walk back toward the restaurant. Melanie and Jake must have gone inside because I don't see them anymore.

As soon as we walk through the door, I make a mad dash for the restroom to fix myself up. I don't look as bad as I thought, so I quickly wipe some eyeliner that has smudged. I need to pull myself together. I take three deep breaths and walk out of the bathroom to face a restaurant full of strangers.

"Stop right there," Angie yells as soon as I walk out of the restroom. Alexander is standing next to her still looking completely shocked. I'm not even sure what's happening right now. I may or may not have ended things with him. Obviously, he found Angie for me.

"I don't want to talk," I say under my breath. "I need to be networking right now."

She folds her arms. "Fine—but we will be talking later."

I nod and walk away, leaving my best friend and my (maybe) boyfriend behind.

∼

The opening is a success and so is Summer Interiors. After the scene I just made in public, I still manage to meet and greet guests. I manage to avoid Angie's glares and that's one conversation I'm not looking forward to having. The strangest thing I notice is that Melanie and Jake have been talking most of the night—I can only imagine what they've been talking about. I guess following my little meltdown they must have come inside together.

Poor Alexander looks like a little lost puppy and that's another conversation I need to have. My heart is breaking each time I look at him because I want to be with him. But I also deserve to have all of his heart. I shouldn't have to share him with a high maintenance ex-wife or a needy assistant and I need to explain this to him. Suddenly I remember a conversation I had with Mrs. Rothera shortly after I started seeing him. She told me to be honest with him and demand the same in return. I owe it to him to tell him how I'm feeling.

The night is beginning to wind down and Nick joins me on the couch in the lobby where I have been sitting sorting through some contacts (and avoiding certain people). "Well done, Summer, your decorating was definitely a huge hit."

I give him a sheepish smile. "I appreciate that, and thank you again for this opportunity."

He shakes his head. "No thanks are needed. Alexander raved about you and that was good enough for me."

I force back a few tears that must have been lingering.

"You know he's pretty crazy about you," he says with a wink. "Just don't tell him I told you that," he whispers.

I force a smile. "You don't have to do this," I interrupt him. "I know Helena and him will always have that connection."

He cocks his head to the side. "Sure, they'll always be friends, but what does she have to do with this?"

"Friends? Don't you mean soul mates?" I say, repeating Caroline's description. Before he has a chance to respond, Angie interrupts us

"I'm sorry, but may I have a quick word with Summer? It's very important."

Nick excuses himself to walk a few of his guests out.

"Okay, let's hear it," she demands, folding her arms. "Alexander is beside himself right now."

I throw my head back and exhale loudly, and then I unload all the events that have transpired over the course of the evening.

She quietly listens and takes a few seconds to process everything I just told her.

"Let me get this straight," she says, holding up her hand. "You saw him with an arm around her and you flipped out."

I shake my head. "You don't get it, Ang. I'm fooling myself if I think they are finished. Even if things are good for us now, if they are soul mates, they will find their way back to each other."

She shakes her head. "You need to stop. Stop listening to

everyone, including Caroline, Melanie, Mrs. Rothera, and even me."

What? My mouth drops open. I've known Angie a long time and she's never told me *not* to listen to her.

"I'm serious," she says without yelling for a change. "Talk to Alexander and work things out. You guys are good together."

She gives me a tight hug and joins Brett who's been waiting patiently for her as usual. I stand up and scan the restaurant to see if I can find Alexander. Sure enough, he's sitting at the bar looking at his phone. I admit I have to catch my breath; sometimes I forget how gorgeous he is. I gather up all my courage and walk toward him.

"Hi," I say awkwardly.

He quickly turns toward me.

"Hey. I thought you left."

I shake my head. "Um . . . I was wondering if I could still get a ride home with you."

The corner of his mouth turns up into a half smile. "Of course. The car should be here any minute."

We spend the next few minutes saying our good-byes to Nick and Caroline and a few other people. I don't see Helena, Melanie, or Jake. Maybe they all took a trip together somewhere far, far away? A girl can dream, right?

Chapter Twelve

Another Valentine's Day in the books and I definitely didn't expect an ending like this. Alexander and I are quiet for about ten minutes after leaving the restaurant. I know I need be honest with him about how I'm feeling. I owe him that much.

"I'm so sorry about tonight," he says, interrupting my thoughts. "I ruined what should have been a huge night for you."

I can't bring myself to look at him. Maybe a part of me is embarrassed at how I acted.

"Well, while we're apologizing, I should have talked to you before overreacting," I say, still not looking at him. "I guess I've been listening to too many people, and then seeing you and Helena . . ." I trail off.

"Summer, I swear to you that it was completely innocent. I meant it when I told you that I want to be with you. Helena is my past; you are my future."

I stare out the car window and watch the city lights fading into the distance.

"I want that, too," I say softly. "But I don't want to feel like I will always have to share you. Maybe you have too many people in your life who require a lot of your attention."

He nods his head. "If you're referring to Melanie, I've taken steps to change that. I was going to tell you this tonight but... well, I haven't had a chance." He pauses. "I've finally rented out an office space, which means Melanie will not be at the house anymore. I realize that it's caused a lot of strain in my life and this change was needed. And it should have been done a long time ago."

Wow. I don't know what to say. I appreciate that he's finally recognized how deeply immersed she is in his life and in mine.

"I really have tried with her," I insist.

He reaches over and takes my hand. "I know you have and that's why I knew this had to be done. I want to do whatever it takes to make our relationship work."

My heart is practically beating out of my chest. As soon as he took my hand, I felt an electric current go through my body. The thing is I don't doubt his feelings for me one bit. I know he cares about me. I just don't know if he realizes that Helena isn't going anywhere and it's not fair of me to make him choose.

"I know you care about me," I tell him. "But I also know that I will never be a match for what you share with Helena. There is something so deep there that I don't think you realize it."

He lets out a frustrated sigh. "You are so stubborn. Yes, I had something wonderful with Helena but it's over. I'm with you . . . I want to be with you . . . I'm in love with you," he exclaims.

My mouth falls open. Did he just say . . . ? Up until this very moment neither of us has said the L word.

He nervously runs his hand through his hair. "That wasn't how I planned to tell you," he says quietly. He reaches under the seat and produces a small bag and hands it to me.

My eyes grow wide as I take the bag from him. I reach inside and pull out a small white box. When I open it, I find a stunning pair of princess cut diamond earrings.

I gasp.

"Happy Valentine's Day and happy opening night," he whispers. "I was planning on giving these to you after the opening when we could officially start our own Valentine's celebration."

I hold the earrings in my hand as I try to wrap my brain around everything that has happened.

"They're amazing," I whisper.

"I was planning on telling you that I loved you but I was waiting for the right moment. Now I'm telling you that I'm committed to our relationship."

Once again, a tear falls down my cheek. "I want that more than anything," I say through my tears. "I'm just scared."

"Because of what happened with Jake?" he asks.

I nod quickly. "Do you blame me? And then seeing the four of you together tonight was just too much. It just feels like the odds are stacked against us, and I'm not ready to go through more heartache just yet."

He pulls me into his lap. "Just give me a chance to prove how good this can be," he whispers into my hair. "Let me show you."

Wow. Talk about being conflicted. My heart is telling me to let go and take a chance, but all those voices from everyone around me are in my head. I wonder what Mrs. Rothera would say.

"At least think about it? I'm not trying to pressure you."

We sit in silence for the remainder of the drive home. I rest my head on his shoulder while every scenario of what-if goes through my mind.

In the meantime, I finally check my phone and sure enough there's a text from Mrs. Rothera.

Happy Valentine's Day! Enjoy yourself and don't worry.

Suddenly I remember something I told Mrs. Rothera last year. I told her that I didn't want to know what was going to happen in the future and that I was content where I am in the present. And I don't know what's going to happen—maybe things won't work out with Alexander or maybe they will. I can't stop living my life because I'm afraid of what might happen in the future.

When we arrive at Alexander's house, neither of us makes a move to get out of the car. Of course I don't want to go back into the cold, but I also don't want to leave Alexander.

"Let me walk you to your car," he says, opening the door. I sit still for a few minutes before getting out.

"I don't want to leave yet," I tell him.

His eyes grow wide. "I don't want you to leave either," he replies

Without saying a word, I throw all caution to the wind and wrap my arms around his neck. He holds me tightly and kisses me with more passion than I have ever felt before.

"Please be patient with me," I whisper in between his kisses. As afraid as I am, I know I'm not ready to give him up just yet.

He leans his forehead on mine. "I promise. Happy Valentine's Day, Summer."

"Happy Valentine's Day," I repeat. He takes my hand and kisses it. He then smiles and leads me into the house and out of the winter cold.

THE END

To Spring with Love

A Novella

Melissa Baldwin

About To Spring With Love

Summer Peters is thrilled to be done with the frigid winter. Spring is in the air, and she's ready for a fresh new start. Her career is thriving, she's searching for a new place to live, and she's finally ready to take her relationship with Alexander Williams to the next level.

What she doesn't expect is to be blindsided by Alexander's assistant, Melanie, who seems to be up to her old tricks, even stooping as low as dating Summer's ex-boyfriend, Jake. Once again, Summer is faced with the dilemma of having to share Alexander with a woman who's out to destroy their relationship.

To add to these challenges, she receives devastating news from her best friend, Angie. At a critical time when she may need her best friend the most, she learns Angie may not be there for her. She quickly realizes that she may need to lean on someone she never expected during this time of change.

Continue to follow Summer on her wild one-year journey in this third book of the Seasons of Summer Novella Series. Stay tuned for the final installment coming Summer 2017.

This is a work of fiction. Names, characters, places, and incidents either are the product of the author's imagination or are used fictitiously, and any resemblance to actual persons, living or dead, business establishments, events, or locales is entirely coincidental.

Copyright © 2017 Melissa Baldwin
All rights reserved.

ISBN: 0692916431
ISBN 13: 978-0692916438

Formatted by Karan & Co. Author Solutions

I dedicate this book to you, the person reading this. Thank you for your support and for taking time out of your life to read my stories. I hope this book brings a smile to your face and makes you laugh out loud. Stay tuned for more fun coming your way!

Chapter One

$\mathcal{A}$h . . . I have really missed the sun. I absolutely love when spring comes, especially being able to sit outside and not worry about my toes falling off from frostbite. I probably should move to a warmer climate but my life is here in Connecticut. Speaking of moving, I'm finally looking at a few new places this afternoon.

I've been so busy with my company, Summer Interiors, that my moving plans have fallen by the wayside, and I'm sure my landlord, Mrs. Rothera, is happy about this. I think she actually likes having me there. It's not that I don't like where I live, I do. But with my apartment comes a reminder of my former relationship and a landlord who likes to give unsolicited advice. Let's just say it seems a little crowded (and I'm not talking about the space).

My friend Angie thinks I'm subconsciously waiting for one of two things to happen, either an invitation to move in with my boyfriend or a marriage proposal. She tends to be slightly overdramatic because I doubt either of these will happen any time soon.

Don't get me wrong, I would love to live in my boyfriend's house because it's exactly what I picture my dream house would be. I still think both of those options may be a bit premature, even though we've both come a long way. When we got together last fall, we were both recently out of relationships, so we decided to take things slow. I was especially cautious because my heart was broken and my breakup was one-sided, and it wasn't my side.

I'm still so cautious that I still haven't said the L word, even after he blurted it out after a tumultuous Valentine's date. Alexander, being the amazing guy he is, says that he's patient and will wait until I'm ready. I know I have very strong feelings for him, but for some reason, I still can't bring myself to admit these yet.

"Let's do this," Angie says cheerfully, interrupting my daydream. She seems to be in a great mood. Not that I blame her, after months of frigid winter the mild temperatures are having a great impact on everyone.

"We'll go soon," I tell her. "Just have a seat for a few minutes and enjoy the sunshine." I'm expecting a lecture from her on my levels of procrastination, but she surprises me when she sits down and orders a latte.

"So, I have some news," she yells. Angie talks really loudly, so it always seems like she's yelling even when she's not. "I think Brett's going to propose to me."

My mouth drops open. "What? How do you know?"

"Well, I don't exactly, but Mrs. Rothera says something big is about to happen, and Brett has been acting funny. He says he's planning a surprise trip for us."

I shake my head. "Why don't you let him surprise you? Don't ruin it for him."

She rolls her eyes. "I'm not ruining anything, and you know I hate surprises."

I lean over and give her a hug. "This is so exciting. When's the trip?"

Angie's smile starts to fade. "What's she doing here? Is she following you now?"

"Who?" I turn around to see whom she's looking at. Sure enough, it's Alexander's assistant, Melanie, aka my archnemesis, sitting at a table by herself.

I groan and turn back around in my chair. I even put my sunglasses on in hopes that she doesn't recognize me. "I doubt she's following me. I actually haven't seen her in a while since Alexander practically banished her from his house. I'm sure she has a voodoo doll with my name on it, though."

Angie starts to giggle. "Probably. Maybe we should invite her to join us."

I snort. "Um, that's definitely not happening. I'm not spending this beautiful day with that . . ."

"No freaking way," Angie interrupts me. She has an absolutely horrified look on her face.

"What now?" I exclaim.

I spin around again, but this time I see that Melanie is no longer by herself. Someone has joined her and that someone just happens to be my ex-boyfriend, Jake. The same ex-boyfriend who blindsided me by ending our relationship last summer.

"Do they know each other?" she asks in a loud whisper. At least she isn't yelling across the café anymore.

My mind wanders back to Valentine's night on a cold New York City street when Melanie walked outside to find me in Jake's arms. It was completely innocent as he was trying to comfort me. I thought she was going to run to Alexander and make a scene, but it didn't go down that way. I remember running down the street to clear my head, leaving Jake and Melanie standing alone.

"I think they do," I reply absently.

"Do you think she's up to something?" Angie asks.

I take a long sip of my coffee. "I don't know, but I'm going to find out."

Angie folds her arms and stares me down. It almost feels like she's my mother and she's waiting for me to crack and admit I've done something bad. Like that time in high school when I snuck out of my window in the middle of the night to go watch movies at my friend's house.

I admit I can't look her in the eye right now.

"Okay, Ang, why are you staring at me like that?" I ask defensively.

She breaks her dead stare long enough to sip her latte.

"Does that bother you?"

"Does what bother me?"

She rolls her eyes. "Seeing Jake with someone else."

Okay, maybe it does bother me a little, but I'm not sure if it bothers me that Jake is with another woman or the fact that the woman is Melanie. Melanie has made it her mission to cause issues in my relationship with Alexander. Up until recently, she's been in my face daily, and according to Alexander's ex-wife, this isn't new behavior for her.

"If you're implying that I'm jealous, I'm not," I snap.

"Calm down," she says, rolling her eyes.

I look over my shoulder once more and notice that Melanie is flirtatiously laughing. I've never heard her laugh like that before. Jake is smiling and clearly enjoying himself.

I scowl. I wonder if this is another ploy in her bag of tricks to drag me away from Alexander. Maybe she thinks I will get jealous and go back to Jake. He's told me on a few occasions that he has regrets about the way things ended between us. (The way *he* ended things.)

"I think it's time to go," I say quickly.

Angie nods, trying to hide her smile.

"Shut up," I say through my frustration.

We're able to escape the café without either Melanie or Jake seeing us, at least I don't think they saw us. When I looked back at them before leaving, they appeared to be pretty deep in their conversation. Honestly, if Jake keeps Melanie busy so she's out of my life, then that's better for me.

～

Next time I go apartment hunting, I'm going alone. Not that I mind having Angie with me but I think the pressure's getting to me. I'm not sure what it is I'm looking for in a new apartment, but I'm not having much luck. To add to my rising stress level, I certainly don't need Angie hanging over my shoulder suggesting I just ask Alexander if I can move in with him. Not even the topic of her possible engagement could distract her from Alexander and my dream home (aka his home).

When I finally get home, the last thing I want is a visit from my landlord. Of course, I'm in my apartment for approximately three minutes when I hear six familiar knocks on my door. (She always knocks six times.) I let out a loud sigh as I make my way to the door. I could totally lie and claim I was in the shower, but I know she wouldn't buy it. And of course, there's that whole psychic thing. She's for real, too, and I'm not talking about those TV commercials where they charge you eight dollars a minute for your phone call.

"I'm sorry to bother you," she says, as she pushes past me and walks into my apartment. She doesn't seem the least bit sorry. "I just had to show you these photos I found online. Since we've finished the living room and kitchen, I think I would like to go ahead with the bedrooms now instead of waiting."

I just finished decorating a few rooms in her apartment, and it wasn't an easy task. In fact, it was quite the opposite since she changed her mind more times than I can count. She said she wanted to hold off on the bedrooms, but I guess she's changed her mind already. Figures.

"I know I said I wanted to wait, but everything looks so new and fresh that I'm ready do it all."

I grit my teeth. The problem with Mrs. Rothera is that I don't know if I should try to pretend because I feel like she can see right through me.

"And since you will be moving out soon, I should take advantage of you living here for as long as I can," she adds.

I shrug my shoulders. "Maybe."

She gives me a curious look. "Is there a problem?"

I sit down at the table. "Not a problem exactly. I just haven't had any luck finding a place yet."

One corner of her mouth curls up, and it looks like she's smiling. She hasn't been happy about me moving out, which I can understand. I'm sure it can be stressful finding new tenants, and good ones for that matter.

"That's a shame. I'm sure you'll find something," she says unconvincingly.

She joins me at the table. "Can I ask what else has you so distracted?"

I hate to ask her for any kind of advice because she will take it and run. I've been very vocal that I have no desire to hear any details about my future. But, I don't think asking for advice is the same thing.

"My friend Angie says I should ask Alexander to move in with him." I pause. "Remember, I'm asking for your advice, not a reading. I'm not sure if it's too soon..."

"Much too soon," she interrupts. "It's best that you don't take that kind of a step so early in your relationship."

I nod. "Thank you. I agree."

She closes her eyes for a few seconds, and then opens them again. Her blank stare is kind of creeping me out.

"Anyway, I really need to get some work done. It's been a long day." I jump up from the chair and make my way toward the door. Thankfully, she follows me. "Make a list of some ideas for the bedrooms, and I will stop by later this week."

She pats me on the shoulder on her way out the door. "That would be wonderful."

Before I have a chance to close the door, she holds her arm out. "Oh, and don't forget you're welcome to stay here for as long as you need."

I force a smile and thank her before closing the door.

Chapter Two

I can't help but stare at Alexander's face. Seriously, my man is so gorgeous. I remember the first time I searched Alexander Williams online. And no, I'm not a crazy stalker; I was actually doing research before our first meeting. I admit I didn't expect him to be so attractive. I had a picture in my mind of a man, maybe mid-fifties, kind of a recluse who was looking to redecorate his drafty old house. Imagine how surprised I was to find out he was a mid-thirties, recently divorced man who just happened to look like Clark Kent, aka Superman.

Staring at him definitely helps to keep me from getting irritated that Melanie has already called him two times since we arrived at the restaurant. I have no doubt she knows he's with me.

"Tell him I will schedule a conference call in the morning," he says.

I swirl my wine around while I semi-patiently wait for him to finish his call.

He puts his phone down. "I'm sorry. We're in the middle of an acquisition, so everything is a bit more urgent."

Everything is urgent to Melanie, I think to myself.

"Tell me about the apartments you looked at. Was there anything good?"

I shake my head. "Unfortunately, no."

It's very possible I'm being extra picky when it comes to moving. Maybe this is a sign that I shouldn't move?

"I don't know. I'm starting to think I should just stay where I am for now."

Right at that moment, Alexander's phone rings again. He lets out an exasperated sigh.

"I'm not answering it," he insists.

Although I appreciate his gesture, I know he needs to answer it.

"It's okay," I tell him.

He grabs my hand and kisses it before picking up his phone. He doesn't let go of my hand.

"Yes, Melanie." He pauses. "That's perfect. Yes, schedule it."

As soon as he hangs up, I watch the phone intently, waiting for it to ring again.

"Melanie says she's sorry for all the phone calls and she will leave me alone for the rest of the evening."

Sure she is. All of a sudden, the image of her and Jake at the café flashes through my head.

"That reminds me, Angie and I saw Melanie at the café yesterday," I tell him.

He tears off a piece of a roll and puts it in his mouth.

"Really? How did that go? Any punches thrown?" he asks, raising an eyebrow.

I giggle. "No, but I don't think she saw us. She seemed . . . preoccupied."

He gives me a funny look. "What do you mean?"

I shift around in my chair. I immediately regret bringing this up.

"It's not a big deal. We were just surprised when we saw the person she was with."

"Who was it?" he asks curiously. Now I definitely have his attention.

I bit my lower lip. "I'm sure it's not a big deal, but she was with Jake."

He looks completely shocked. "Jake? You mean your ex-boyfriend, Jake?"

I nod. "Yeah. I remember seeing them talking at the restaurant opening and . . . anyway, I don't think they saw us. We left shortly after they arrived."

Alexander doesn't say anything. Perhaps this is the news he needed to hear to make him realize how much Melanie dislikes me? Why else would she be meeting with my ex-boyfriend?

"Do you think they're seeing each other?" he asks.

I shrug my shoulders. "I don't know. But it would be strange if they were, considering the situation." And by situation, I mean the fact that she's in love with Alexander and I'm the other woman. Not to mention Jake has been going out of his way to rectify what happened last summer.

He stares off into the distance. I probably shouldn't have said anything.

"Yes, it would be strange. Of course, I have no right to tell Melanie whom she can be involved with, but considering the history here, I don't think it's appropriate."

Hah! *Take that, Melanie.* Unfortunately, I can see how distracted Alexander is, and I only have myself to blame. I barely had his attention before, and now he's completely shut down.

"Can we just forget about them for the rest of the evening?" I plead.

Without saying a word, he leans over and kisses me. Our dinner date ends up being very nice, and shockingly, Melanie keeps her promise. There isn't one more phone call from her.

The only awkward moment of the night is when I mention Helena's apartment. Helena is Alexander's ex-wife; a few months ago, she asked me to redecorate her apartment. After I finally agreed, I visited her Tribeca apartment only to be met with a wall dedicated to memories of her life with Alexander. Following our meeting, I sent her the contract and she has yet to send it back to me. Both Angie and my friend Gina think she was playing me the whole time. They think she had no intention of hiring me and she used it as a way to make me jealous of her past with Alexander.

"Helena is known for her procrastination. The last time I saw her she told me she would be contacting you to finalize everything."

The truth is I don't want to decorate Helena's apartment. If I had my way, she would be completely out of our lives. Unfortunately, that's never going to happen since Alexander and Helena have the same best friends. She's part of the package whether I like it or not.

"It's fine. I've got plenty to keep me busy," I reply.

The subject of Helena is still a sensitive subject between us. After being reminded of their intense relationship and seeing them interact, I was almost ready to end my relationship with Alexander. This all happened at the opening of a restaurant I decorated. Needless to say, I may have overreacted slightly, but I can't help the way I feel.

"I have another referral for you," he says, changing the subject.

I place my hand on his cheek. My business has tripled since I decorated Alexander's house, and I know I owe it all to him. Another new client is just what I need since I'm sure I won't be doing business with Helena.

"That's awesome. Who?"

He smiles excitedly. "My parents."

His parents? Is it really time to meet the parents? I don't know why this freaks me out so much. I haven't thought about introducing my family to Alexander yet. And I'm sure they aren't ready either after the situation with Jake. Although, my father was quite pleased when Jake and I broke up. He never liked him anyway, and I'm still not sure why.

"Your parents need a decorator?"

He nods. "Yes. But, I'm actually the one hiring you. Their fiftieth wedding anniversary is coming up, and I would like to do it for them as a gift."

"So, it's a surprise?"

I don't have a good feeling about this. I would never go into someone's home and change things around without them being in agreement.

"Oh no, they know about it. So, if you're interested, they've invited us to dinner and you can sit down with my mom to discuss ideas. That is, if you want the job?"

This is his way of introducing me to his parents? This should make me feel more secure in our relationship, but for some reason, it doesn't.

~

"You're making that poor man wait? I would bet fifty bucks that you're the first woman to do that."

My friend Gina has no inner monologue.

"I just want to make sure the timing is right. We've had a lot of roadblocks in our way already."

She's leaning back in her chair with her feet up on the desk. "He's already told you he's in love with you, so why haven't you told him? You're going to give him a complex."

I roll my eyes.

"He knows I'm being cautious, and he's fine with that."

She's looking at her phone, so I'm not sure if she's still listening or if I've bored her already.

"Does this have anything to do with Jake?" she asks.

I look up from my laptop screen.

"Why would this have anything to do with Jake?"

She shrugs.

"Angie told me you guys saw him with Alexander's assistant. That girl never gives up, does she?"

Even though we all think she's using Jake to get to me, it's very possible that they're really seeing each other, and I can't do anything about it. Alexander certainly didn't like the idea, so I don't think I've heard the end of it. If anything, her being distracted is certainly better for my relationship.

"I don't know what's going on between them. I'm expecting Alexander to find out. He was not happy when I told them we saw them together."

Gina puts her feet down on the floor.

"Was he mad?"

"Not exactly mad, but he did say he thought it was inappropriate."

She purses her lips.

"Huh. Maybe he's jealous."

What does she mean by that?

I laugh. "Why would he be jealous that she was with Jake?"

She gives me a look that clearly says she thinks I'm being naïve. I've seen this look before.

"Not necessarily that she was with Jake, just that she was with another man in general."

Seriously? She thinks Alexander is jealous that Melanie was out with someone. I'm sure she has dated people in the time she's worked for him. Right?

"All I'm saying is that men can be very territorial over their employees, and even though he may not be interested in her in a romantic way, he may not want another man to step in and take her attention away from him. And let's be honest, I'm sure he likes the attention she gives him. I certainly wouldn't mind having someone at my beck and call every day."

As crazy as this sounds, she may be onto something here. Alexander is extremely dependent on Melanie, so much that he's kept her around even after she caused issues in his marriage.

"Well, I for one hope she finds someone else," I insist. "Then maybe she will get out of our lives."

Gina raises her eyebrows.

"Even if that someone is Jake?"

I scowl. "Yes."

Thankfully, Gina has an appointment, so we end this conversation. My mind starts to wander to Melanie and her romantic history. I wonder if she's dated anyone in the few years she's worked for Alexander. I know how completely devoted she is to him, so I'm guessing she hasn't. What are the chances she's finally found someone else and that someone just happens to be my ex-boyfriend? Ugh. This just gets more and more complicated.

Chapter Three

I love how it feels when I complete a project. There is such an overwhelming feeling of accomplishment, and I love when my clients are happy. I just finished decorating a home for the son of Brad Cooper. Mr. Cooper was one of the first clients Summer Interiors had, and he also happens to be Jake's boss. I was a little nervous when he contacted me about working on a second project with him, especially considering Jake and I are no longer together. Thankfully, the project was a huge success, and I can add another beautiful home to my portfolio.

Ever since I was a little girl I knew I wanted to be an interior decorator. I will never forget when my mom bought a Victorian floral couch for her formal living room. She let me help her pick out the color for the walls. We painted the room a very pale pink to bring out the pink tones in the couch. This was in the '80s of course. Some of my favorite memories are of visiting furniture stores and model homes to check out the décor. My brother and I would walk down the rows in the store and pretend we lived there.

The best part of my job is going into a building for the first time and seeing it as a blank canvas. So, why am I so nervous when Alexander sends me some pictures of his parents' home? The home is very nice, a little outdated but nothing too horrible. Of course, I want to make a good impression on his parents without suggesting they change things they may love about their home.

There's a knock at my door, and I glance at the time. It's a bit early for Mrs. Rothera, considering she tends to sleep in. She doesn't use alarms of any kind because she claims they disturb the natural rhythm of the body or something like that.

When I answer the door, I find Angie standing there, and I immediately notice that something is off. It's not unusual for her to show up at my door at this time of day, but today she's not herself.

"What's the matter?" I ask worriedly.

She holds up a tray of coffee cups and a box of donuts.

I raise my eyebrows as I hold the door open for her to come in. She puts everything on the coffee table and falls dramatically down on the couch.

"Are you planning on talking to me or should I guess why you look so devastated?"

She opens her coffee cup and dumps in a few creamers and sugar.

"Of course I'm going to talk, why else would I be here?" she wails.

Angie can be slightly overdramatic, so I sit next to her on the couch and open the donut box.

"We're moving," she blurts out.

I give her a curious look. "What? Who's moving?"

She hangs her head while playing with her coffee cup. "Brett and I are moving . . . to Florida."

I sit still for few seconds as I try to collect my thoughts. I let her words register in my brain, my best friend is moving . . . and to Florida?

"Hold on," I exclaim. "Why don't you start at the beginning?"

She reaches for a chocolate donut and takes a huge bite. After she devours the entire thing, she lets out a deep sigh.

"Remember when I told you that Mrs. Rothera said something big was happening. Well, I thought Brett was going to propose, so I finally asked him why he's been acting so strange. He says he was planning a trip to Orlando for us so he could tell me about the new job offer. He's asked me to go with him, and of course I said yes."

I must be in shock. Angie is moving to sunny, warm Florida. Also known as the home of Disney World, humidity, and alligators.

"Of course, I can run Friendship Travel from anywhere, so it's not that big of a deal for me. And just think, now you can come visit during the winter months and we can go to Disney World and the beach."

I nod slowly.

"Summer? Are you okay?"

I feel like crying. What am I going to do without my best friend?

"Yeah. When is this move happening?"

She frowns. "Within the next few months, he wants to find a house and get settled before the school year starts."

"I had no idea he was looking for a new job. Especially not thousands of miles away," I say softly.

She shrugs. "We've talked about it in the past, but I figured it would be a while." She stops and reaches for another donut.

I have to wonder if Angie is really happy about this. Yes, she can work her business from anywhere, but her life is here.

"Brett's dad is there and so are Isabella and Antonietta and their families. It's really a good move, and let's face it, this past winter was a killer."

I can't disagree with her about the winter, it was miserable. But I'm a little surprised she wants to live near her sisters. It's not that she doesn't get along with them, but they tend to be slightly overbearing.

"Wow." That's all I can say at this point.

"I know it's a shock, but it's going to be okay. And you have a terrific future ahead of you with Alexander."

I sigh as I take another donut out of the box. "I wish I was as confident about my relationship as you are."

She shakes her head. "Why do you say that? Does this have to do with Helena again?"

I shake my head. "No. I'm probably overreacting."

"Probably," she interrupts.

I scowl. "I was talking to Gina and she said something that got me thinking."

"Gina?"

I give a half smile. "I know, right? Anyway, she asked if I thought Alexander was jealous that Melanie was out with Jake. I never thought about it before, but what if Alexander likes having Melanie there whenever he needs something? Maybe he doesn't want to have to share her."

Angie listens intently. "I could see that, but I don't think that has anything to do with your relationship with Alexander."

I groan and cover my face with a pillow. "You can't leave. How am I ever going to survive without you?"

She laughs. "You'll be fine. But there is one thing you have to do for me."

I raise my eyebrows. I'm hesitant to agree to anything Angie says without knowing what it is.

"Promise me we will always spend Halloween together," she begs.

And that's all it takes for me to start the ugly cry, which makes Angie start the ugly cry. I can only imagine what people would think if they walked in to find us binging on donuts and crying.

"I'm really happy for you," I tell her after I pull myself together. "And a little jealous."

She laughs. "You could join us."

That's actually tempting, but with my career really starting to take off, I have no plans to leave Connecticut anytime soon.

Angie ends up staying for the majority of the day, and we spend most of the afternoon taking a trip down memory lane. We spend hours looking through yearbooks and photo albums. I can't believe that in a few months Angie will be thousands of miles away. Sometimes I wish I could run away to Disney World, too. Of course, I'm really happy for her and Brett. I'm expecting the proposal isn't far behind.

Several hours later, I'm finally firing up my laptop when Alexander calls.

"Hey, babe. How was your day?"

I sigh loudly. "Very unproductive. I was just going to do some research for your parents' house."

Of course, Alexander can sense my distress, so I tell him all about Angie's news and he's very understanding as always.

"I'm sorry. I know how close you two are."

Ugh. I remember when Angie went away to summer camp one year. I was lost without her and that was only for two weeks. This is going to be a whole new experience for me.

"Yeah, it's going to be hard. But I know life changes and people move on. I'm happy for her."

Alexander tells me about his day, and I start to zone out. He mentions Melanie but nothing about her and Jake. I'm curious if he asked her, but I don't want to be the one to bring it up.

"Is anything else bothering you or is it just Angie's news?"

Crap. Did I miss something he said?

"What?" I say absently.

He laughs. "I can always tell when you aren't listening."

I cringe.

"I'm sorry. I zoned out for a second."

Just then, there's a knock at my door. Crap. Mrs. Rothera is right on time as usual. I've been so distracted by Angie that I almost forgot she was supposed to stop by tonight.

"Ugh. This is exactly why I need to move," I say out loud.

"What?" he asks curiously.

"Mrs. Rothera. She wants to go over more decorating ideas."

He laughs. "I'll let you take care of that. Call me later."

I start to dig through the mess that is all over my apartment. I had all my ideas for her in a folder.

"Be right there," I call. I rush to the door and pull it open. Although, it's not Mrs. Rothera at the door, it's Jake.

Chapter Four

I'm definitely not expecting Jake to be standing outside the door when I open it. The last time he was here didn't go so well, so I'm not sure why he would come back.

"Jake. What are you doing here?"

He shoves his hands in his pockets and rocks back on his heels. "I'm sorry to stop in unexpectedly. I was in the neighborhood, and well . . . there's something I wanted to talk to you about."

Seriously? He couldn't just text or even call me?

"Okay, but I only have a few minutes. Mrs. Rothera should be here any minute."

He frowns. Mrs. Rothera doesn't care for Jake and he knows it. He walks in my apartment and starts talking right away.

"This is awkward, but I feel like I owe it to you to tell you in person."

I fold my arms tightly against my chest. I already have a feeling this has to do with Melanie.

"I've started seeing someone and . . ."

"You're seeing Melanie," I interrupt.

He opens his eyes wider. "Yes, how did you know?"

I tell him about seeing them at the café, and he looks surprised. I guess they didn't see us after all.

"Who you choose to date is your business, Jake," I say flatly.

He nods. "I know, but being that you're seeing her boss, I felt I owed it to you to be honest. And you made it clear that we would never have a chance again."

I purse my lips. I'm not sure what that has to do with him seeing Melanie. I'm trying to decide if I should warn him about her unhealthy attachment to Alexander.

"Melanie is very devoted to Alexander," I say carefully.

He nods. "I know. We've talked about him a great deal. And you."

Me?

"What could Melanie possibly say about me?"

He shrugs. "She told me how protective she is of Alexander and how she had reservations about him getting involved again so quickly after his divorce. She's not just his assistant—she's his friend."

I bite my tongue a little harder in order to stop myself from bashing Melanie. That would be completely immature and petty. Of course, it would be fun, too, but that's not the point.

"I told her that you're a good person and that you would never do anything to hurt him . . . or anyone." He trails off. There is the familiar expression of guilt on his face that I've seen before.

"Yes, I would never hurt Alexander, and from what I know about his divorce, it was a mutual decision."

He shrugs. "Yes, but she initiated it."

Okay, I'm not trying to get into a discussion about Alexander's past relationship.

"I appreciate you stopping by Jake, but I need to get some work done. It's been a very long, emotional day."

He eyes me curiously. "Everything okay?"

I exhale. "It will be. I just found out Angie and Brett are moving to Florida."

His mouth drops open. "Really? That's definitely surprising news."

I don't answer him. He knows Angie doesn't like him either because of what he did to me.

Mrs. Rothera knocks on the door before I'm able to kick Jake out. I groan as I know she will be very curious as to why he's back in my apartment again.

"Crap."

He holds up his hands. "Should I escape through a window?"

I shrug. "That's not a bad idea. Thanks for stopping by."

When I open the door, Jake says a quick hello to Mrs. Rothera before he practically races out of my apartment.

"It's not what it looks like," I say quickly before she has a chance to give me one of her famous looks of disapproval.

She smiles. "I didn't say anything."

I close the door behind her. "You didn't, but I know what you're thinking."

I pick up my laptop from my desk and bring it to the couch where she's patiently waiting. I open the folder on my desktop that I have set up for her. She's being very quiet, so quiet that it's freaking me out a little. Normally, she's rambling on about all kinds of nonsense.

"I'm sorry I don't have all of this ready for you; it's been a hectic day."

She raises an eyebrow. "Anything I can help with?"

I shake my head. "I found out Angie's moving out of state. I'm just a little sad."

She gives me a sympathetic look.

"Oh dear, that's a shame."

I hang my head. "Yeah, I don't know what I will do without her."

She pats me on the arm. "Well, you have me. I mean, in case you ever need someone to talk to."

I give her a grateful smile. "I appreciate that."

And I do appreciate it. As frustrated as I get with her always popping in, I know she means well. I turn the computer toward her so she can see the color scheme I picked out for her guest room.

"And as far as Jake goes, he just came by to tell me he's seeing someone. It doesn't bother me, but it's kind of an awkward situation."

She nods. "Of course he did. He's looking for your approval."

I snort. "I'm not sure I can give him that because he's seeing Melanie. I don't know if that's a good thing or not."

Mrs. Rothera knows all about Melanie and my complicated relationship. In fact, Melanie was the one who told her I was looking for a new place. This didn't go over well with Alexander, but somehow she managed to talk her way out of it as usual.

She's busy scrolling through my ideas on the computer. I'm wondering if she already knew about Melanie and Jake. I still don't know if she has any client-psychic confidentiality agreements.

"You should give him your blessing. That way he knows without a doubt you've moved on."

I nod. "I have moved on." I pause. "But you're right, I need to give them my blessing. And I'm glad Melanie has someone to distract her, even if it is Jake. Sometimes I feel like I have to share Alexander. It's frustrating."

I don't know why I suddenly feel the need to unload on her. I usually try to stay reserved when talking to her.

"Just be careful," she says wistfully.

"Be careful about what?" I ask.

She has a very pensive expression on her face. It's almost as if she's watching something unfold.

"Don't try too hard to push her out. There may not be romantic feelings for her, but she's important to him."

My mind wanders back to what Gina said. Maybe Alexander is jealous, and maybe he really doesn't want to share Melanie with anyone else

∼

Mrs. Rothera finally leaves after what feels like hours, but she was actually only here for about an hour and a half. I must be really struggling with the news of Angie moving because I didn't mind her company at all tonight.

I finally crawl into bed around one o'clock after talking to Alexander for a few minutes. As I lie in my bed, I think about everything that has happened in my life since last summer. I remember this time last year Jake and I were in a very committed relationship. I truly believed we had a great future ahead of us.

Things sure have changed and I have moved on, so it would be silly to not expect Jake to do the same. Alexander is an amazing man, and I believe he loves me. Despite everything that has happened between us, I'm happy that he's bringing me home to meet his family.

I really should listen to what Angie said. We could have an

awesome future ahead of us, and it's up to me to push past my insecurities and focus on that. I want to tell him how I feel about him and that I love him, too. I stretch out and pull the covers tightly around me. Spring is in the air and it's time for a fresh start and for me that means a fresh new attitude.

Chapter Five

I'm definitely a different person when the sun is out. The more I think about it, I could totally move to Florida. I'm sitting at an outdoor table at Starbucks (outdoors!), and it's glorious. As I look around, I can see that the other customers are enjoying the weather just as much as I am. Spring has come at the perfect time.

I'm busy prepping for my big night tonight, aka the night I meet Alexander's parents. I shouldn't be that worried because parents usually like me. Jake's mom and stepdad live in Boston, but I met them twice and they told Jake he should propose right away. Yeah, that certainly didn't go like they had hoped.

I asked Alexander if I had anything to worry about, and he insisted they couldn't wait to meet me.

I haven't seen Alexander in almost a week because he's been traveling for work, so I'm beyond ready for our reunion. He still hasn't mentioned anything about Melanie and Jake, and I haven't brought it up either. I'm really trying hard to have a fresh new outlook and focus on our future together. Alexander being the awesome boyfriend he is agreed to let me host a good-bye party for Angie and Brett at his house.

I spend the remainder of the morning contacting potential clients from referrals, and the best part is that I stay outside the entire time.

I change my outfit four times before finally deciding on a cute and classy high-low dress with wedges. I'm just putting on my jewelry when there's a knock at the door. Alexander is leaning against the doorframe when I open the door.

"Hi. I'm so . . ."

Before I finish talking, Alexander scoops me up in his arms and kisses me as if his life depended on it. After he places me back down on the ground, he closes his eyes and puts his forehead to mine.

"I've missed you," he whispers softly. "Next time, you have to join me because I hate being away from you for that long."

I wrap my arms around his neck. "I think that can be arranged."

His lips press hard against mine, and I know I'm going to need to touch up my makeup, but I don't care.

I run my fingers slowly down his biceps. "Do you think your mom would be devastated if we canceled on her? We could stay here."

He throws his head back. "Don't tempt me. As much as I love my parents, I would rather spend the evening alone with you."

I head to the bathroom to fix my makeup. Alexander comes up behind me and wraps his arms around my waist.

"I was serious, though, what would you say about coming with me on my next trip? I want to spend time with you without any distractions."

I smile. "I think it sounds perfect, sign me up."

We start kissing again, and I finally push him out of the bathroom so I can make myself presentable again.

∼

What is only an hour drive feels like five hours. The knots in my stomach are getting increasingly tighter as we get closer. Alexander's talking a mile a minute about work and his recent trip. I'm trying to be the supportive girlfriend, but I'm too busy obsessing over every possible scenario that could happen tonight. I'm also making a mental list of possible excuses I can use to make a quick getaway, should I need to. I even texted Angie and asked her to be on standby in case I call with some kind of fake emergency. Of course, she thinks I'm losing it and maybe I am. I'm bringing a gorgeous bouquet of fresh flowers and a bottle of wine. I was always taught it's important to never show up empty-handed, especially the first time you're meeting your boyfriend's parents.

"You're very quiet," Alexander says, reaching for my hand. "You really don't have to be nervous. My parents are not that scary, well, maybe my mom's a little scary, but only because she's the one who always caught me getting into trouble."

I laugh nervously. "I know. I just want to make a good impression."

He kisses my hand. "You will, and I know they're going to love your ideas for the house."

"Well, I would like to get to know them before I just walk in there and start changing things. That wouldn't the best way to win them over."

A few minutes later, we pull into a long driveway on the right side of a charming two-story brick home. I have to admit it's even more stunning in person. The first thing I notice are the tall white pillars on both sides of the door and white shutters at every window. I notice that fresh bushes and flowers have been planted around the front porch, another reason I love springtime.

"Here we are," Alexander announces loudly.

I take a few deep breaths and get out of the car. There's a large wooden deck on the backside of the house. We walk up a few steps toward two French doors. Alexander holds my hand tightly in his. I take a few breaths and plaster a big smile on my face.

A taller, older version of Alexander greets us at the door. He's obviously Alexander's father, and I'm amazed at how much they look alike. Now I know what Alexander will look like in a few years, and it's definitely a good thing.

"Hello, son," he says, holding out his hand to shake.

"Hello, Father." Alexander shakes his hand, and then they hug in the typical manly kind of way. They're both smiling, so this must be some kind of inside joke I don't know about.

We all walk into the house, and immediately I start looking around to get decorating ideas. As usual, it's fun and exciting to see a brand new blank canvas.

"And who did you bring with you today?" he asks, looking past Alexander toward me.

Alexander smiles proudly.

"Dad, I would like you to meet my amazing girlfriend, Summer Peters."

Of course, I start to blush.

"It's wonderful to meet you, Mr. Williams," I say politely.

"It's very nice to meet you. I've heard quite a bit about you. And please call me Rick."

We follow Rick down a hallway and into the spacious kitchen. I immediately get excited at the possibility of giving this kitchen a fresh new start. The walls are painted a very pale yellow; it's not ugly, just outdated. The cabinets are oak, very well made, but could use a facelift.

The island is covered with a variety of appetizers, including bruschetta, vegetables, mini quiches, and a cheese platter. There's enough food to feed an army and that's just appetizers. There's a mouth-watering aroma coming from the oven.

"Where's Mom?" Alexander asks, taking a carrot from the vegetable tray. He puts the bottle of wine down on the counter.

"She ran to the market for something, should be back in a few minutes."

I'm still holding the bouquet of flowers, so I hand them to Alexander.

"Let's leave these here. I'm sure Mom will want to put them in a vase."

Rick offers us a drink, and I manage to bite my tongue to stop myself from asking him for a shot of tequila. A few minutes later, he takes us down to the basement where he proudly unveils his new man cave. Apparently, Penny (Alexander's mother) has banished him and his sports memorabilia collection to the basement. His collection is very impressive, full of autographed football helmets, pictures, balls, etc.

"Wow. My father would love this room," I exclaim, looking around at the walls. "He's been a football coach for years."

Rick smiles mischievously. "Giants or Jets fan?"

I laugh. "Jets."

He punches the air. "Good man. Our team doesn't get the accolades they deserve. All those bandwagon fans are so disloyal. I'm a Jets fan for life."

I throw my head back in laughter. "I've heard this before."

Rick puts his arm around Alexander and pretends to whisper in his ear. "I'm liking this girl already, son."

Alexander pretends to whisper back. "Me, too."

I start to blush again. I wonder if I'm going to be blushing all day today.

While Rick and Alexander talk, I walk around and look at his collection. Obviously, I won't be redecorating anything in this basement. I hear my phone buzzing from my bag; Angie's sent me several texts asking how things are going. I excuse myself and walk back upstairs. I don't feel comfortable wandering around the house alone, so I sit down at the table in the kitchen and text her back.

So far so good. Haven't met his mom yet.

I'm just about to send another text when I hear a door shut and see an attractive brunette walking down the hall toward the kitchen carrying two grocery bags. I see she's struggling with the bags, so I rush to help her.

"Let me take one of those for you," I say, grabbing the bag before she drops it.

"Thank you."

We put the bags down and finally come face to face.

"I'm Summer," I say warmly.

For a second, I feel like she's sizing me up. I'm sure it's the typical motherly thing to do, checking out the woman who's taking her place in her son's life. But considering Alexander was married, this shouldn't be a new feeling for her. Add in the fact that her son has hired me to redecorate her home. I didn't even consider the possibility that she could have been close to Helena. What if she feels the same way about Alexander and Helena as his best friends do? They would love nothing more than for them to reconcile.

"You're the decorator."

Okay, so that was a little on the cold side, but I promised Alexander I wouldn't overreact.

And I'm your son's girlfriend but whatever. Of course, I don't say that out loud.

"Yes. I'm not sure if Alexander told you or not but I have my own company, Summer Interiors."

She starts to empty her grocery bags onto the counter.

"Yes, he did, and I've heard very good things. I'm Penny."

I can definitely see why Alexander is so good-looking. Both of his parents are attractive, and they obviously take good care of themselves.

"Where is Alexander?"

"He's downstairs with his father, enjoying the man cave."

She rolls her eyes.

"That doesn't surprise me. He comes home for the first time in months and immediately gets sucked into the basement."

"I didn't get sucked in. I'm right here," Alexander interrupts. He holds out his arms, and Penny rushes to give him a hug.

"My handsome boy," she exclaims, cupping his cheeks with her hands.

It's very sweet to watch them interact. But, I'm a little unsure of Penny and her reception of me. I know it's our first meeting, so I won't read too much into it, but I have a feeling something's off.

"This is a lot of food, Mom," Alexander says, looking at the spread on the island.

She waves her hand back and forth.

"You can never have too much food, and Anna said she may try to stop by."

Anna is Alexander's older sister; he's mentioned her a few times. Apparently, she's a busy mom of four and the PTA President.

After a few glasses of wine and about twenty mini quiches, I'm much more relaxed. When we finally sit down for dinner, I'm so full but I know how much time Penny's put into the meal, so I force myself to take a few bites.

"Mom, this is delicious," Alexander says, as he digs into the pork tenderloin and roasted potatoes.

"Thank you. I got the recipe from Melanie; her food is always a huge hit."

At the mention of Melanie, I start to choke on my potatoes. I can't believe one of my biggest fears may actually happen . . . I'm going to die from choking.

"Summer, are you okay?" Alexander shrieks.

I manage to clear my throat after chugging my entire glass of water.

"Ahem . . . yes, I'm okay. Sorry, it went down wrong."

Once I get over seeing my life flash before my eyes and the embarrassment, it hits me that Penny and Melanie are sharing recipes. It could be nothing, but it makes me start to wonder about Penny's immediate reaction to me. I thought she might have been sizing me up because I'm taking Helena's place, but that may not be the case.

"Penny, everything is delicious," I exclaim. I'm hoping she takes the bait and offers up some more information about Melanie.

"Thank you. Melanie has some fantastic recipes, both the pork and the potatoes. The key lime pie I made for dessert is also her recipe. They're all wonderful."

I glance at Alexander who's practically licking his plate. I think it's pretty clear that Penny and Melanie are friends, and that doesn't bode well for me.

Following dinner, I help Alexander clean up the dishes while his parents set up the fire pit in the backyard.

"Why are you so quiet?"

I shrug my shoulders.

"No. Tell me what's bothering you. Are you not enjoying yourself?"

I turn to face him and lean against the counter.

"I guess your mom and Melanie are friends, huh?"

He opens his mouth to say something, and then immediately closes it.

"Thank you both for helping," Penny interrupts.

Crap. I hope she didn't hear me ask about her friendship with Melanie.

"The coffee is on, and we can have dessert whenever you're ready."

Ugh, how about never. I feel like I'm going to explode. As soon as I heard the food was all from the cookbook of Melanie, I forced myself to eat almost all of it.

"Oh wow. I definitely need to make some room," I exclaim.

Alexander and I make our way outside. The subject of me redecorating hasn't come up, and I'm certainly not going to bring it up. We've talked about Anna and her family, Alexander's job, and Rick and Penny's Alaskan cruise, but nothing about me changing Penny's house. I'm getting the feeling it was all Alexander's idea and she's not really keen on the idea.

The four of us are sitting around the fire. I'm wrapped in a warm blanket, and Alexander has his arm around me.

"So, tell me again how you two met?" Penny asks.

He gives me a loving smile. "I was looking for someone to decorate the new place, and Summer Interiors came very highly recommended from the reviews. Now looking back, there was something that drew me to her. I know it was meant to be."

There I go again, blushing. Luckily, it's dark outside so they won't notice.

"I still remember our first meeting," I say, with a laugh. "When I asked him which rooms he was interested in decorating, he said all of them. I admit I was more excited about working with Alexander than about contracting a new client."

"It was the best business decision I ever made," he says, kissing my forehead.

My heart begins to flutter. It occurs to me that Melanie and Penny may be sharing recipes but Alexander loves me. I need to trust in that.

"Same for me," I say, looking into his eyes.

"That's my boy," Rick says proudly. "Good taste in teams and women." We all start to laugh, including Penny.

Alexander and I finally have a few minutes alone when Penny and Rick bring the coffee cups and plates inside.

"Can you do me a favor?" I whisper.

"Of course."

"Can you not mention the redecorating tonight? If your mom brings it up, that's one thing. I just want them to get to know me as your girlfriend first."

He smiles. "Okay, I won't say anything. At least, not tonight."

Chapter Six

It's been four days since my dinner with Alexander's parents, and he's been so busy with work that I haven't seen him. Today, he's working in town and I'm meeting him at his office for lunch. I'm expecting to run into Melanie for the first time since Jake told me they were dating, and I have no idea how she's going to act toward me. Although, finding out she and Alexander's mother are buddies certainly complicates things a little more. I really shouldn't complain because the family dinner ended up being fine. Of course, the subject of me redecorating never came up, and honestly, I'm okay with that. I finally explained my feelings about it to Alexander and he was very understanding. If Penny and Rick want me to decorate their home, they can ask me themselves.

I've started planning Angie's good-bye party, and I get emotional just thinking about it. She keeps telling me we have plenty of time, but I have a feeling the big move is going to be sooner than we all expect. We've set the date for the party in three weeks, and I've already been sending invitations.

When I arrive at the office, Melanie is sitting at her desk staring at her laptop. I can hear Alexander talking on his phone in his office.

"Hello, Melanie."

She turns around and gives me a half wave, half smile.

"Alexander's on an important call. You may have to wait for a little while, or you can come back if you have something else to do."

I nod and sit down in one of the chairs. It's not surprising that she wants to get rid of me as quickly as possible.

"I'll just wait for now."

She continues working while I silently look at my phone.

"What did you think of Penny and Rick?"

I'm not sure I feel comfortable talking about Alexander's parents with Melanie. What if I say something the wrong way and it gets twisted? She will totally use that against me. Whether she's in a new relationship or not, I know she's still threatened by me.

"They were great."

She gives me a smug smile.

"They are. I got to know them really well when we went to Key West together."

Huh? Key West? She went on a trip with them?

Once again, I'm not going to make a big deal out of this. And even if I am upset, I'm going to pretend I'm *not* upset.

"Oh, by the way, your pork tenderloin recipe was delicious," I say sweetly. I have every intention to kill her with kindness.

She laughs. "Did Penny serve the pork again? She makes it every time they entertain. Did she make the mini quiches this time?

Holy crap. I figured those quiches were from the frozen food section at Costco. I'm not going to tell her I ate twenty of them or that I loved them.

"Yes, they were good."

Once again, we're both quiet. I wonder if there will ever come a time when things aren't awkward between us.

"So, how are things going with Jake?"

She raises an eyebrow.

"Things are good."

I'm totally going to take this opportunity and run with it.

"That's what Jake said when he stopped by. I'm really happy for him . . . for both of you. I hope Jake finds as much happiness as I have with Alexander."

I force myself to keep from laughing at her expression. I think she may be in shock to hear that I'm publicly giving them my blessing. I still believe she was hoping I would get jealous and try to get back together with him. That would have freed Alexander so she could have him all to herself.

"I am happy with him. So much that sometimes it's hard to

concentrate on work. I would love to spend more time with him."

"What makes it so hard to concentrate?" Alexander asks.

He has a worried expression on his face.

"Her new boyfriend," I tease. She glares at me. If looks could kill, I'd probably be dead.

He shakes his head.

"None of that right now. We have to get this acquisition completed. I need you all in right now."

Hearing Alexander talk about not losing Melanie doesn't surprise me, and for some reason, Mrs. Rothera's advice keeps repeating in my head. I can't force Melanie out, and as much as I don't want to, I have to share him. At least for right now.

"You ready?" he asks, dragging me out of my thought.

I nod. "Yep."

"We'll be back in an hour," he tells Melanie. "If you need me, call."

Crap. I'm expecting her to call before we even get in the car.

I can tell Alexander is distracted today, and I know it's because of all he has going on with work. We're almost halfway to the restaurant when he brings up my conversation with Melanie.

"What were you two discussing? It seemed like everyone was on their best behavior and not one punch was thrown."

I give him a half smile. "Actually, we were talking about her and Jake."

This is the first time the subject of Melanie and Jake has come up since they've officially become a couple. It's obvious how uncomfortable Alexander is.

"Yeah, I'm sorry about that. I'm sure it's not easy for you."

The thing is it doesn't bother me as much I thought it would. I think this is a good sign that I'm moving past everything that happened with Jake last summer. If anything, it seems to bother Alexander more than it bothers me.

"Believe it or not, it doesn't really bother me. We're both moving on; that's what's supposed to happen."

Granted, I never expected him to move on with my boyfriend's assistant, but when it comes to things Jake does, I'm not surprised anymore.

"Not to change the subject, but I didn't realize Melanie and your mom were so close, other than sharing recipes."

He shrugs nonchalantly. "Melanie's been working with me for a while. She's met my family on several occasions. I wouldn't say they're friends, though, maybe a message every few months."

"Well, she made it sound like they were very close. She mentioned going on the family trip to Key West."

Alexander looks uncomfortable. "It's not what you think."

"How do you know what I'm thinking?" I ask curiously.

I can see how agitated he's becoming, and maybe I should just drop it. It really isn't important anymore.

"My sister was getting married in Key West, and we were closing a huge deal at work. Melanie came with me, and we spent most of the time working. It wasn't anything more than that."

I look out the window without saying anything.

"Melanie seems to think it was more or she wouldn't have tried to rub it in my face. Well, that and being besties with your mom."

Alexander exhales loudly. "I'm sorry, Summer. I don't know what else to do here. Neither of you like the other, and I'm stuck in the middle."

I feel guilty for a half a second, but I refuse to explain myself again. I can't count how many times I've tried with Melanie. It started with smug comments, selling me out to Mrs. Rothera, and now she's dating my ex-boyfriend. I'm not the one instigating this.

"I never intended to put you in the middle. I do realize she's going to be a major part of our lives. That is unless she lets Jake take over her life."

He frowns. "I appreciate that you understand, and I know how difficult it is. Melanie knows me, she knows my business, and it would be a nightmare trying to train someone else. I need her."

I would be lying if I say that didn't sting a bit.

We finally pull up at the restaurant. Talk about perfect timing. It's now clear that *if* Alexander and I are in this for the long haul I will always be sharing him. I would never make him choose, and honestly, if I did, I'm not sure he would choose me.

Chapter Seven

I stare at my computer screen. I could be dreaming right now, although it feels more like a nightmare. I'm in a state of shock when I see an email from Helena asking for a meeting to discuss the contract. I really believed we were past this and it wasn't happening. I guess I was wrong.

I could tell her my schedule is full and I'm not taking any more clients. That would be the nicer and much more professional way of saying "you snooze, you lose." The problem with this is that my schedule is not that full right now. Other than decorating Mrs. Rothera's bedrooms, I have one other project getting ready to start. And that's all until the summer. I have the time for Helena's apartment, and I can always use the business.

I groan as I send her a response agreeing to the meeting.

I'm sure it's going to be fine. The last thing I heard was that she reconciled with her hot French boyfriend and she's happy in her relationship. And the good thing about decorating her place is I can get rid of all the pictures of her and Alexander. I wouldn't throw them away, but I would pack them safely in a box never to be seen again. Helena was very specific about wanting a fresh new look in her home, and that's what she's going to get. Now if only I can stay sane throughout the whole project, then I will consider it a success.

As much as I'm not looking forward to dealing with Helena and her high-maintenance ways, I've decided it's better than putting up with Melanie. Ugh. I can't believe I'm thinking this way. Helena is truly the lesser of two evils. I pick up the phone to call Alexander.

At first, I don't think Alexander was happy with the idea of me working with her, but he doesn't seem to care now. It could be that he's so preoccupied with work that he doesn't hear me when I tell him about Helena contacting me. I can hear him typing on his laptop and another phone ringing in the background. We get off the phone after talking for maybe three minutes, or rather, I talked for three minutes.

~

"I called it months ago," Gina says smugly. "That girl has had her sights on your man for a while now. She succeeded in getting rid of the wife, and you're next."

Gina, Angie, and I are at dinner, and I just told them about the family dinner and Melanie's claims of being best friends with Penny.

"Gina, why do you have to be so harsh?" Angie yells.

She rolls her eyes. "It's not harsh, it's the facts. I told you that girl was trouble. You know I can make it all go away, don't you?"

Angie and I glance at each other, and she shakes her head. Let's just say Gina's uncle has his own ways of getting people to behave. One call from Gina and my problems with Melanie would probably disappear, which isn't a bad idea. But if that ever got back to Alexander, it would be the end of that.

"Alexander would probably never forgive me for that."

Gina pulls the crust off her piece of Italian bread and dips it in the olive oil.

"So, does this tramp like Alexander or Jake?"

I giggle. "She's not a tramp . . . at least, I don't think she is. I really don't know anything about her personal life, other than she seems to covet the men I'm involved with." I pause. "And to answer your question, I don't know who she likes. If I had to guess, I think she's in love with Alexander and is only using Jake to piss me off and make Alexander jealous."

Gina pounds on the table. "And you're just going to let her get away with this?"

I glance at Angie who's been surprisingly quiet. She looks perplexed.

"What's up with you?" I ask her, clearly ignoring Gina's outburst.

She's playing with the straw in her glass.

"We set our moving date. We're leaving in three weeks."

We're all silent, even Gina who has clearly forgotten about the revenge plot she was planning in her mind.

"I knew it would be sooner than expected," I say sadly. "That's why I set the party so soon. Once you and Brett set your minds on something, it's usually done quickly."

She has a pained look on her face.

"Yeah, we're kind of annoying, aren't we?"

"Hell yeah, you are," Gina chimes in. "It gives us procrastinators a bad rep."

We all laugh. I'm glad Gina's here for the comic relief on what would be a sad afternoon. I hate to say it, but I'd almost rather talk about Gina's possible revenge plan than the fact that my best friend will be thousands of miles away in a few weeks.

"Please, can we talk about something else?" Angie begs.

I may as well take this opportunity to give them the low down on my latest career dilemma.

"Helena requested a meeting to go over the contract I sent her. I guess she wants me to decorate her apartment after all."

"She did?" Angie squawks. "I would've bet she was playing you the whole time."

"Seriously, you mean to tell me there isn't one decorator in all of Manhattan?" Gina adds.

I shrug my shoulders. "I guess since both Alexander and Nick hired me, she wants to follow suit."

While Gina and Angie discuss the possible reasons why Helena is hiring me, I zone out.

So far, this spring isn't turning out the way I had hoped. Melanie is still intertwined in my relationship and now involved with my ex, Helena wants me to be her decorator, and my best friend is leaving in three weeks. Huh, maybe I will just have to look forward to summer.

∽

I arrive at Nick's restaurant earlier than I expected. You never know with New York City traffic. Helena and I agreed to meet here because it's a great central location and the food is amazing, not to mention we know the owners. It also doesn't hurt for her to see some of my work as a reminder that I'm good at what I do.

"Well hello, stranger," Nick says, greeting me at the door. "Where are you hiding my best friend?"

Hmm . . . that's funny. However, it does make me feel better knowing that I'm not the only one who isn't seeing much of Alexander.

"I have no idea, but when you find him, let me know."

He starts to laugh.

"He's closing a huge deal right now, so I'm sure he'll resurface as soon as that's complete."

He nods. "I spoke with him about a week ago, and he sounded really overwhelmed. It will pay off in the end, right?"

"I hope so. He really needs to slow down, but at least he has Melanie to help him."

Okay, so I know that was a sly way of bringing up the fact that Melanie is with my boyfriend more than I am.

Nick gives me a curious look. "Is someone feeling a little insecure in their relationship?"

I laugh. "It wouldn't be the first time. Sometimes it's hard having to share Alexander with Melanie."

He purses his lips. "That's what Helena used to say to Caroline all the time."

Damn, he actually took the bait. I hope this doesn't come back to bite me.

"What do you mean?"

He shakes his head. "First of all, I know what you're thinking. Trust me when I tell you there's nothing romantic between Xander and Melanie. However, he does depend on her . . . probably more than he should and she latches onto that. If anything, I think it gives her some false hope that they could be more someday."

"So, you think he leads her on?"

He shakes his head. "No, he just makes it very obvious how much he depends on her."

I'm just about to ask his advice on how to handle the situation when he's summoned from the kitchen.

When I sit down at our table, I take out my laptop and open the file for Helena. I stare at the screen, but I'm really thinking about what Nick said. Everyone, including Alexander himself, insists there's nothing romantic there, so it just comes down to me being secure enough in how he feels about me.

"Hello, Summer."

I look up to see Helena, the Swedish goddess, standing next to me. She's wearing a gray and white off-the-shoulder sweater, and her hair is up in a half bun on top of her head. She's as stunning as ever.

"Hi," I say cheerfully.

"Thanks for the meeting. I would have contacted you sooner, but my schedule wouldn't allow it. And Jacques and I went on a short holiday."

I smile. I can see how happy she is.

"I'm glad everything worked out for you two."

She nods. "So am I. Shall we look over everything? I have another appointment following this."

Shockingly, Helena and I have a very productive meeting. She seems to be receptive to most of my ideas, or it could be that she's just telling me what I want to hear. And before we end our meeting, she signs the contract. So, I guess this means she's officially my new client. Wow, who would have thought I'd be working with my boyfriend's ex-wife? Oh well, I'm not going to let it concern me. She's moved on and so has Alexander. I'm just going to keep my fingers crossed that everything will go smoothly.

Chapter Eight

The last few days have been exhausting. Ever since Angie announced that they were moving in a few weeks, I've been in full party planning mode. The planning has helped to distract me from the sadness of her leaving. I even rented a karaoke machine as a throwback to our college days. We loved going to karaoke night, so I thought it would be a fun way to celebrate. I feel like I could sleep for days, so when I arrive home from the city, I'm ready to crash. Until I see the note Mrs. Rothera left for me on my door.

Please stop by my place when you get home.

-Mrs. R

I groan loudly. On the other hand, if I look on the bright side, at least she didn't come to my apartment unannounced. I'm sure this has something to do with her apartment; maybe she's changed her mind on the style already. Based on the last project I did with her, she changed her mind at least four different times, so it's probably that time.

I shouldn't complain because our last interaction went really well. I actually enjoyed her company.

And if she asks me how my apartment search is going, she'll be happy to know that I haven't had time to look for a new place in days, so as of right now, I'm not going anywhere.

I slowly make my way back downstairs, and when I approach the door, I hear music playing. This isn't the first time I've heard this music. It's a weird mixture of sounds, like different instruments, chanting, and humming. She claims this is meditation music but to me it sounds like a bunch of noise. I knock loudly on the door, and sure enough, she answers a few seconds later. I have no idea how she hears me when that music is playing, but she does every time.

"Sorry to bother you. I just got your note."

She has a very calm and serene look on her face. I guess the meditation noise-music works.

"Thank you for coming," she says calmly, actually it sounds more like she's singing. I walk into her dark living room, and she quickly turns on the lights.

"I wanted to talk to you about my bedroom. I'm just not feeling what we discussed."

I knew it. I take my tablet out of my bag to get ready to jot down her new ideas. At least I didn't put a lot of time into this yet.

"I hope you don't think I'm being difficult."

I stare at my tablet trying not to make any kind of eye contact with her. I'm not going to answer that. It's probably better than trying to lie my way out of it.

"What did you have in mind instead of the Moroccan?" I ask, changing the subject before she asks me again.

She sits down and begins taking slow, deep breaths. What the hell is she doing? It looks like she's going into labor.

"I'm thinking the islands of the South Pacific. Maybe some palms, floral, bamboo. Oh, maybe I should get an aquarium? That would definitely give it an island feel."

An aquarium? She can't be serious. I quickly type up the notes as she's talking.

"Okay, I will get started on this."

I head for the door when she stops me.

"Forgive me for asking, but you seem very concerned about something."

I laugh loudly. "When am I not concerned? It seems like I'm always worrying about something."

Mrs. Rothera doesn't seem to find this as funny as I do.

"Angie's leaving in a few weeks, and I guess I've been going through a rough time thinking about her being so far away."

She nods her head, but I know she can see right through me. All of a sudden, something comes over me and I feel the need to completely unload on her. It feels as if the words begin to pour out of my mouth like vomit.

"And there's the whole thing with Alexander and Melanie . . .

again." As soon as I say it out loud, I immediately hope I don't regret it.

"Ah yes, but the last I heard there wasn't an Alexander and Melanie. I thought she was dating Jake."

I roll my eyes.

"She *is* dating Jake. For what reasons, I don't know other than in an attempt to make me jealous. Anyway, regardless of whom she's dating, she's Alexander's assistant and that's a big deal to him."

"You're afraid you're going to lose him, aren't you? You're afraid he's going to move on like Jake did."

I rub my forehead. "I guess so. The thing is Alexander has already told me he loves me. And I'm the one who hasn't said it back to him yet."

She tries to hide her smile. I know she's enjoying the fact I'm finally confiding in her.

"Do you love Alexander?"

I take a deep breath and lean my head back. I know how I feel about him, but for some reason I'm holding back on admitting my feelings out loud and to myself.

"It's difficult to open up your heart after it's been broken," she adds. "You're entitled to feel this way."

"It's very difficult. And yes, I do love Alexander, and that terrifies me."

After I say it, I feel like a weight has been lifted off my shoulders. I'm actually wondering if Mrs. Rothera put something in the air. She's always using different kinds of essential oils, and maybe tonight she's put some kind of calming blend into the air. Holy crap, maybe she's drugging me. Maybe it's a truth serum or love potion? Either way, I actually finally admitted it. I'm in love with Alexander. But now what? Am I going to be okay with Melanie always being here? I thought I was okay with it. I guess I had just accepted it because we were just casually dating, but now this is serious. This is my future . . . our future, and I really need to think hard about this before I let myself get in any deeper.

"You need to tell him how you feel," Mrs. Rothera demands. I almost forgot I was still in her apartment. Seriously, what did she put in the air?

"You mean that I'm in love with him."

She nods slowly. "Yes—but also how you're feeling about the situation with Melanie."

I frown. "I've done this already. He knows how I feel."

"He knows you're not sure you want to move forward in this relationship?"

I furrow my brow. "I never said that."

"You didn't have to say it. You're having a lot of doubts and have been for a while. There's another woman in his life—maybe not in the same manner as you, but she's there and it doesn't appear she will be going anywhere. Unless, you speak up."

This really sucks. How am I supposed to tell him I love him, and then tell him he needs to choose between us? Is that really fair to him? But is it fair to me?

"You told me I shouldn't push her out," I remind her.

"I did tell you that. But if it's weighing on you this much, you can't stay silent. You're visibly distraught about it, and I believe you can do it in a way that's not *forcing* him to choose. Just be honest and let it come from the heart."

~

I finally crawl into bed after what seems like one of the longest days of my life. Mrs. Rothera was really helpful tonight, and now I feel super guilty for being so negative toward her. Yes, she's nosy and sometimes the unsolicited advice is too much. But, she also cares about people, and for some reason she especially cares about me. Tonight, she acted like a supportive friend and not a nosy neighbor-psychic. And she swore up and down she didn't release any kind of soothing chemical into the air.

Now comes the million-dollar question: When do I talk to Alexander about my concerns? Right now, he's so busy with this acquisition I think it will just add to his stress levels. I certainly don't want to be the cause of that.

In the meantime, I can put all my attention into my projects for both Mrs. Rothera and Helena, and of course, Angie's good-bye party. I also can't forget about finding a new place to live—I still want a fresh new start, but I need to find the right place to start over. I'm not going to rush into anything, because I'm learning that rushing into things is not the best idea.

Chapter Nine

Sometimes all you need is a good shopping trip to clear your mind. And for me, this is exactly what I need. Gina was supposed to meet me to shop for a going away present for Angie, but something urgent suddenly came up and with Gina that could be anything. As I walk through the mall, I'm kind of glad she canceled. It gives me a chance to really think. It's not like I haven't thought about how to handle the Alexander-Melanie situation, it's practically been monopolizing every waking moment I have. The good news is when I spoke to him this morning he told me they would finally be wrapping up this deal today and tomorrow, and we're having dinner tomorrow night to celebrate. I'm not sure if that's the right time to have our little talk or if I should wait, but I've never been very good about keep things bottled up inside. And usually I'm so transparent I end up blabbing my feelings anyway. The other night with Mrs. Rothera is the perfect example of this.

I would normally talk to Angie about this, but she's so busy with the move and I don't want to give her anything more to worry about. As it is, she's been sending me multiple texts checking up on me every day. I feel like the little child whose best friend is moving away. I have this image of myself hugging a stuffed animal and chasing after the moving van as it drives down the street. Seriously, I'm an adult and I need to act like one. It's okay (and natural) to be sad, but I can't let it consume my whole life. Things change and people move on. This is just part of life.

I'm in Pottery Barn looking for something for Angie's new place when I see Melanie.

Crap! This is the last thing I want right now. I try to hide behind a tall display of throw pillows but I'm too late.

"Summer?"

I crawl out from behind the pillows and try to act surprised to see her. I know she caught me trying to hide from her.

"Oh, hi, Melanie," I say, trying to sound surprised to see her.

Ugh, I'm really not a good liar.

"Looking for something back there?" she asks smugly. I wonder if I'd get arrested if I accidentally punched her. I know that's not the mature way to handle this, but it was just a random thought.

I ignore her snarky comment and change the subject away from me trying to hide from her.

"Hey, congrats on the acquisition. Alexander told me it's being finalized today."

Her smugness seems to disappear for a moment. "Yes, we did

it. Alexander was so sweet and gave me the rest of the day off today."

"You guys worked really hard. I'm sure it's well deserved."

She nods. "So, what are you doing? Are you here to get Penny a birthday present, too?"

Penny—it doesn't take a genius to know she's talking about Alexander's mom. Of course, I didn't know it was her birthday.

"No, actually a good-bye present for Angie. She's moving soon, and I wanted to get her something for her new home."

"I guess great minds think alike. Penny loves this store."

I force a smile. Maybe I'm making a huge deal out of nothing. So what if she and Penny are friends. She's allowed to be friends with whomever she wants. That doesn't change how Alexander feels about me.

"Who doesn't love Pottery Barn?" I say loudly.

Of course, I immediately think of the episode of *Friends* where Phoebe hates Pottery Barn. I start to giggle, and Melanie gives me a funny look.

"Sorry, I just remembered something funny."

Obviously, she doesn't remember the episode.

"Well, I better get back to shopping," I say awkwardly.

I start to walk away, and she follows me. Really? What else does this girl want from me? "Did you need something else?" I ask, looking back at her.

She glares at me. "You really don't like me, do you?"

She really wants to do this now—in the middle of Pottery Barn.

"I never said that," I say calmly.

She snorts. "Come on, it's no secret how we feel about each other. Sure, we try to play nice for Alexander's sake, but it is what it is."

Okay, so I don't disagree with her, but I'm still not sure what she's trying to accomplish by doing this now.

"The fact is you're Alexander's assistant and I'm his girlfriend. We have no choice but to coexist."

"And you hate that."

I grit my teeth. "What do you want, Melanie? What's the point of your infatuation with Alexander anyway? I thought you were dating Jake, remember Jake, my ex-boyfriend?"

She gives me a wicked smile. "You mean the one who broke up with you."

That was a low blow. In this situation, I could do one of two things: I could start screaming at her in the middle of Pottery Barn and maybe something childish like pulling her hair, or I could calmly and rationally walk away and include it in my conversation with Alexander. I have to do what I have to do.

"Yes, Jake and I broke up. Of course, I was disappointed at first, but then I met Alexander and . . . well, you know the rest."

It's my turn to give her a smug smile and remind her that

Alexander and I are in relationship despite her many previous attempts to break up our relationship.

I decide to leave the store and get away from Melanie before I do or say something I can't take back. Now I wish Gina had met me after all. She would have had no mercy on Melanie, and of course, I could easily remind Alexander that I can't control what Gina does. I've finally decided that enough is enough, we all tried to make it work, but it's obviously not going to. What the next step is, I don't know.

∽

"Are you serious? Oh man, I wish I was there," Gina yells.

After my escape from Pottery Barn, I went to the office I share with Gina and told her about my run-in with Melanie.

"She probably wouldn't have acted like that if you were there. She's really good at making it look like she's completely innocent."

"I can't believe she brought up the fact that Jake broke up with you. Just proves what a bitch she really is."

I don't disagree.

"There's something that's bothering me, though," I say. "She just doesn't seem to be that into Jake. It's almost like . . ."

"Like what?" she asks.

"I don't know—I'm just starting to wonder if they're really dating."

"You think it's a setup?"

I shrug my shoulders.

"It might be. Maybe they plotted this whole thing to make Alexander and me jealous? I wouldn't put it past Melanie, but I would be surprised if Jake did something like this."

She has a disgusted look on her face. "I wouldn't be surprised at all. He's been trying to win you back for a while."

Gina answers a call, and I rock back and forth in my chair. Could they really be faking this? Jake was so convincing when he showed up at my apartment to tell me, but what if that was his way of trying to make me jealous? And Melanie would stop at nothing to get Alexander's attention, including make him worry he could possibly lose her to an exciting new relationship.

If this theory doesn't pan out, it's still very obvious that Melanie is not that into Jake. And if that's true and she's just playing Jake . . . well, let's just say I'm a firm believer in karma.

"So, what's the plan?" Gina asks.

I bite my lip. I don't know, but somehow I need to find out the truth. This could be the only way to prove what Melanie is really capable of.

"And what if you're wrong?"

"If I'm wrong and things go south for Alexander and me, well then, I guess we were never meant to be anyway."

Chapter Ten

Alexander always goes out of his way to make everything perfect. When I arrive at his house, I'm greeted with candles and Chinese lanterns hanging outside on the deck. He has a table set up outside, and he ordered dinner from my favorite Greek restaurant. I look around and I'm completely speechless. Another reason I love spring so much is being able to enjoy evenings like this.

I find Alexander in his office.

"Everything looks amazing," I say, leaning against the doorframe.

He looks up from his laptop. I walk behind his desk and lean down to give him a kiss. He quickly pulls me into his lap and kisses me with more force than usual.

"I've missed you," he whispers.

I cup his chin with my hand and kiss him again. "I've missed you more."

I sit in his lap for a while, and he tells me all about the big win for his company. I knew it was important, but I had no idea just how important. The way Alexander makes it sound, this deal has set them up for five years. I can see the relief on his face and he's back to his normal self. He's in such good mood I don't know if I have the heart to bring up my issues with Melanie.

"You hungry?" he asks.

I nod, and we make our way outside to the romantic dinner he has planned for us.

I'm just digging into my Greek salad when he asks me what's been happening with me. I laugh nervously because I don't know where to start between signing the contract with Helena, Angie moving soon, my love for him, and last but not least the almost-brawl with Melanie in Pottery Barn.

"I suppose I should give you the bad news first." I pause. "Well, it's not completely bad news, but it may come with some uncomfortable feelings and emotions."

He gives me a curious look.

"Okay, give me the news."

I take a sip of my wine. "Helena and I met at Nick's for lunch and to discuss the contract."

He raises his eyebrows. "Did she sign it?"

I nod quickly.

"She did, finally."

"So you're going to decorate my ex-wife's home?" he asks with a fake laugh. "Never in a million years did I see that one coming."

I cringe. "Neither did I, but this is all your fault. You went and referred me out to all your friends and you have the same friends as Helena. Don't get me wrong, I appreciate all the referrals, but truthfully, I didn't think she was going to go through with it and hire me. And she seems kind of . . . easy to work with."

He sips his wine. "I guess love does that to people. It makes you strive to be a better person. I'm glad she's found that someone new, and I wish her all the happiness in the world. Just like I've found with you."

I take a deep breath. It's now or never. This perfect weather and this amazing setup makes me want to tell him how I feel. I'm so nervous my palms are sweating and my mouth is dry. I shouldn't be this nervous, he's already told me how he feels, so I know he will be happy. I don't have to worry about rejection.

"I'm so sorry I've been unavailable lately. I promise it won't be like that all the time, some deals require more time and attention."

"You don't have to explain anything," I insist. "I know how important your work is."

He takes my hand in his. "Not as important as you. I know I've already told you this, but I love you, Summer."

I close my eyes and take a deep breath. "I love you, too."

The next few minutes are so surreal. I'm about to explain my feelings more in depth when he jumps out of his chair and pulls me into his arms.

"Whoa. If I had known you would have had this kind of reaction, I would have said it sooner."

He laughs. "You needed time and I respect that. I wasn't going to push you even though I couldn't wait for you to say it. Do you know how happy I am right now?"

I can see how happy he is, and I feel the same way. Truthfully, I haven't felt this happy in a long time. Even though in the back of my mind I know we still need to talk about Melanie. Sure, things are good now and we're having a wonderful night together, but what happens the next time a big project comes up or the next time Melanie tries to get under my skin. We need to have this conversation, but not tonight. I don't want to be the one to mess this up.

After dinner, Alexander puts *Grease 2* (our favorite movie) on and we curl up on the couch together. I've decided that I need to do everything I can to make this work. A man like Alexander doesn't come along every day. If anything, I should probably admire and respect his loyalty. He's definitely been loyal to Melanie, and she has to him.

Normally, I would be breaking out into song and dance to "Cool Rider" but my mind is still wandering.

"Hey, are you all right?"

I stare at him for a second.

"What? Oh yeah, just daydreaming."

He looks concerned and sits up.

"You had a very worried look on your face."

Hmm . . . I guess I didn't try hard enough to hide my distraction.

He pauses the movie and turns to face me. Crap! He's going to do this now. Why couldn't I just enjoy our evening instead of overthinking everything?

"You know I can tell by your expression. Something has you worried."

I cringe. He won't believe me if I say nothing's wrong. Now is my chance, and I need to do this in the kindest way I possibly can.

"I didn't want to talk about this tonight. Everything has been so perfect." I look down at my hands in order to avoid his curious stare.

"You know you can tell me anything."

I nod slowly. Here goes nothing.

"Did Melanie tell you we ran into each other in Pottery Barn?"

"Noooo. Did something happen between you two?"

I tell him all about our run-in except I leave out the part about me hiding behind the pillows. He listens intently as I explain my feelings.

"I'm not trying to give you an ultimatum, but I don't see how this is going to work. We've all tried, and things aren't any better between us."

Alexander is silent. He doesn't look mad, but he is visibly upset.

"Summer, are you asking me to let Melanie go?"

I grit my teeth. How do I answer this? Yes, this would be ideal unless there was some way she would lay off but it never stops.

"I'm not going to force you to do anything," I say bluntly. "But if you have another suggestion, I'm all ears. I've told you how I feel about you, and I want more than anything for this to work out between us. I just don't want to feel like I come second in your life."

"You don't," he insists. "I told you I was sorry I've been so busy."

"It's not about your work," I interrupt. "It's Melanie. And how she can't separate being your assistant and butting in to your personal life. She went out of her way to tell me she was at the store to buy your mom a birthday present."

"That's my fault. I've been so busy that I haven't had a chance to shop for her. The gift is from me, not from Melanie."

I shake my head. "See what I mean. She could have told me that, but she conveniently left that part out because she was trying so hard to make me believe she's buddies with Penny."

I know this is all making sense to him. I can almost see the wheels turning in his brain.

"Okay, I will talk to her."

I snort. "Again? Sure, things will get better for a while, and then it will happen all over again. She's got it out for me. Don't forget she told Mrs. Rothera about me moving out. Oh, and I don't believe she and Jake are really dating. I think it's all a ploy they set up to make us jealous." I don't know where this comes from, but I'm on a roll. I've come this far, I might as well put it all out there.

He puts his face in his hands. "Do you really believe they would pretend to be in a relationship?"

I fold my arms defensively. "I wouldn't put anything past either of them at this point."

It's obvious that the mood has changed once again at the mention of Melanie. This is exactly the point I'm trying to make. How long is this going to go on? Are we going to spend the remainder of our relationship arguing over this? As bummed as I am that this conversation has ruined our night, it had to be done.

"Please say something," I beg.

He's still looking at the carpet.

"I understand where you're coming from, and I never wanted you to feel like you come second. I don't know how many times I have to apologize for her behavior, but you're right. Something has to change."

My heart starts beating a mile a minute, and my mouth is dry. Would he really choose her? Maybe deep down he really does have feelings for her and doesn't realize it?

He puts his hand on my cheek. "I promise you everything's going to be okay."

I really wish I could believe him. In the meantime, I need to get to the bottom of this lingering question, and there's only one person who can answer it for me. Jake.

Chapter Eleven

Jake seemed really happy to get my phone call, and when I asked him to meet me, he seemed very eager. I didn't tell Alexander I was going to contact him, but I need to find out what Melanie is up to.

After our amazing evening together ended up being not so amazing, Alexander promised me he would fix everything. I don't know what he meant by that, but I'm hoping we can finally get some kind of resolution. I barely got any sleep last night thinking about all of this and about what I need to say to Jake.

I'm sitting outside (of course, any excuse to enjoy the good weather) at the same café where Angie and I saw Jake and Melanie together. I arrived a little early so I could follow up on some emails and finalize a few things for Angie's party. When I look up, I see Jake walking toward the table.

Show time.

"Hi, Jake. Thanks for meeting me."

He gives me a warm smile. "Of course. I was glad to hear from you."

He sits down and orders a drink. After a bit of small talk, he cuts to the chase.

"So, what did you want to talk about?" He's practically on the edge of his chair. I wonder what he's expecting me to say.

"Well, first of all, I hope Melanie doesn't get upset about you being here."

He gets a funny look on his face. "Why would she be upset?"

I cringe. "Let's just say Melanie and I probably won't be allowed back into Pottery Barn."

"What do you mean?"

I give him a curious look. "She didn't tell you about this?"

He shakes his head. "Um . . . no."

Of course she didn't tell him. I wouldn't be surprised if they haven't spoken in days.

"What happened?"

I tell him about our altercation. He looks angry when I tell him about what she said about him breaking up with me.

"I don't understand why she would say that."

I snort. "Oh, I can answer that, because she loves to get under my skin any chance she can get."

He looks away and doesn't say anything. Here's my chance to finally get to the bottom of all of this.

"Is everything all right with you two?"

He looks back at me. "Yeah. Why do you ask?"

I shrug my shoulders. "I don't know. Despite everything that happened with us, I want you to be happy. Just because Melanie and I don't get along doesn't mean I don't wish you well."

He folds his hands on the table. "I still wish I could take it all back. I know I've told you this before but I would give anything to change last summer. I made the biggest mistake of my life when I ended things with you."

I reach across the table and put my hands on his.

"I know. Unfortunately, we can't change the past even if we wanted to."

He takes my hands in his. "There's always a chance. And don't you want someone who will be devoted to you and only you."

I knew it. Wait until I tell Angie and Gina.

"I'm confused. First of all, Alexander is devoted to me and you're with Melanie now."

He shakes his head. "I'm not seeing Melanie. We went out a few times, but it just wasn't meant to be. She's in love with Alexander and I'm . . . well, I'm still in love with you."

It's my turn to be speechless. I'm not surprised to hear him say he's in love with me, but I am a little surprised to hear him say that Melanie is in love with Alexander. She obviously shared this bit of information with him.

"So, you two have been lying this whole time?"

"The whole thing was a stupid idea," he interrupts. "We started talking at the restaurant opening, and it was really cool. After we got to talking, we admitted that we had feelings for other people. Melanie came up with the idea to try to make you guys jealous, and I went along with it."

I shake my head. "Jake, you even came to my apartment to tell me you were seeing her."

"I know. Anyway, it obviously didn't go as planned and I just decided to back off. She's been trying to keep it going because Alexander didn't like the idea at all. She thinks he's finally showing his true feelings."

I laugh loudly. "He's been worried about how it was affecting me."

"Summer, don't you see it?" he asks. "Doesn't it bother you that she's always there?"

There's no way I'm admitting anything to him. By him going along with this plan, he's just proven to me that he can't be trusted. He will probably run back to Melanie with everything I tell him.

"She's his assistant, that's it. He loves me, and I'm in love with him."

Jake nods his head. "I'm sorry I lied to you and for everything." He pauses. "I truly hope it works out the way you want it to. I wish you nothing but happiness."

"Thanks."

A few minutes later, I make up an excuse to leave, because truthfully, the sight of him disgusts me. Now that I have this information I'm prepared for whatever happens next. I can only hope that Alexander loves me enough to make the right decision.

∼

"We told you they were playing you," Angie says loudly. I pretend to cover my ears, and she throws piece of crumpled paper at me. Ugh. I'm really going to miss teasing her about how loud she is.

Gina is leaning back in her chair, smacking her gum as usual. "Both of them are scum. Now can I make a call?"

"No," Angie and I yell at the same time. We all start laughing.

"I appreciate the gesture, but I don't think threats of cement shoes are the answer."

She grins.

"So, what are you going to do?" Angie asks.

I exhale. "I'm going to wait on Alexander. He says he's going to take care of it, and I have to trust him."

"He will. That man loves you," Angie insists.

I smile. "I know. I just hope that's enough." I stop. "Anyway, let's talk about something else, like this good-bye bash we're having. I have a few fun surprises planned."

Tears well up in Angie's eyes. "I just can't believe we're talking about this."

I clear my throat and try my best to keep myself from crying.

"You're the one who's ditching us for sunshine and theme parks, so you only have yourself to blame," Gina says sarcastically.

Leave it to Gina to take an emotional moment and turn it into a joke, but it worked. Angie starts laughing before her tears begin to fall. Unfortunately, I know this is just the beginning of the tears.

Chapter Twelve

I'm rushing around trying to finish the last-minute details for this party. I'm really not that great at party planning. That's always been Angie's thing. Tonight is the good-bye party for Angie and Brett, and there are going to be even more surprises than I was planning. Brett called me a few nights ago and told me he was planning to propose to Angie. We have it all set up for him to pop the question tonight at the party. Angie doesn't really like surprises, but I have no doubt she won't mind this one. I really appreciate him trusting me enough to tell me. Of course, I promised him I would keep it a surprise and so far so good.

Alexander has been working in his office for most of the day while I've been dealing with caterers and decorations. At least the karaoke is ready to go. I'm so tempted to jump right in and completely butcher some Britney Spears and Christina Aguilera songs.

Alexander hasn't mentioned Melanie since our conversation last week. Of course, we've both been so busy we haven't seen that much of each other either. Once the party is over I'm going to have to sit down and talk to him. He needs to know about Melanie and Jake and their master plan to try to break us up.

"Awe. Everything looks so nice," Angie says loudly. "Not as great as my Halloween party but a close second."

I giggle. "Thanks. I'm glad I could make you proud."

I notice Brett standing behind her looking super pale. I can see how nervous he is already.

"I can't believe the last time we were all here together was Halloween," she says sadly. "A lot has happened since then."

I nod.

"Oh, I have to go say hi to Vinny. I'll be right back."

While Angie greets her cousin, who is also bartending for us, Brett pulls me outside on the deck.

"Are we all set?" he whispers loudly. "I'm freaking out. Do you think she's going to say yes?"

I start laughing.

"Of course. Relax."

He motions for me to follow him. Once we are a good distance away from the French doors, he takes a small box out of his pocket. I gasp when he opens it to show me the beautiful engagement ring.

I squeal in delight. "She's going to love it."

He relaxes a little. "You sure?"

"Yes."

"What are you two up to?" Angie asks.

Both Brett and I jump when we hear her voice. He shoves the box into his pocket.

We both turn around as she slowly wanders over to join us.

"We aren't up to anything," I reply. "I was just having a private talk with Brett, reminding him that he better take good care of you for me or else."

She gives us a skeptical look but doesn't question me. Whew. That was close.

"Welcome, everyone."

Alexander is standing in the doorway munching on chips and salsa.

"Look who it is," Angie says excitedly. She runs over to give him a hug, and Brett is right behind her to shake his hand.

"Since Summer just gave Brett a lecture about taking care of me, it's my turn."

She drags Alexander back inside the house. Brett gives me a grateful smile and follows them.

This is crazy; my best friend is about to get engaged. I could stand here and cry or I could go inside and get this party started. I watch Alexander talking to my friends, and he fits in so perfectly. He looks at me and gives me a wink, reminding me of how much I adore him.

The guests slowly trickle in, and it's a great turnout. Angie and Brett obviously have a lot of friends, so Brett's going to have quite the audience for his big proposal. The karaoke machine is a huge hit. Angie and Gina don't waste any time performing several songs. I even join them in singing "I Will Survive."

Alexander comes up behind me, wrapping his arms around my waist. "Having fun?"

I give him a kiss on the cheek. "Yes. I was just thinking that soon I wouldn't be seeing Angie every day or even every other day. It's just surreal."

Alexander nuzzles into my neck. "I understand. But you still have me."

Before I have a chance to respond, Brett interrupts us.

"I'm ready."

Suddenly, my adrenaline kicks in and I quietly call all the guests into the living room.

Angie and her cousin just finish a very poor rendition of "I Got You Babe," when Brett takes the microphone.

Here we go.

Alexander joins me and wraps his arm around me. Brett begins by thanking everyone for coming.

"Angie and I appreciate you all and the roles you've played in our lives. We hope we have a lot of visitors in Florida."

Angie nods in agreement.

"Before we get back to partying, I wanted to say one more thing." He turns to Angie and grabs both her hands.

"What the hell is happening?" Gina says in my ear.

I shrug my shoulders and give her a knowing look.

"Oh my gosh," she says, putting her hand to her mouth.

"Angie, I know this was a very difficult decision to leave our lives behind and start fresh. You've already made me happier than I could imagine."

His voice is trembling, and he's obviously terrified. He drops to one knee, and the guests gasp.

"There's only one more thing you could do to complete my life and that would be if you agree to marry me."

Angie is speechless, which I've never seen before. The room is so quiet you could hear a pin drop.

"Are you kidding? Of course I'll marry you," she yells.

The crowd erupts in cheers and applause. There are a few tears shed—some by me.

"That was great. Good for them," Alexander says, after the crowd begins to disperse.

"I wish them a lot of luck. Marriage can be hard, but it can be fantastic, too."

Of course, I know he's referring to his marriage to Helena.

"I'm so happy for them," I say excitedly.

"Me, too. I'm sure they'll have a long and successful marriage. Some people aren't meant to be married, but I have a feeling they're going to make it."

Well, that's interesting. Is he referring to himself and Helena or just himself? Of course, we've never talked about marriage at all. It's much too early in our relationship for that kind of a conversation, and we have other issues to work through before that.

"Summer, you knew about this and didn't tell me? You know I hate surprises," Angie squeals. I give her a big hug and congratulate her and Brett.

"Only for a few days," I say with a giggle. "I would never have been able to keep that to myself for that long. And you have to admit, this surprise was pretty great."

"Let's see the rock," Gina says, interrupting us. She studies Angie's left hand very carefully for several seconds. "Oh yeah, that's a good one."

"You're moving and engaged," I say excitedly. "It's an exciting time for you."

She pulls me into another tight hug. We both get a little choked up, but before we have a chance to talk about this emotional moment, she's approached by several of the other guests. I stand back and watch, and I couldn't be happier for her. Spring has certainly brought her a fresh new start.

∾

As much as I love a good party, I really dislike the cleanup. Alexander, Gina, Vinny, Brett, and Angie all stay to help clean up. Of course, we save the karaoke machine for last.

"Do you see what's happening over there?" Angie whispers.

I look in the direction she's pointing and sure enough Gina

and Vinny have their heads together and they seem to be in deep discussion.

My mouth drops open. "Whoa. I would have never thought of that."

Angie's face falls.

"I can't believe I'm not going to be here for all of this. You and Alexander are on your way to the next step, and now Gina and Vinny are flirting. I'm going to miss everything."

I grab her hand and remind her of the gorgeous bling on her finger.

"You're making a fresh start with the love of your life. Enjoy it."

She nods. "You will always be my best friend, Summer, no matter how far apart we are."

I give her a big hug. "Of course."

"And will you promise me that you will let yourself be happy with Alexander?" she says loudly.

I shush her, but luckily no one is around to hear us.

"I'm trying. Hopefully, we can get everything sorted out with this Melanie situation."

"It will all work out. I know it," she insists.

I wish I could be as sure as she is.

Chapter Thirteen

I open my eyes to the sun streaming in the window. For a second, I don't even know where I am. Suddenly, I remember that after the good-bye party it was so late I ended up staying at Alexander's.

After I get ready, I wander downstairs to find Alexander sitting on the deck. He's drinking coffee and working on his laptop.

"Good morning," he says cheerfully.

Hah! It's already almost noon. I never sleep this late.

"I'm sorry I slept so late. I guess I needed the rest."

He grabs my hand and pulls me down to kiss me.

"I'm sure you did. You worked hard on that party."

I pour myself a cup of coffee and stir in some sugar and cream.

"Are you working?" I ask, pointing at his laptop.

He rolls his eyes.

"Just following up on a few things. I'll be done soon, and then I'm all yours."

I hate to ruin another good day but I need to address the elephant in the room. I wish I had his ability to avoid it, but that's just not me.

"I was hoping we could talk."

He looks up from his laptop and gets a worried look on his face.

"Okay."

I try to swallow the lump in my throat.

"I met up with Jake a few days ago, and he told me a few things. First of all, I was right, he and Melanie are not seeing each other. They pretended to be together to try to make us jealous and ultimately break us up."

Alexander stares at me as if I'm speaking in another language.

"I know it's hard for you to believe that Melanie is capable of these things, but I assure you she is. Jake also told me that he was still in love with me and that Melanie is in love with you."

I wait for Alexander to say something . . . anything.

"Please say something."

"I'm so sorry," he says sadly.

Okay, that's something. But what's he apologizing for?

"I let this get out of hand. I appreciate Melanie for all her service over the years. I guess I never believed it would get to this level."

"Have you spoken to her since our conversation?" I ask.

He nods.

"She insisted that what happened in Pottery Barn was a misunderstanding. She actually told me she was happy with Jake and things were progressing for them."

"She was trying to make you jealous," I interrupt.

Really? A misunderstanding. What kind of hold does she have over him? I have to give her credit because she's a master manipulator.

"I've been so unfair to you, Summer. I promise I will take care of this once and for all. Can I ask just ask one more thing of you?"

I stare at his gorgeous face, and I can see the sincerity in his eyes. Suddenly, Angie's words play over in my head about letting myself be happy with him.

"Yes."

"Can you give me a little more time? This is going to be a huge change in my life."

I don't say anything.

He pulls his chair over to mine and puts his hands on mine.

"Do you trust my feelings for you?"

Ugh. Of course I do, but I don't know if that's enough.

"I trust that you love me, but I believed Jake loved me, too. I gave him almost two years of my life."

He shakes his head. "I'm not like Jake."

I look away to avoid his eye contact. "I feel so guilty about forcing you to make this choice."

He takes my chin in his hand and turns my head to look back at him.

"Don't feel guilty. I'm going to prove to you how committed I am to making this work."

He gently pulls me into his arms. I close my eyes as I breathe in his scent. I have to have faith in him and in us. I need to believe that I'm making the right decision for my future and for this season in my life.

"I have a feeling things are just going to get better from here."

I smile. "Me, too."

We spend the rest of the afternoon enjoying each other and this beautiful spring day.

THE END

Return to Summer

A Novella

Melissa Baldwin

About Return to Summer

Summertime has arrived and things aren't only heating up outside for Summer Peters. After a rocky spring, Summer thinks she's finally moved on from the heartache of last year. She's found a new place to live, her company has new clients, and her relationship with Alexander Williams is going strong, despite the desperate attempts by others to sabotage it.

Just when Summer thinks everything is finally falling into place, she receives another crushing blow, and this time it could even affect her business. Summer knows it's finally time to put a stop to the one thing that threatens her happiness, even though it requires a difficult decision in order to do this. Will this season bring her everything she's always wanted or will history repeat itself?

Find out how Summer's one-year journey ends in this final installment of the Seasons of Summer Novella Series.

This is a work of fiction. Names, characters, places, and incidents either are the product of the author's imagination or are used fictitiously, and any resemblance to actual persons, living or dead, business establishments, events, or locales is entirely coincidental.

Copyright © 2017 Melissa Baldwin
All rights reserved.

ISBN: 0692931120
ISBN13: 978-0692931127

Formatted by Karan & Co. Author Solutions

I dedicate this book to my little brothers and sisters—Richie, Christopher, Adam, Michael, Celestial, Star . . . and to Joseph in heaven.

Keep your eyes open.

Chapter One

I'm fanning myself with my menu. Summer has arrived, and as much as I love it, I'm never prepared for the brutal heat waves. I open my planner and look through the pages for the next few months. Hopefully me, or rather, my company, Summer Interiors is going to be really busy. It's been quite a year for me, and even as difficult as things have gotten, I wouldn't change anything.

The most exciting thing happening in my life is that after several months of searching, I've found a new apartment. The plan is to move in next month, assuming nothing else gets in the way. Unfortunately, little things seem to keep popping up that make me wonder if this move is a mistake, but I've finally found a place that's the right location and the right price.

The sound of my phone ringing distracts me from my thoughts of moving, and I smile when I see it's my best friend Angie calling.

"I finally get to talk to a real live person," I say sarcastically.

She giggles. "Me, too. I can't believe I haven't even been gone two months yet."

Angie recently moved to Florida. It was unexpected, so we're all still trying to get used to it (me especially). I may or may not have thrown a tantrum, but true best friends are hard to come by. Everyone knows that.

"I know. It feels like an eternity since we've been able to talk."

Angie and I have both been busy, and other than texting, we haven't been able to catch up.

"Well, you're missing a brutal heat wave right now," I tell her while continuing to fan myself. It's so hot that I'm tempted to pour this whole glass of ice water over my head, but I doubt the patrons of this café came here for a wet T-shirt contest. Except maybe the three guys in designer suits who are sitting at the bar. They've been checking out every woman who walks through the door.

She starts to laugh. "Don't talk to me about a heat wave. It's ninety-eight degrees right now, and the only break we will get is when the afternoon thunderstorms roll in."

I have to admit that sounds miserable but I know when winter comes I will be wishing I was there with her.

"What are you up to?" she asks. I close my planner and hold the cold glass of water up to my head.

"I'm waiting on Helena . . . again."

Helena is one of my clients. Summer Interiors has been

redecorating her apartment, when I can get in touch with her. She also happens to be my boyfriend's ex-wife, but that's another story. Thankfully, I was able to remove the shrine of their life together from her living room. I admit I used some serious reverse psychology to get her to take it down. Who would have thought she would fall for my lecture on new beginnings and feng shui?

"How's that going?" Angie asks.

"Surprisingly well. She's been much easier to work with than I expected, other than waiting on her like right now."

This is true. I struggled with the decision of working with her, especially after one of her and Alexander's best friends told me they were soul mates and would get back together eventually. We had a few obstacles, but surprisingly she's been one of my easier clients.

"That's good. And how's Alexander?"

I smile to myself. I feel like a giddy teenager when I think about him. We've been together since October, and despite some rocky times, things are good right now.

"He's great."

"And Melanie?"

I sigh. Melanie (Alexander's assistant) would be the one area of our relationship that isn't great.

"She's still here," I say through gritted teeth.

"How can that be? After everything."

I continue to fan myself and take a sip of my water.

"Because she begged him to let her stay. She swore she would never meddle in our lives again and this was the best job she ever had. She laid it on thick, tears and all, and he fell for it. But, I have to admit she's stuck to her word . . . so far anyway."

She groans. "Well, keep your eye on her."

I snort. "Oh trust me, Melanie is not going to make any more trouble for us."

I'm so involved in my conversation that I don't notice Helena has finally arrived.

"Oh, I wouldn't be so sure of that if I were you, love," Helena says, she has a look of dread on her face. "Melanie is diabolical, and you must never let your guard down."

She sits down across from me.

"Hey, Ang, Helena's here. I'll give you a call back later." I quickly hang up, barely giving Angie a chance to say good-bye.

I'm not surprised by Helena's reaction to Melanie; there's certainly no love lost between them.

"I was just talking to my best friend, and she asked me about Melanie. I know there's a lot of bad blood between you."

She folds her arms.

"You don't know the full story, do you?"

I give her a curious look. "About you and Melanie?"

She raises her eyebrows. "I think it's about time for you to hear what really happened with my marriage to Xander. Then, you'll fully understand who Melanie is and who you're dealing with."

My heart sinks at the possibility that there could be more to this whole thing than what I already know. Since the first day I met Alexander and our—ahem—instant attraction to one another began, Melanie has been the constant dark cloud hanging over our relationship.

"Alexander has made things very clear to her. Honestly, I'm not expecting to have any more issues."

Helena orders a bottle of San Pellegrino.

"If only it were that simple," she says, a hint of sarcasm in her voice. "As you know, Xander and I had an amazing marriage."

I furrow my brow. I really hope this isn't going to be another monologue about the perfect marriage of Alexander and Helena Williams. I can't even count how many times I've heard about how passionate and intense their connection was. They never came out and told me the details about their sex life, but I can read between the lines. The story is they grew apart as the intensity began to fade. In addition to that, Melanie's constant presence put a strain on their marriage. And after almost a year with Alexander, I totally understand how that could happen.

"Mmmhmm," I say, while trying not to make eye contact. I'm silently praying this conversation isn't going to get awkward.

"I can't even count the number of times Xander would talk to her over and over again and things would get better . . . for a time."

This is nothing new. I've heard this before.

"Melanie would create different situations or a crisis that would require Alexander's immediate attention. That was her way of dragging him away, and it usually worked. It didn't help that he was trying to grow his business at the time. This made everything urgent and Melanie knew that."

I listen intently as Helena relives the events that lead to her marriage falling apart.

"Then, there were the photographs."

Photographs? What's she talking about?

"What photos?" I ask, suddenly feeling nauseous. Helena came to the States from Sweden to model, but I don't think she's referring to photos from her modeling days.

She gets a pained look on her face.

"One day, I had lunch with a friend from university. It was completely innocent," she trails off. "Not long after our meeting, some photos surfaced of my friend and me in what appeared to be an intimate encounter. To this day, I believe she was behind those photos. She wanted to destroy my reputation and my marriage."

"Wait. You think she took them?"

She sips her Pellegrino and nods her head. "I'm not sure she took them herself, but I believe she was behind the whole thing. It was obvious they were doctored, and even Alexander could see that."

I'm completely speechless.

"Anyhow, I accused her, which made Xander very upset with me. Let's just say she accomplished exactly what she wanted."

Wow. Okay, so I knew Melanie was a jealous, but I never thought she would stoop as low as fabricating photos to sabotage Alexander's marriage. Maybe I should ask Helena about Melanie's relationship with Alexander's mom. I haven't even touched on this subject. That was another whole issue that happened a few months ago when Melanie rejoiced in getting under my skin by pretending to besties with his mom. I'm not proud to admit we almost had a brawl at Pottery Barn, not one of my finest moments.

"My point is you should not let your guard down when it comes to Melanie. Even if Alexander has assured you that he has it under control." Helena says, dragging me out of my thoughts.

I nod my head slowly.

Before I know it, Helena has moved on to talking about her apartment and abandoned all talk about Melanie. Of course, I'm still thinking about it. The problem is there is nothing I can do about it except wait and see what happens. I can't believe I have to sit here and wait for the possibility of someone sabotaging my relationship.

"Oh, and we have to change the rugs in the guest bathroom," she demands, as if her life depended on it. "That spoiled, self-absorbed Valynn has the same ones. The last thing I want is for her to think I copied her."

I zone out while Helena continues rambling about her *friend* Valynn and her bathroom rug.

Why do I feel like I'm waiting for the inevitable when it comes to Melanie? One thing is for sure, Helena may have let her succeed in destroying her relationship but I won't. I will do whatever it takes to make sure she doesn't come between Alexander and me.

Chapter Two

I don't know what I was thinking? I look around at the sea of boxes, newspaper, and junk I've somehow accumulated over the years. I have no idea how or when I got this stuff? And do I really need nine flower vases? Probably not.

It's actually been somewhat of an emotional experience packing up my apartment. Especially when I come across a box of things from my eighteen months with Jake. I even saved the napkin from our first date. (Lame, I know.) If I had a backyard, I would totally do a bonfire. I continue to sort through the random items in the box—a small stuffed animal he won at a carnival, some clothes, and an envelope at the bottom of the box.

I sit down, leaning up against the wall. I hold the envelope in my hands like it's an important document. I contemplate opening it or just throwing it away.

Unfortunately, my curiosity gets the best of me. When I

finally open it, I remember exactly why I saved it. It's a card from our sixth-month anniversary, and Jake wrote the sweetest note about how much richer his life was having me in it. Reading this, I would have never suspected that a year later he would blindside me by dumping me while on a vacation. A few months ago, this note would have brought me to tears, but not anymore. This is probably because I'm finally feeling more secure with Alexander. It's been difficult to not be paranoid in my new relationship after what happened with Jake. And of course, Melanie's involvement doesn't help.

I take a deep breath and slowly tear the card in half. Who would have thought it would feel this amazing to throw something away? I feel as if I just climbed to the top of Mount Everest. I'm about to text Angie, and then catch myself. I know I can still text her, but it's not like we can meet up at the coffee shop to celebrate my huge breakthrough. Alexander is in LA for work this week, and suddenly I feel very lonely. I want to share my news with someone. Hmm . . . there is someone I can tell, but I'm not sure I want to open that can of worms tonight. After much thought, I abandon my packing and make my way downstairs. I can hear the sound of ocean waves crashing through the door, so I knock loudly. The music stops, and a few seconds later my landlord, Mrs. Rothera, opens the door.

"Hiya," she says warmly. She gives me a questioning look, and I'm pretty sure she's watching my aura or body language to figure out the reason for my unexpected visit. I try not to make too many visits to her because it's usually somewhat of an ordeal. As nice as Mrs. Rothera is, she tends to stick her nose into my personal life and offer up a dose of unsolicited advice. Although, I guess that's what psychics do.

Yep, she's a psychic. She's legit, too; at least, that's what I've heard from all my friends who have had readings from her. I haven't actually had a reading because the thought of knowing stuff about my future makes me nervous. She's given me hints here and there but that's as far as I've let it go.

"Am I bothering you?"

She shakes her head and pulls me through the door.

"You know you're always welcome here." She pauses. "Hopefully, you've come to tell me that you've changed your mind about moving out?"

I laugh nervously. "Not exactly. Actually, I was looking through some boxes tonight and I found something . . . a note from Jake."

She raises her eyebrows.

"And?"

"And, it didn't bother me. In fact, I threw it away. For the first time in almost a year I feel like I've finally moved on from my heartbreak. I think I've finally turned a corner."

She nods slowly, and I know her well enough to know she has something to say.

"Good for you. How does it feel?"

I smile. "It feels amazing. It almost feels like it was exactly what I needed to close this chapter of my life."

I know I'm being really dramatic over throwing away an old card, but doing this reminds me of how far I've come.

Mrs. Rothera closes her eyes and sits very still. I really hate it when she does this. One of these days I'm afraid she's going to open her eyes and claim she's someone else, as in someone else will take over her body. For some reason, I always think about that scene in the movie *Ghost* where the spirit jumps into the psychic's body to talk to his wife.

I'm relieved when Mrs. Rothera opens her eyes and she's still herself.

"Anyway, I'm proud of you." She quickly stands up and walks toward the door. "I hate to do this but I have to get to my meditation and turn in early tonight."

Wait. What the hell just happened?

"Oh, okay." I reluctantly stand up.

"Thanks for listening."

She gives me a half smile. "Of course. Keep me posted on the moving plans."

I barely have a chance to say good night before she shuts the door in my face. I'm so confused right now. I don't think Mrs. Rothera has ever rushed me out like that before. She must really be upset about me moving, but I can't let that distract me from my plans. If throwing away the letter proves anything, it's that I know I'm ready to move forward with my life and I couldn't be happier about it.

∽

"One more day, baby. I can't wait to wrap my arms around you."

I'm sitting in the office I share with my friend Gina, and I'm trying to tone down my giddiness. I absolutely love talking to Alexander on the phone. He has the sexiest voice, and of course when he says things like this, it totally makes my heart race.

"One day is too long," I whine.

I glance over my shoulder to see Gina making gagging motions. Like she has room to talk. She hooked up with Angie's cousin Vinny at the good-bye party I threw for Angie and Brett. I know for a fact they are very open with their PDA—kissing, wandering hands, and who knows what else has gone down in public places.

"Are you still planning to meet me at the house?" he asks.

"I sure am. I have a meeting with a client, but I plan to head over there right after."

"Good because I will be ready to spend the whole evening with you."

When we get off the phone, my face hurts from smiling so much.

"You two are so adorable. It's almost nauseating," Gina says playfully.

I roll my eyes. "Don't even start in on me. You and Vinny are lucky you haven't been arrested for public indecency."

She shrugs her shoulders. Typical Gina, I know she wouldn't care if she were arrested. Although, I'm sure she never would be. Her family is well connected with the law enforcement in our small Connecticut town, not to mention even more connected in New York City. Whether that's good or bad I'm not clear, and I don't ask.

"Speaking of nauseating, I have to tell you about what I found last night. You're going to be so proud of me."

I tell her all about finding the box of Jake's things and ripping up the note. She gives me a high five, but she definitely isn't as excited as I am about it. I guess it's hard for other people to understand exactly how big of a deal this is for me.

"So, you finally realize that Jake did you a favor by showing you what an ass he is."

I giggle. "I guess so. I was so excited I needed to tell someone, so I went downstairs to tell Mrs. Rothera."

She gives me a funny look. "Really?"

"I know, right? Anyway, at first she was really nice. Invited me in like she usually does, and then she got weird."

"What do you mean weird? Weirder than she usually is?"

I love Gina's honesty. No matter how brutal it is, I can always count on her to give it to me straight.

"I can't explain it. One minute we were just talking, then she closed her eyes, and then she rushed me out."

As I tell her what happened, it makes me even more confused. Maybe she had some kind of vision or weird psychic moment. She knows I don't like to hear things about my future so maybe she wanted to get rid of me before she blurted something out.

"Are you going to ask her what happened?" Gina asks, barely

looking up from her phone. It's obvious she's losing interest in our conversation.

"We'll see. She's probably still mad that I'm moving out."

After how strange she was acting last night, I really hope that's all it is.

Chapter Three

I really enjoy my job, but sometimes I end up with the most difficult clients, and unfortunately you never know until you start working with them. I know this comes with the territory and not everyone is going to be flexible and easy. My newest client, Valerie, is definitely difficult. She contacted me about a month ago and insisted that she had picked Summer Interiors over *several* other interior decorators. According to her, my company has been the talk of the town and she knew she *had* to work with me because she only works with the best. I appreciate her stroking my ego but that should have been a red flag for me.

Don't get me wrong, she was very nice, but the moment I set foot in her home, she became super high maintenance.

The biggest issue we're having is that she picks out the most expensive décor, and then complains about the cost of everything. Not to mention she calls or texts me several times a day with random, unimportant questions. A few occasions have been so irritating I've considered telling her I can't work with her anymore. The problem is she's already recommended me to quite a few of her friends. I continue to remind myself that if I can work with Alexander's ex-wife, I can certainly work with Valerie and her unreasonable requests. After a particular frustrating day searching for the exact mirror she wants for her formal living room, I'm more than ready to see Alexander later tonight.

"This one is close, but it's still not the exact frame I'm looking for," Valerie whines. I contemplate throwing the laptop against the wall but refrain from expressing my frustration in such a childish manner.

"We will find it, don't worry," I say, trying to reassure her.

I zone out as she continues scrolling through pictures on her quest to find this perfect, one-of-a-kind mirror. My thoughts bounce back and forth between my move and Mrs. Rothera's odd behavior from the other night. I'm still so confused about why she flipped the switch so quickly. Maybe I should take Gina's advice and ask her about it.

"Wait. This is it," Valerie shouts, snapping me out of my thoughts.

I'm about to jump up and cheer, but I stop myself. I've already been short with her today, and I need to maintain my stellar reputation. (Her description, not mine.)

"Awesome," I say, glancing at the mirror. Honestly, it looks exactly like the thirty other mirrors we've looked at.

"It's perfect, don't you think?"

I purse my lips. "Absolutely."

She's about to say something when she gets a text message. She glances at her phone and a strange expression comes across her face.

"I have to make a quick phone call. I'll be right back."

She rushes off to the kitchen, so I start to gather up my things. I glance at the time and my pulse picks up, only a few more hours until Alexander arrives home. I reach for my bag and accidently knock over my glass of water. Crap!

I quickly move my laptop out of the path of the flood and rush to the kitchen to get a towel. I stop in my tracks when I overhear Valerie on the phone.

"Don't worry, Mel. I got this," she whispers. "Yes. You know you can count on me."

Mel? For some reason Melanie pops into my head. Could she be talking to Melanie—as in my arch nemesis? Maybe I'm just being paranoid, but it wouldn't be surprising if she knew Melanie. She told me she was referred through a friend of a friend.

I hear her say good-bye, so I count to three and hurry into the kitchen.

"Hey, Valerie," I call. "Can I have a towel? I'm so clumsy. I just spilled my water."

Her eyes grow wide as if she was just caught her robbing a bank. She had to be talking to Melanie, otherwise she wouldn't look so guilty.

"Oh . . . um . . . sure," she says nervously. She hands me a few towels, and then follows me back to the dining room to help me clean up the mess.

I leave about fifteen minutes later without any explanation for the secret phone call. Whoever Valerie was talking to, she obviously didn't want me to hear.

I spend my entire ride home (to Alexander's home) giving myself a pep talk. I refuse to let this worry me, and I certainly refuse to let it affect my evening with Alexander. Melanie has ruined one too many nights we've had together and from now on that's going to change.

∽

After making myself a cup of tea, I curl up on Alexander's couch with my laptop while I wait semi-patiently for him to get home from his trip. Of course, his flight is delayed, so I have several hours to kill before he's home. I decide to use this time to search some ideas for decorating my new apartment. I find it funny that I have no issues decorating other people's homes, but when it comes to my own home, I stare at a blank page.

I lose interest pretty quickly and start to think about Valerie whispering on the phone today. I decide to look up Valerie's online profile and pictures. I know I'm totally trolling, but if Helena is right, then I need to keep an eye on Melanie and that would include her friends. Sure enough, Melanie is listed on Valerie's contact list. I know that doesn't guarantee that she was talking to her on the phone today, but she was definitely whispering for some reason, not to mention she left the room rather abruptly.

I must doze off because the next thing I know someone is touching my face. When I open my eyes, I see Alexander sitting on the edge of the couch leaning over me.

I practically jump up and wrap my arms around his neck.

"Mmmm . . . this is exactly what I've been waiting for," he says into my neck.

When I finally loosen my grip and pull away, he takes my face in his hands and kisses me gently.

"I'm sorry it's so late," he says, rubbing his eyes. "Today was one of the longest travel days I've ever had. And I was extra impatient to see you, so that made the day even longer." He sits down, pulling my legs onto his lap, and leans his head on the back of the couch.

I start to run my hand through his hair. One thing's for sure, I will never get tired of looking at him. With his dark hair and blue eyes, he could be Superman's twin.

"Why don't you go to sleep? We can talk tomorrow," I tell him.

He shakes his head, but I can see the exhaustion. He's trying to stay awake for me.

"It's okay," I tell him. "You can barely keep your eyes open."

"Okay, but on one condition," he mumbles.

I smile. "Condition? What condition is that?"

"You stay with me tonight," he begs. "Please."

I smile. "There's no place I'd rather be."

As I lie still, listening to Alexander's gentle snoring, I can't help but feel incredibly happy. Being in love will do that to you, and I guess I never thought I could feel this way again after what Jake did. Boy was I wrong.

Tonight didn't go the way I had hoped, being that I spent maybe twenty minutes with Alexander before he crashed, but I still feel grateful. This is exactly the point I've been waiting to get to because no matter what Melanie tries to pull, I'm more than ready for my future, a future with Alexander.

∼

I wish I could stay here all day. It's a beautiful morning, and I'm sitting on Alexander's patio planning out my day. The only thing that would make it more perfect would be to spend it *with* Alexander. Unfortunately, he's been on the phone most of the morning. I know it's his first day back in town after a week so I can't expect him to spend the entire day lounging around with me, although that would be awesome.

"I'm sorry," Alexander says, interrupting my thoughts. "I'm supposed to be out here having breakfast with you."

I force a smile. This isn't the exact homecoming I was hoping for, but I'm certainly not going to make him feel bad about it.

"It's okay."

He shakes his head. "No, it's not. I can at least take a break during breakfast. I told Melanie to hold calls until later."

A few months ago, she would've been calling him every two minutes, but since Alexander had his long talk with her, she's been more respectful of his personal life. This gives me hope that Helena is wrong and we've turned a corner once and for all.

"What are your plans for the day?" he asks, taking a sip of his coffee.

"Well, I have to try to get some packing done, and I have a few things to do for my new client."

"Oh yeah. Which new client is this?"

I groan. "Her name is Valerie Watson. I totally regret taking her on as a client. It's been a month and we haven't made any progress. We just keep going around in circles."

He makes a face. "Mmmhmm . . . I know Valerie, and yes, she can be a lot to take."

I give him a curious look. "How do you know her?"

He gives me a thoughtful look.

"You know I don't even remember where I met her, probably some social event. She's one of Melanie's good friends."

A-ha. I knew Valerie was talking to Melanie yesterday. That would make sense as to why she looked so guilty when I walked into the kitchen. Valerie and Melanie are besties, how cute. Ugh.

"Summer?"

Alexander interrupts my thoughts.

"Sorry. I was . . ."

I just can't tell him about my theory. I promised I would trust him and let him handle Melanie. But this makes me wonder why Valerie hired me and whether is Melanie involved?

Alexander looks skeptical. "You got awfully quiet all of a sudden. You might as well tell me what's going on in that brain of yours."

I laugh nervously. "It's not a big deal. I just overheard Valerie on the phone yesterday. She was whispering and . . . well, I think she was talking to Melanie."

"And?"

I shrug my shoulders. He looks totally confused.

"What did you hear?"

Crap. I knew I would regret this. I promised him I wouldn't let it get to me anymore.

"She said, 'you count on me' and that she 'would take care of it.'" I pause. "I don't know what she was talking about, but she was whispering, and she had the look of sheer panic on her face when I walked in."

Alexander is quiet, which makes me nervous. He's either thinking about Valerie's conversation or he's thinking that I've completely lost my mind. Or maybe both?

He reaches over and takes my hand. "Baby, I promised you that Melanie wouldn't be interfering in our relationship anymore. I made myself very clear to her, so I don't think she would dare try anything."

I nod slowly. "I know, and things have been better. I just had a weird feeling yesterday."

He pulls my hand up to his lips and kisses it. "I love you, and I'm committed to you. Nothing is going to get in the way of that." I give him a grateful smile.

"So, give me an update on the moving plans. How has Mrs. Rothera been?"

Wow. He changed the subject fast.

The mention of Mrs. Rothera totally reminds me of her strange behavior while I was at her apartment.

"Interesting you should ask. I thought she was doing okay until the other night."

I explain how she abruptly rushed me out of her apartment.

"She loves having you there. Which I can totally understand, if you were living with me I would never want you to leave."

I start to choke on my orange juice. This is the first time there has been any mention of me living with Alexander except for when Angie was convinced he was going to ask me to move in. Obviously that never happened.

"Are you okay?" he asks, patting me on the back.

"Um . . . yeah," I say, clearing my throat.

"She will have to get used to the idea because moving day will be here before we know it."

Before Alexander can say anything else, his phone starts ringing. I guess that's a sign that our intimate breakfast is over.

I begin to zone out again while Alexander takes his call. The truth is I don't want to read too much into what Alexander said. He was probably speaking hypothetically because we've never discussed me moving in and he's never asked. And it's not like I would want to rush anything. Things are good the way they are right now.

Chapter Four

"I told you," Angie says loudly. I have to pull the phone away from my ear. I swear sometimes she's so loud I feel like I could hear her from thousands of miles away, without the phone.

"Why don't you just bring it up to him? You know you want to."

I just finished telling her what Alexander said about me living with him, and I'm definitely not surprised by her reaction.

"I'm not going to bring it up. I don't think he meant anything by it. It was totally hypothetical," I say cautiously.

"What if it wasn't? What if he was giving you that hint to feel you out?"

I stretch out on my bed and throw my arm over my eyes.

"And how many times have you told me that he never liked any of the apartments you picked out? Weren't they all too far away or too small or too old?"

I cringe. I did mention his constant disapproval of the apartments I've looked at, and Angie practically has a photographic memory. She can probably remember what she was wearing the second day of high school.

"Yes, he did, but that was mostly me. It took me forever to find a place I liked. And for your information, he doesn't have an issue with the apartment I finally decided on, so your theory really doesn't hold up." Of course, he hasn't seen my new apartment yet, but I don't tell her that.

"On another note, I have a feeling Melanie is up to her old tricks. And she's bringing in reinforcements again."

This is a good way to change the subject from the topic of me moving in with Alexander.

"What did she do this time?" I can tell by the tone in her voice that she's not surprised and she's quickly becoming disinterested in the never-ending saga of Melanie. Not that I blame her, because I'm over it, too.

"I'm not exactly sure, but I have a weird feeling about my new client."

I tell her about walking in on Valerie's conversation and about her being friends with Melanie.

"Summer, this is ridiculous," she shouts. "Alexander needs to get rid of her once and for all. How long are you going to put up with it?"

I don't say anything. This is not the first conversation we've had about this, and I can't say I disagree with her.

"He talked to her already and things have been better." I trail off. "And I don't know for sure that Valerie and she are up to anything. It was just strange."

"Come on. You know better than that, you wouldn't have this feeling if it were nothing. Remember what happened with Jake? She even pretended to be in a relationship with your ex. It doesn't get much more twisted than that."

"Well, what should I do then?"

I don't know why I'm asking Angie what I should do. She'll probably tell me to hire a private investigator or something completely over-the-top like that.

"Well, first you need to find out if there's something to all of this, and then when you have the proof that this Valerie is up to something, you need to give Alexander an ultimatum."

An ultimatum? As in Melanie goes once and for all?

"You know I can't make him choose. We've already been through this."

"That's crazy. You absolutely can ask him to choose. How long are you going to let her be a hindrance in your relationship?"

I groan.

"Summer, I have to go. Just think about it, okay?"

As soon as I hang up, I realize that familiar feeling of uncertainty has crept up again. I know Angie is looking out for me, but she may be taking things overboard. I'm not saying that I haven't thought about it. There have been several instances when I've almost told Alexander that Melanie needs to go or I go. I just don't want to jump to a conclusion without any proof. And things have been better lately; she's definitely been keeping her distance. For now, I need to live up to this fantastic reputation that Valerie keeps referring to, and hopefully I will find out if there is anything to that phone call.

～

I look around my living room and I have to admit I'm proud of myself. In the corner are four neatly packed boxes. I've wrapped the fragile items and purged quite a few things. Everyday I get a little closer to my move. And speaking of my move, it's been days since I've seen Mrs. Rothera. I'm sure she's been trying to ignore all the noise of me moving things around, one of the joys of living in a downstairs apartment. I probably should check in on her, especially after our last interaction. As frustrating as she can be, I'm going to miss her. I hop off the couch and make my way downstairs. For some reason, tonight it feels like I'm walking into a storm. I don't hear any weird music or the sound of tambourines coming from her apartment, but I still knock loudly on the door. She could be in some deep meditation, so I wait patiently. A few minutes go by and she doesn't answer. Maybe she's out? I head back upstairs, but for some reason I can't shake this strange feeling. Mrs. Rothera is clearly avoiding me, and I want to know why.

When I get back to my apartment, I don't return to my packing. I pick up my phone and try calling Mrs. Rothera. The call goes straight to voicemail, so I leave her a short message letting her know I stopped by and want to chat with her.

I stretch out on the couch and send a text to Alexander. He said he would be in and out of meetings all day but hopefully he's finished by now.

Not even two minutes go by when my phone rings. I smile to myself.

"Hey, babe. I was just thinking about you."

"Oh really?" I reply flirtatiously.

"Yes, I was thinking about taking you to dinner to make up for our interrupted breakfast."

I look around my apartment, and I know I should continue packing, but an evening out with Alexander is so much more enticing."

"I would love it."

I quickly get off the phone so I can get ready. I don't mention Mrs. Rothera to Alexander yet. I can't stress myself over nothing, and if she is upset about me moving I can't control that. I've been planning this for a while and I'm confident this is the right step for my future.

~

"Babe, you look perfect," Alexander says, wrapping me up in his arms. Now that he's here I'm even more excited for a night out with him. No jetlag, no work, and no Melanie.

He looks around my apartment.

"Wow, look at this place. It's starting to look empty."

I nod. "Yep. I will be out of here before I know it."

He sits down on the couch and stretches his arms out. "So, when do I get to see your new place?"

I smile as I sit down on the edge of the couch.

"We could check it out after dinner?"

"Let's do it."

On our way out the door, we run into Mrs. Rothera. I'm not sure why, but she looks surprised to see me or maybe she's disappointed? How long did she think she was going to avoid me? I do live in her building, right downstairs from her. The crazy thing is that a few short weeks ago I couldn't get away from her.

"Hi, Mrs. Rothera, I just left you a message."

"I'm sorry. I haven't checked my messages yet," she replies coldly.

I wave my hand. "It's fine. I just wanted to make sure you're okay. It seems like we keep missing each other."

She awkwardly checks her mailbox, which is empty. I would stake my life on it that she already picked up her mail hours ago.

"I'm doing just fine. I've been caught up in my work."

I glance at Alexander who's stayed quiet. He raises his eyebrows at me.

"We probably should get going," he says, pointedly. "Good night, Mrs. Rothera."

She smiles warmly at him. "Have a nice evening."

Once we're safely in the car, I ask Alexander if he thinks Mrs. Rothera was acting strange.

"She definitely didn't seem like herself."

That at least makes me feel better knowing I'm not imagining her odd behavior.

"It's weird, isn't it? She's normally so much more engaging. The Mrs. Rothera I know would be asking us every detail about our night."

Alexander makes a face.

"Well, she knows how you feel about all the psychic stuff, so maybe she's respecting that?"

I chew on my bottom lip.

"Maybe, but why now all of a sudden?" I pause. "No, there's more to it. I think she's been avoiding me on purpose."

Alexander casually changes the subject. I know he doesn't want to spend another evening talking about my landlord and neither do I.

After a wonderful and *uninterrupted* dinner, I give Alexander directions to my new apartment. I'm so excited for him to see it I can barely sit still. This will prove to Angie that he doesn't have an issue with every apartment I choose. And why is it a big deal anyway? We don't need to live together to prove we're committed to each other.

"Turn here and the complex is on the right. Isn't this area gorgeous? All fresh and new?"

Alexander laughs nervously. I'm not sure what's so funny.

"It's a great place, Sum."

I give him a curious look.

"Why are you laughing?"

"Don't freak out okay."

Crap. Everyone knows when someone tells you not to freak out the first thing you do is freak out.

"What?"

"Melanie lives here."

Shit.

I put my face in my hands and shake my head. Okay, before I curl up into the fetal position, this really isn't a big deal. So she lives here in this complex. It's a big place, and what are the chances I will see her? Probably never.

"That's fine," I reply nonchalantly. "Um, do you know which building she's in?"

He gives me a side-glance.

"Which building are you in?"

I punch him on the arm. "Very funny. I'm in building eight, apartment one zero one. I finally have a downstairs apartment."

Alexander covers his mouth with his hand. Oh, please no.

"Don't even joke about that," I shout. He hasn't said anything yet, but I know he's probably going to make some joke about Melanie living next door to me.

"Melanie lives in building eight, apartment two zero three."

"Haha. Okay, you've had your fun." I roll my eyes.

But then I notice that he's not laughing anymore.

And there it is. All my joy is sucked out in a matter of seconds. Alexander must notice that I'm practically on the verge of tears. I know I shouldn't let it bother me, but seriously? Will I ever be free of this woman? Is she going to be a permanent fixture in my life? What about when Alexander comes over? Is she going to stop by all the time? Suddenly, Angie's ultimatum idea isn't looking so bad.

"Babe, don't let it get you down. I'm sure you'll never see each other."

This is crazy. Alexander may not have a problem with this apartment, but I certainly do. I would prefer to be as far away from Melanie as possible.

I shrug my shoulders. "I guess. Maybe I can switch apartments. I will call the leasing office first thing in the morning."

This really sucks because I really liked the location of my apartment. It's right on the edge of the complex. next to the woods with a beautiful view.

"Come on. I don't think you need to do that," he insists.

Am I being completely ridiculous? Maybe I am.

"I'll think about it."

He parks the car in front of building eight, and I stare at the building where Melanie and I will be neighbors. Ugh, that sounds completely miserable.

Alexander reaches for my hand.

"I'm sorry. This is all my fault."

I can't disagree with him. Unfortunately, his unorthodox working relationship with Melanie has led us to this point. I stare out the window and think about this new obstacle (at least, an obstacle in my mind) in the way of my move.

"I'm being ridiculous, I know."

He leans his head back against the seat. "It's okay. But I have an idea how to solve all of this."

I give him a curious look.

"What's your idea?"

All of a sudden, my phone starts to ring. Talk about bad timing.

I search for my phone in my bag, and as soon as I see it's a call from Mrs. Rothera I have a feeling I should answer it.

"Hello."

"Hello, Summer. I'm sorry to bother you on your date. I just wanted to let you know I received your message, and I was hoping we could sit down and chat tomorrow. I would like to settle the details of your move."

I look out the window at my new home, and suddenly I'm filled with doubt.

"Um . . . okay. I have a meeting with a client in the morning, but I will be available later in the afternoon."

Hopefully by then I will be feeling better about my decision. I'm starting to sweat. It could be the humidity or it could be my nerves. Either way this is really happening, so I better be sure about my decision.

"I'm sorry," I apologize to Alexander. "Believe it or not, it sounds like Mrs. Rothera is ready for me to leave. We're meeting tomorrow to discuss everything."

I sigh loudly. "I need a vacation."

"Let's do it," he exclaims.

I stare at him blankly. Is he asking me to go on vacation with him? Not that I wouldn't love to go somewhere with him alone—away from Melanie, Helena, Jake, and Mrs. Rothera. The one thing holding me back is the last summer vacation I took with a man; it didn't turn out so great.

"Are you serious?"

He throws his head back in laughter.

"Of course I'm serious. Where would you like to go?"

"Hah. Where don't I want to go?" The past few summers we've gone to Angie's aunt's beach house, but this year we have no plans since Angie's moved. "I don't know, anywhere alone with you would be amazing."

He gives a thoughtful look. "Okay, you pick the location and we'll book it."

I'm so excited I can hardly stand it. I love summertime, and I can't wait to enjoy our first vacation together. The rest of the evening we discuss our vacation, and this is the perfect distraction to keep me from stressing about Melanie being my neighbor.

Chapter Five

This really sucks. As soon as my fantastic evening ends I start worrying again. It feels like that's all I've been doing since last summer. Constantly looking over my shoulder—waiting for something to interfere with my happiness.

How am I going to live in the same building as Melanie? I wouldn't put it past her to use this to her advantage, another tool to worm her way into my personal life. She's already proven that she will take whatever drastic measures she needs in order to keep herself in Alexander's life.

As soon as I wake up, I make myself a cup of coffee and place a call to the leasing office at the complex. I practically beg them to let me rent a different apartment. If I were there in person, I would probably be on my knees begging. Unfortunately, they don't have any other apartments available for another six months, and they offer to add me to a waiting list. I strongly consider resorting to tears and bribes but I refrain. I don't have long to worry because I have to get ready for my appointment with Valerie. For the first time since I took this job, I'm looking forward to our meeting but only because I need to figure out what she's up to.

As soon as I finish getting ready, I receive text from Alexander.

Good morning. Have I told you how much I love you?

My stomach does a back flip.

You haven't this morning.

A few seconds later, my phone rings.

"Good morning."

"Good morning to you. How are you feeling this morning?"

I groan.

"I'm okay, but unfortunately the apartment complex doesn't have any available units for another six months. So, either I break the contract I just signed or Melanie and I will be neighbors?" I pause, waiting for his response, but he doesn't say anything. I can hear him typing something on his laptop.

"Anyway, I'll figure something out. How are you?"

"Hectic morning, of course. But the reason I'm calling, other than to hear your voice, is to invite you to dinner again, only this time it's at my parents' house. Saturday night—will you be my date?"

Hmm . . . his parents. I've met Penny and Rick once and it was a bit awkward. But only because Alexander had the brilliant idea to *hire* me to redecorate their home as an anniversary gift. Let's just say Penny wasn't too keen on the idea of her son's new girlfriend walking in and changing around the house she's lived in for twenty-something years. Then, there was the whole thing with the menu being straight from the cookbook of Melanie. I didn't feel too confident on the impression I made even though Alexander said it went well.

"I would love to be your date. What's the occasion?"

"No special occasion. I guess Penny's just looking for another excuse to cook."

I grit my teeth.

"Sounds great."

I hold back my sarcastic comment about trying another one of Melanie's extraordinary recipes.

~

"Are you sure there isn't too much gray?" Valerie asks for the hundredth time. I'm seriously contemplating sticking my pen in my eye, just so I have an excuse to leave. I can't believe this, she picked out all the colors (most of them different shades of gray) and now she's questioning her choices.

"I don't. In fact, I think the schemes work really well together."

Suddenly, a thought pops into my head.

"In fact, I've been looking at a similar color scheme for my new place." I scroll through my files on my laptop. "This is what I was looking at, although now I need to decide if I'm actually going to move."

Valerie gives me a curious look.

"What do you mean? Why wouldn't you move?"

I frown. "Unfortunately, I found out there might be an issue with my apartment. Well, not exactly the apartment, more like a neighbor."

"Oh," Valerie says disappointedly.

It's obvious she's already lost interest, so I know I need to throw out more hints.

"Yeah, I just found out my boyfriend's assistant lives in the building I'm moving into, and unfortunately we don't exactly get along."

And that's all I needed to say to reel her back in.

"You're moving into the same building?"

I nod. "Yes. Can you believe it? What are the chances?"

She chews on her bottom lip. "So, it sounds like you have a complicated relationship with this girl?"

I let out a loud sigh.

"I guess you could say that," I reply. "But, things have been better lately. Hopefully, we've all moved on. And things are really, really amazing with Alexander. I'm a very lucky girl."

Valerie looks as if she's mentally taking notes of everything I say.

"Can I tell you a secret?" I whisper. I don't know why I'm whispering, but it definitely makes me sound more dramatic.

"Yes. Definitely," she replies, more eagerly than I expected.

This is awesome. I'm going to lay it on thick.

"Truthfully, I'm hoping my boyfriend will ask me to move in with him. He's dropped a few subtle hints."

Her eyes grow wide.

"Really? That surprises me that you would want to give up your independence."

What does she mean by that?

"I don't think moving in with him would take away my independence."

She shrugs her shoulders. "I don't know. It sounds like you have a great thing right now. And you don't strike me as the type to let another woman scare you away . . . from the apartment."

And that's all the information I'm going to give her for today.

"I'm so sorry," I exclaim. "Here I am supposed to be decorating your home, and I'm talking about my personal life. That's so unprofessional of me."

She places her hand on mine. "Don't apologize. Just because you're decorating my house doesn't mean we can't be friends. You can talk to me about anything."

Hah. Friends? She's good.

"I appreciate that. It's been difficult lately since my best friend moved to Florida."

She pats my shoulder. "Well, you have me."

I guide her back to discussing her paint selections and off the subject of my personal life. Thankfully, she follows my lead.

On my way home, I start to wonder if Valerie really is up to anything. Maybe I'm completely wrong. Have I become so paranoid that I've let my insecurities control my life? There is one way to find out, and I'm meeting up with her this afternoon. Maybe I should give in and take advantage of having my own personal psychic right downstairs.

Chapter Six

I wonder if I'm getting sick. That's all I need right now. It's either that or I'm having hot flashes from the rising temperatures. Maybe I wouldn't want to live in Florida after all? I sit down on the couch with a cold drink and my laptop while I wait for Mrs. Rothera to come over. I'm just about to send Helena an email when I hear six knocks at my door. Mrs. Rothera always knocks six times.

"Hi," I say cheerfully.

"Hello, Summer," she says. She sounds so formal, so different than usual.

I invite her in and offer her something to drink.

"No thank you."

We sit down at the table, and she produces a few sheets of paper from a manila envelope.

"I'm assuming you're still planning to move at the end of the month?" She glances around the apartment and at my four measly packed boxes in the corner of the room.

I nod slowly. "That's my plan, at least I think so. I just have to figure out how to get past my latest roadblock."

She raises an eyebrow. "Roadblock?"

I let out a loud sigh. "Yes, unfortunately the perfect apartment I found isn't so perfect after all."

She purses her lips. "Oh?"

"This is probably going to sound ridiculous, and I wish it didn't bother me, but I found out that Melanie and I are going to be neighbors. I guess I'm starting to wonder if this is another sign to keep me from moving?"

I can tell she wants to say something.

"Summer, do you want me to tell you what I think?"

I nod. And this time I mean it. I need direction or at least someone to tell me I'm being completely ridiculous.

Her expression turns very serious. "Moving into that apartment is a mistake."

I had a feeling she was going to say that,

"Mrs. Rothera, can I ask you something?"

"Yes," she says, raising one eyebrow.

"Why have you been avoiding me these last few weeks? The last time I was at your apartment you rushed me out without any explanation."

She frowns.

"You aren't going to like hearing this. But, I'm concerned for you."

She's right, I don't want to hear this. In fact, this is exactly what I wanted to avoid.

"I have an uneasy feeling about your move and the negative forces that could affect your happiness. I know how heartbroken you were following your last relationship and . . ."

"Thank you," I interrupt. "I really do appreciate your concern."

She's about to say something else, but she stops.

"It's never going to end, is it?" I ask. "Angie thinks it's time to give Alexander an ultimatum."

Mrs. Rothera is quiet. So quiet that it's starting to scare me.

"I think you need to do whatever will make you happy. Do you know what that is?"

I nod. "I thought I could handle this. But between Helena's warnings and now this new client, who also happens to be good friends with Melanie, it never stops."

"Well, there's your answer."

Crap. I was hoping it wouldn't get to this point.

"Thank you for being a good friend. I'm sorry if I've been difficult."

She laughs.

"You're not the first person to be uncomfortable with my . . . unique qualities."

Now, it's my turn to laugh.

"That's an interesting description."

She shrugs as she stands up. "Anyway, I'll leave you to your work. Just think about what I said before you make your final decision about moving."

"I will."

After she leaves, I stare blankly at my computer screen. I should be working on Helena's dining room, but instead, I'm contemplating how I'm going to break the news to Alexander.

∼

I'm very quiet as we drive to Alexander's parents' house. I've spent the past few days contacting new potential clients that it hasn't given me much time to think (or obsess) about my move or Melanie. Which is probably a good thing.

"Hey. You sure you're okay?" he asks. "Please tell me you aren't worried about seeing my parents again."

I shake my head.

"It's not that. I'm just distracted."

He reaches over and puts his hand on my leg.

"What did you decide about the apartment?"

I groan.

"I have no idea. According to Mrs. Rothera, it would be a very bad idea for me to move in there."

"Are you serious? You're not going to listen to that, are you?"

I stare out the window, and thankfully, we turn onto his parents' street.

"I'm not sure what I'm doing yet."

When he pulls into their long drive, he doesn't turn off the car.

"Summer, I'm worried. You seem distant. Is there something else going on?"

Just then, his father and niece knock on his car window.

"Hi, you two."

Alexander makes a face.

"I would really like to finish this conversation later."

I nod. "Okay."

"I love you."

I give him a grateful smile. "I love you, too."

∼

I really like Alexander's sister Anna. She's friendly and down to earth. She gives me a warm hug as soon as we walk in the house. Which is more than I can say for Penny.

I don't know what it is, but I have a feeling Alexander's mother doesn't care for me.

She's standing over the stove, stirring a big pot of marinara sauce.

"Hello, Summer." She gives me one of those quick cheek

kisses. The kind where your cheeks touch and you make a kiss sound.

"Hey, Mom," Alexander says, giving her a hug.

I stand back and watch their interaction. It's very obvious she adores her son. It makes me wonder what kind of relationship she had with Helena?

I can hear Rick playing with Alexander's adorable six-year-old niece Kelsey, and Anna's husband Rob is holding eighteen-month-old Elise.

"Would you two mind setting the table? Oh, and there will be eight of us tonight."

Alexander nods, and then gives her a curious look.

"Eight? There are only seven of us, unless you're planning on allowing Elise to play with your good china."

Penny smiles. "No, I've invited Melanie to join us tonight. She was so helpful with the meal planning for the church banquet last week."

I watch as all the color drains from Alexander's face. He looks in my direction and gives me an apologetic look.

The crazy thing is I'm not surprised Penny invited Melanie—not at all. I have no doubt Melanie has been talking to Penny about me. I'm sure she does it in a very sly and innocent way, because that's what she does.

"Is there a problem?" Penny asks. She must have noticed the awkward silence between Alexander and me.

"No problem at all, Penny," I announce loudly. "Please show me the dishes you would like to use."

Alexander and I follow Penny into her formal dining room, a room that would definitely benefit from a facelift by Summer Interiors. The walls are covered in dated floral print wallpaper, which is peeling in some spots. The cream curtains are faded and dingy. The furniture is very nice, obviously made of good sturdy oak.

"You can use this china," Penny says, opening the cabinet. "The silver is in the drawer."

She rushes back to the kitchen, leaving Alexander and me alone. I don't say anything as I very carefully pull out the good china. The last thing I need to do is break one.

"Sum, I promise I had no idea."

I nod slowly.

"I know you didn't. But I'd say it's obvious that Melanie and your mother have more of a relationship than just sharing recipes."

He drops his head. The last time we discussed this he insisted they just shared recipes from time to time.

"Let's just discuss it later," I whisper. I have a strong feeling there are listening ears from the kitchen.

We set the table in silence, and I head back to the kitchen to help in any way I can.

"Summer. I had a chance to take a look at your website," Anna says with a smile. "You do beautiful work."

I grin widely. "Thank you. I love my job."

At that moment, we're interrupted by a knock at the door. Penny wipes her hands and hurries to answer it. Anna walks by me and squeezes my hand. I give her a grateful smile. As soon as I hear Melanie's voice, I cringe.

"I made the raspberry cheesecake and a turtle cheesecake. Since that's Alexander's favorite."

"You're wonderful. Thank you," Penny gushes.

I awkwardly lean on the counter when they join us in the kitchen.

"Hi, everyone," Melanie says.

Anna, Alexander, and I all say hello at the same time. Melanie immediately starts discussing work with Alexander, going out of her way to ignore my presence.

I stand awkwardly off to the side, feeling completely out of place. I can't help but wonder how I got to this point? The truth is it's partly my fault, because I allowed this to go on. Helena is right. Angie is right. I don't want to wake up years down the road with this other person affecting my relationship.

"Okay, everyone to the dining room," Penny shouts, dragging me out of my thoughts.

Alexander puts his arm around me and guides me to the dining room. I look around and a thought crosses my mind. I guess this is how it will always be, one big happy family that obviously includes Melanie.

Chapter Seven

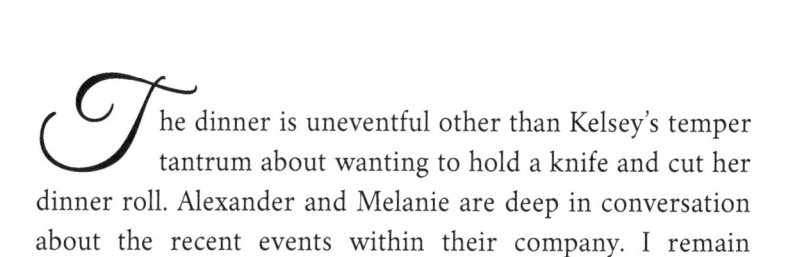

The dinner is uneventful other than Kelsey's temper tantrum about wanting to hold a knife and cut her dinner roll. Alexander and Melanie are deep in conversation about the recent events within their company. I remain mostly quiet, picking at my food.

"Melanie, before I forget, please thank your friend Valerie for that pastry chef recommendation," Penny says. "The desserts were a huge hit at the banquet."

Thanks to Penny, I finally have the answer I've been hoping for since the day I heard Valerie whispering on the phone. It's at this exact moment everything comes crashing down—for Melanie.

"Valerie? As in Valerie Watson?" I interrupt, raising my voice to a level that probably isn't suitable for one of Penny's dinners.

Penny, Alexander, and Melanie all look at me. I guess I was

yelling or maybe they're looking at me because it's the first time I've spoken a word since we sat down at the table.

Melanie's eyes grow wide. "Um, yes."

"Summer, do you know Valerie?" Penny asks.

I glare at Melanie. She makes every effort to avoid making eye contact with me, even pretending to choke on her wine.

"I do know Valerie. In fact, she just hired me to decorate her home."

"What a small world?" Penny says, as she folds her napkin into a small square.

"It really is," I say. My tone is so sarcastic I have no doubt Alexander has caught on. "Valerie told me she was referred through a friend. Was that you, Melanie?"

I look at Alexander out of the corner of my eye. He's watching our conversation intently. I think I see a few beads of sweat on his forehead.

Melanie shifts around in her chair. All eyes are on her now.

"Oh, um, I didn't realize you were decorating her house," she stutters. Ha! There's no way for her to escape this conversation, except maybe a sudden bathroom emergency.

I fold my arms.

"Really? Alexander says you two are good friends. You really had no idea I was her decorator?"

I watch as Melanie continues to squirm.

"You know, I think I did mention you had decorated Alexander's home—and did a fantastic job."

I force a smile.

"Well, I should be thanking you then . . . for the referral."

Melanie nods as everyone else at the table sits quietly, listening to our conversation. The only sound is coming from Kelsey's iPad.

"You're welcome, but I don't know that I did anything," she says, fumbling over her words.

I look at Alexander once again, hoping he will say something.

"Penny, let me help you with the dishes," Melanie exclaims, finally finding the perfect excuse to end our conversation. She's been caught, and she knows it.

She and Penny pick up several dishes and head off to the kitchen.

"Summer, would you like to help me get Elise changed?" Anna asks. I could kiss her right now. And yes, I would rather change a toddler's dirty diaper than wash dishes with Melanie any day.

Alexander joins Rick and Rob in their discussion about preseason football, although he looks slightly nauseous.

A few minutes later, I'm standing next to Anna as she gently lays Elise on the bed in Penny's bright yellow guest room.

"Are you okay?"

I let out a loud sigh. I feel very comfortable with Anna, so it doesn't surprise me when I suddenly unload all my pent-up frustration.

"I don't know if I can do this—deal with Melanie, not change the baby."

She smiles. "I know what you were referring to."

"I really thought I could," I continue, as I rub my temples. "I respect Alexander and his career, but I can't go on like this."

I decide to tell her about what I overheard when Valerie was on the phone.

"So, what do you think is the purpose of Valerie hiring you?" she asks.

I shrug. "I'm not exactly sure. Maybe it's some diabolical plan to sabotage my business? Or maybe she's planning on accusing me of something horrible, anything to break up Alexander and me. According to Helena, Melanie's capable of anything."

She raises her eyebrows. "So, you've met Helena?"

I roll my eyes. "Oh yeah, I'm actually redecorating her apartment."

Anna throws her head back in laughter.

"I'm sorry I'm laughing. Being with my kids all the time, I don't get this kind of excitement often."

I can't help but laugh as well.

"Seriously, I couldn't make this stuff up if I tried. My best friend, Angie, says she doesn't understand how I get myself into these messes, but here I am."

Anna puts a pair of Minnie Mouse pajamas on Elise, while making faces at her. Elise giggles in delight.

"Speaking of Helena? Did you all get along with her?"

I've been dying to know what Alexander's family thought of Helena and their divorce.

Anna makes a face. "We didn't see much of them during their marriage, but when we did she was always pleasant. Not overly warm, but pleasant. I just don't believe she ever had any desire to be a part of this family."

Hmmm . . . this is interesting.

"Well, according to her, Melanie was a major factor in their marriage breaking up."

She nods as if she already knew that.

"I'm sure she was. Melanie's involvement in Alexander's life is not an ideal situation. I would *never* tolerate Rob having an assistant who's so immersed in our personal lives. So, I can see where you're coming from." She pauses, picking up Elise. "And as far as my mother, it's nothing personal toward you. She and Melanie have similar interests, especially with the cooking thing. Helena never really made an effort to form a bond with her and I believe Mom always wanted that with the woman Alexander ended up with."

"Everything all right in here?" Alexander interrupts.

Anna and I glance at each other.

"I'll let you two talk." She hurries out of the room with Elise over her shoulder.

I make myself busy folding the baby blankets Anna left in the room. Alexander and I are silent for a few seconds. I'm not sure what it is, but something feels different between us and I don't like it.

"Summer, I'm so sorry about everything that happened at dinner. There has to be some kind of explanation for Valerie. Summer Interiors is becoming quite popular so . . ."

"What?" I interrupt, raising my voice once again. "Alexander, do you hear yourself? Why can't you just admit that Melanie is purposely trying to cause problems? She couldn't even explain her connection to Valerie. If that isn't a red flag, then I don't know what is."

He stares at the floor.

"And you don't think it's odd that she accepted a dinner invitation tonight knowing we would be here too?"

Silence.

I need to get the hell out of here.

"I'm ready to go home."

"Summer . . ."

"I want to go home," I reply calmly.

The next few minutes happen so quickly I feel like I'm outside of my body watching it. I quickly gather my things and say my good-byes to Alexander's family, giving them the ever-convenient excuse that I don't feel well. Anna gives me a tight hug while Penny offers me an aspirin.

I glance at Melanie before we leave. I contemplate the ways I could wipe the smug expression off her face. Instead, I walk out without saying a word to her. Unfortunately, she may succeed in doing what she's wanted since the first day I showed up to decorate Alexander's home. I know what I need to do now, and I can already feel my heart breaking even worse than it did last summer when Jake left me alone on the beach.

~

I silently stare out the window as we make our way back to my apartment. My mind is racing with hundreds of different thoughts. Thankfully, Alexander respects the fact that I don't want to talk right now. I will have plenty to say to him soon enough.

I know I've finally reached my breaking point. I wonder if this is how Helena felt. The only difference is she walked away from a marriage of four years . . . and what some of her friends say, the greatest love story of all time. Gag.

We almost make it back to my apartment when Alexander breaks the horrible silence in the car. The tension is so thick I contemplate opening my window.

"Please talk to me."

I take a deep breath. "What do you want me to say? Do you want me to tell you I'll just stand back while you have another discussion with Melanie? Are you going to threaten her to stay out of our lives again? Or are you going to tell me that Melanie and your mother barely know each other, when it's obvious they have more of a relationship than you thought?" I pause, before continuing with my monologue. "Is tonight an example of how dinners with your family are going to always be? I thought I could handle being your girlfriend while you have this assistant so involved in almost every aspect of your life. It's just not going to work . . . so . . ." I take a deep breath as I fight back the tears. "It's time for you to choose—Melanie or me?"

As hard as I was trying to fight back the tears, they make their way out of my eyes and down my cheeks. I know I'm making the right decision. I love Alexander, but I also know that I will never be completely happy if things continue the way they are. I would hate to be years into our relationship and this situation slowly destroy us as it did with Helena.

Alexander is gripping the steering wheel so tightly that his knuckles are turning white. He slowly pulls up in front of my apartment building and puts the car into park. The tears are still rolling down my cheeks, but I'm not sobbing. I'm surprisingly calm despite the huge rock in the pit of my stomach.

"Please don't do this," he says, his voice barely over a whisper. "I don't want to lose you or lose what we have."

I wipe my cheeks with both my hands.

I look at his face for the first the time since we left his parents' house. His normally confident exterior is gone, and he looks completely distraught. I wouldn't be surprised if he started crying along with me. Once again, I begin to doubt this decision. Maybe I'm the one being inconsiderate, insecure, and selfish? I close my eyes and suddenly I feel as if a slide show of the past ten months begins to play for me. I can see Melanie interrupting our close moments, the nonstop phone calls, plotting with Jake to break us up, telling Mrs. Rothera about my decision to move, convincing Valerie to hire me, and antagonizing me about her relationship with Penny and Alexander's family.

Of course, Helena's words begin repeating in my mind. Melanie destroyed their marriage of four years; she's capable of anything. At least I can say I made an effort in the beginning, and I was willing to coexist with her in Alexander's life.

Alexander grabs my hand and holds on to it for dear life.

"I will do whatever it takes to show you that you come first in my life. In fact, I was . . ." He inhales deeply. "I was going to ask you to move in with me, especially since you've hit so many obstacles with your moving plans. I'm ready to take the next step with you and really begin our life together."

He hasn't let go of my hand, and the truth is I don't want him to let go of it—ever. And I would love nothing more than to take the next step in our relationship. Not to mention it would solve a lot of issues for me. But, moving in with him isn't going to solve the biggest issue in our relationship.

"I wish that was enough," I say softly. "But us living together won't fix the way we disagree about Melanie and her constant presence in our lives. And it really concerns me that you can't see the effect she's had on your life. She destroyed your marriage."

He shakes his head. "That's not entirely true. Helena and I rushed into our marriage; we barely knew each other even when we were married. It wasn't going to last with or without Melanie."

I purse my lips. "Okay, but you can't tell me she had *nothing* to do with your issues."

"Oh no, she did."

"Do you see what I'm saying? I'm not willing to risk it. I don't want to be years into our relationship and still arguing over this."

He nods. "Okay."

I'm not sure what he means by okay. Okay—as in he agrees? Okay—as in he chooses me? Or okay—as in he's letting me go? The rock in my stomach seems to be growing and I start to feel like I can't breathe. I grab my bag, throw the car door open, and take off running toward my apartment.

"Summer," Alexander yells, jumping out of the car.

The tears are falling again, and just as I reach my building, the door flies open and Mrs. Rothera appears with her arms outstretched. Without thinking, I run into her arms and begin sobbing on her shoulder.

"Summer," Alexander calls again, finally catching up to me.

"Just give her some space," Mrs. Rothera says softly. "Go home and think about everything. You two can talk in the morning."

"But, I have to . . ."

"Go home and decide," she tells him.

I unwind myself from her arms and run into the building, not looking back at Alexander. I've made my decision, now it's time for him to make his.

Chapter Eight

I don't usually binge on anything. In fact, I'm pretty healthy overall, but for some reason, relationship drama turns me into a raging sugar addict. Last summer, when Jake dumped me and left me at the beach, I ate my way through several boxes of Little Debbie Swiss Cake Rolls thanks to Angie's endless stash of junk food.

Unfortunately, Angie's no longer here, so I have to settle for the stale Oreos in my pantry. I'm sure I look completely pathetic right now with my tear-stained face, hugging the package of cookies as if my life depended on it. I'm so thankful Mrs. Rothera hasn't knocked on my door wanting to talk. I hope she takes her own advice and leaves me alone.

After I calm down, I curl up on the couch and replay the last few minutes with Alexander. The worst part is that even after everything I said to him, he still couldn't tell me he would choose me. I guess that should tell me something. I look out the window to see if by some crazy chance he's still out there, but he's gone. My mind begins to wander again . . . did I make the right decision or did I just destroy the best thing that's ever happened to me? A few seconds later, there's a knock at my door. I don't need to be a psychic to know who it is.

"Be right there," I call.

I quickly throw away the now empty package of Oreos and grab a paper towel to wipe my face. I open the door to find Mrs. Rothera holding a tray. I smell peppermint, so I'm sure it's something to calm me down. And who knows what else she put in there? I know how crazy this sounds, but there have a been a few occasions when I thought Mrs. Rothera was mixing magic potions.

"I'm sorry to bother you. I just wanted to drop this off. It's tea, a calming blend, perfect to help you relax and get some sleep."

Ha, I knew it.

"Thanks," I say, eyeing the teapot with caution.

She's staring at me, which is making me nervous.

"Um, if you don't mind, I kind of want to be alone."

She nods her head slowly, and I get the feeling she's not surprised by the events of tonight.

"I understand."

She turns and starts to walk away.

"Wait," I yell.

She stops dead in her tracks as if she was expecting me to stop her.

"Actually, I'd like you to come in."

She follows me into my apartment. I place the tray of magic tea down on the table. I have no intention of ingesting her crazy concoction.

"I suppose you know what happened with Alexander."

She fidgets with her rings.

"I don't know the exact details, but I have a pretty good idea."

I chew on my bottom lip.

"I finally told Alexander he needed to choose between Melanie and me." I try to swallow the lump in my throat. Unfortunately, once again I fail at holding back the tears. "Anyway, I guess it was just a matter of time," I say, through my tears. "It's obvious he's not ready to let her go from his life."

I wasn't planning to unload all my emotional turmoil on Mrs. Rothera. I was saving that for a phone call to Angie.

"You need to believe that everything will work out the way it's supposed to. The universe will bring you the life you're meant to have."

I appreciate her trying to help, but this is not what I want to hear right now. What I want is for her to tell me that Alexander will realize what needs to be done. Honestly, is it really that difficult to find a new assistant? I know Melanie does a great job and she knows his business inside out, but I'm sure life would go on without her.

"She's getting exactly what she wanted all along," I wail. "Remember when she came to see you for advice and you told her she wouldn't have a future with Alexander?"

She looks at the floor. "Summer, I haven't been completely honest with you."

My heart sinks into my stomach. Those are some of the worst words anyone can say, other than "it's over" or "let's just be friends." Either way, I know I'm not going to like what she's about to say.

"Okay."

She clears her throat.

"Even though I *believe* there's no future for Melanie and Alexander, I still encouraged her to go after what she wanted. It wouldn't be fair of me not to, and I thought she would give up as time went on and your relationship with him grew deeper."

I don't respond to her admission because I just don't know what to say. Yes, I would have hoped she would be on my side, but I haven't exactly taken any of her advice seriously, so I should never have assumed she had my back.

"There's something else."

Seriously? What a way to kick me when I'm down.

"It's not a secret that I don't want you to move."

Ha. The only way it would be less of a secret is if she was shouting it from the roof.

"I know you don't, but I've given you plenty of time to find a new tenant."

She shakes her head. "Do you think this is about rent money?"

I'm confused. "Yeah."

"It's never been about the money." She looks down at her hands, now neatly folded in her lap. "The truth is I'm very lonely. I've enjoyed having you here. And that's also why I hired you to decorate my apartment, and why I changed my mind on décor so many times."

Ahhh . . . this is all starting to make sense.

"I knew you weren't going to stay forever, but I was hoping you would stay a little while longer, so I . . . I helped Melanie come up with a plan to cause some issues for you. I thought if you were having trouble in your business you may not want to have the stress of moving on top of everything."

Whoa. I'm completing dumbfounded right now. Is she for real?

"What do you mean you came up with a plan?"

Before she can respond, I figure it out for myself.

"Valerie."

She hangs her head. "I'm so embarrassed."

"What exactly was going to happen with this plan?" I ask through my gritted teeth. All my tears are gone, and I can actually feel my blood pressure rising by the second.

She lets out a huge sigh. "Melanie came to me desperate for advice. She's so head over heels in love with Alexander, and she's still holding out hope that things will finally happen for them. In her mind, she can do and say anything and he still won't let her go. She believes the reason he won't let her go is because he has feelings for her deep down."

I put my face in my hands. Nothing would surprise me at this point. Maybe he does have feelings for her.

Mrs. Rothera continues talking. "Melanie wanted your attention on something other than Alexander, and I wanted your attention on something other than moving. I know how important your work is to you, so we thought..."

"Hold on," I say, putting my hand up. "*You* were going to sabotage my business?"

She looks horrified that I would suggest such a thing. "No, not at all. We just wanted to distract you."

This is the most insane thing I've ever heard. I was right all along about Valerie, and I was right about that phone call. And the worst part is that no matter what I say, I don't think Alexander would believe me.

One thing's for sure, I would have never thought that Mrs. Rothera would go along with something like this.

"Can you please go?" I say calmly.

I don't know if I'm technically allowed to kick my landlord out of my apartment, but considering this new information, I feel it's justified.

"I truly am sorry," she says, hanging her head.

"Please go. I can't handle any more of this tonight."

She makes her way toward the door but stops before she leaves.

"For what it's worth, Alexander does love you and you could have a beautiful life together."

I close the door behind her. First of all, I don't believe anything she says, and if Alexander loves me as much as he says, he would respect me enough to take my feelings into account.

And after tonight, I don't have faith that's going to happen.

Chapter Nine

"What the hell is going on? I move away and everything falls apart," Angie yells. It's one o'clock in the morning when she finally returns my calls. Yes, calls, as in many urgent calls.

"So, are you two officially broken up?"

I sigh. "I don't know what we are. I finally took your advice and gave him an ultimatum, but I was so emotional that I didn't even give him a chance to talk. He did ask me to move in with him, though."

"What?" she yells (this time she's actually yelling).

I tell her about our conversation.

"I knew it. He's wanted you to move in with him this whole time."

I rub my eyes. I'm so emotionally drained from this night, but I know I won't be able to get any sleep.

"Yeah. But when I asked him to choose between us, he just avoided it. He's not ready to give her up, and I don't want to share him anymore, so I'm not sure where that leaves us. Moving in together is the worst thing that could happen."

I begin to cry once again.

"Oh, Sum, I'm so sorry I'm not there."

"I know." I blow my nose loudly.

"Maybe you need to get away for a few days," Angie exclaims. "When's the last time you took some time off?"

I dab the corner of my eyes. "Um, that would be last summer when we were all at the beach."

"Oh."

"Yep. And we all know how that vacation ended." I pause. "Alexander and I were just talking about taking a trip. That's definitely not happening any time soon."

Angie is quiet, which doesn't happen often.

"Ang, you still there?"

"Yes, I was just thinking—why don't you come here for a few days, just to clear your head? A few days on a Florida beach can do wonders."

That doesn't sound like a bad idea. I'm at a good place with my clients and getting away from everything and everyone sounds pretty great.

"Summer."

"I'll do it. I will look at flights tonight. A few days in Florida are exactly what I need."

∼

After getting off the phone with Angie, I book a flight to Florida for next weekend. I wouldn't normally just take off, but I know I need this. Despite minimal sleep, I make sure I'm out of my apartment as soon as the sun comes up. I have no interest in seeing Mrs. Rothera this morning. It's actually a beautiful summer morning, so I sit outside at my favorite café with a coffee and my laptop.

Before making any more travel plans, I follow up on an order for Helena and send her a text letting her know I will be out of town for a few days. Now, if only I can figure out how to handle this situation with Valerie. I don't know whether I should confront her or just fire myself as her decorator. Honestly, I wonder how far she was going to take her act. I suppose I should have caught on sooner when she changed her mind on everything she chose. I feel so stupid.

I lean back in my chair and take a sip of my first cup of coffee. I have no doubt I will need more than one cup to make it through the day after maybe three hours of sleep. I haven't heard a word from Alexander since I asked him to leave last night, and I'm not sure if that's good or bad. In a perfect world, he's letting Melanie go right this second.

I must be so deep in thought I don't notice someone calling my name. Either that or I'm beyond exhausted and have fallen asleep with my eyes open.

"Summer."

I look up from my laptop to see Jake standing next to me. He's wearing a tight Adidas shirt, running shorts, and a baseball cap. I can't deny that I still find him physically attractive.

"Summer," he repeats. "You okay?"

"What? Oh yeah, I just didn't get much sleep last night."

He sits down on the edge of the chair across from me. Huh, that's funny because I don't remember inviting him to sit with me. Unless I was asleep . . .

"Do you mind if I sit?"

He must have read my mind.

"I have a lot of work to get done," I say, pretending to open a file on my laptop.

He gives me a curious look. "You sure you're okay?"

"Yep. Just a lot going on before I leave town for a few days. So, if you don't mind . . ."

He doesn't move from his chair, obviously not taking my hint.

"Jake, what do you want?"

He puts both hands around his coffee cup and tightens his lips.

"What do I want? That's a loaded question."

Crap. I totally walked into this one.

"Actually, I've had a lot of time to think about this the past few months. And what I want the most is for you to be happy." He stops and takes a deep breath. "I made the biggest mistake of my life last summer, and I regret it more than you know. But, you deserve better than me, you deserve to be treated like you're the most important person in the universe. I failed at that, and I don't blame you for not taking me back."

Wow. For the first time since last summer I believe he has remorse for hurting me like he did.

He stands up from the chair and picks up his coffee. "Make sure Alexander takes good care of you."

He's about to walk away, but I stop him.

"Thank you, Jake. I hope you find whatever it is you're looking for."

He smiles. "Me, too."

After he leaves, I think about one of the things he said. I do deserve to be treated like the most important person in the world. And because of this, I know I made the right decision by asking Alexander to choose. The truth is it's not fair to Melanie or me if our situation continues this way.

Surprisingly, I'm glad I saw Jake. This was the closure I've been looking for since we broke up. I do wish him happiness despite how much he hurt me, and I know I can't let that hurt define my future.

∽

"I want to go with you," Gina wails.

I giggle. "Really? Do you really think you will be able to pry yourself away from Vinny for an entire weekend?"

She scowls.

"What's that supposed to mean? Of course I can."

I raise my eyebrows because I can't remember the last time I saw her, and I know she's been spending her every waking moment with Vinny.

"Don't get defensive. You're welcome to come if you want."

She folds her arms. I know she won't go through with it unless Vinny joins her. Of course, Angie and Vinny are cousins so he just may. Great. And then it will be me with the two happy couples. Ugh.

"I knew that girl was trouble since day one. You just let me know and we can get that problem taken care of, if you know what I mean."

I laugh. Of course I know what she means.

"Thanks, I'll let you know."

"And what about that landlord of yours? We might as well take care of her, too."

I force a smile.

"I appreciate it, Gina." I pause. "I do need your help with something, though. I need to find a place to live. I cancelled my contract at the new complex. There was no way in hell I was going to live in the same building as Melanie."

She gives me a thoughtful look. "You could stay with me, it would be tight but . . ."

"Thanks, girl, but your tiny studio is definitely not big enough for both of us."

This is a nice way of telling her I would never live with her.

Not only is her place the size of a shoebox, but also she's a complete slob.

"Does Alexander know you're taking a trip?"

I shake my head.

"No. I haven't spoken to him since I asked him to leave last night."

Gina's face softens from her normally tough exterior, and she pats my shoulder.

"Don't worry about it. He'll do the right thing."

I shrug my shoulders.

"I saw Jake earlier today. He said something that got me thinking."

Gina's eyes grow wide. "No way. Don't you dare think about it," she demands.

I laugh. "Very funny. Don't worry, we're not getting back together. In fact, I think we both finally got the closure we needed."

Relief washes over her face. "Oh good. Don't scare me like that. What exactly did Jake say? He doesn't exactly exude eloquence."

I snort. Gina has never been a Jake fan.

"He told me he wanted me to be happy and that I should be treated like the most important person in the universe. That just reminded me that I don't feel that way when Melanie is in the picture."

She frowns. "Well, as much as I hate to agree with anything that comes out of Jake's mouth, he has a point."

"Yes, he does . . . believe it or not, I actually feel better after talking to him."

Gina begins to make gagging noises.

"At least he didn't mention your *amazing* decorating magic and try to manipulate you into giving him another chance."

I roll my eyes. Jake used to tell everyone that I had some kind of decorating magic. Gina thought it was annoying, and she continues to bring it up to this day.

"Nope. I believe that chapter is finally closed. We're both moving on once and for all."

Chapter Ten

This may be the longest I've gone without talking to Alexander since the day we met. It's been three long days since the horrific dinner at his parents' house. I've managed to avoid him, which has been absolute torture because I miss him so much. He's tried calling and has texted several times. Of course, none of his texts mention my ultimatum. Even though it's been hard, I'm proud of myself for staying strong. I keep reminding myself that until he makes up his mind I have nothing to say to him.

In each message, he tells me how much he loves me and that we will get past this. This morning he left me a message about having to go to Boston for two days, but he wants to talk when he gets back, the same day I leave for Florida.

My trip to Florida is the only bright spot in my life right now, and I'm counting the minutes until my escape from reality. I've also managed to avoid all contact with Mrs. Rothera by staying late at my office, going to the mall, and going to Starbucks. Basically, anything that will keep me out past her bedtime. The good news is I'm hopeful I will be out of this mess sooner than I expected. Gina has a friend who's looking for someone to rent her house. I've already set up a time to meet her when I return from my trip.

In the meantime, I'm completely dreading my meeting this morning with Valerie.

I'm sure she's spoken to Melanie by now, but she didn't mention it when I asked to meet. My plan is to just come out and confront her. I'm hoping she tells me the truth, but I'm not going to hold my breath. Anyway, it really doesn't matter because I have a feeling she's no longer going to be a client an hour from now.

As soon as I arrive I know something's different. She seems more relaxed than she usually is. Unfortunately, we're not alone—Melanie is sitting at the kitchen table, ready to pounce. Normally, this would throw me off but not today. I think deep down I had a feeling something like this would happen.

"Hello, Melanie," I say formally.

"Summer."

I look back and forth between the two of them, waiting for someone to break the ice.

"Summer, I'm glad you asked to meet today because I wanted to talk to you," Valerie says, being the first to break the tension.

"I asked Melanie here so we could all discuss and get everything out in the open."

I glance at Melanie who's trying very hard to pretend she cares, but she's doing a crappy job.

Valerie sits down at the table next to Melanie. I'm still standing—just in case I have to make a quick getaway.

"I know what you must be thinking," Valerie starts.

"Do you?" I interrupt. "I'm surprised you don't want to wait for your third conspirator. Shouldn't Mrs. Rothera be here?"

Both women look completely shocked. I'm not sure if they're shocked I called them out or shocked that I know she was in on this, too.

"But please, let's *discuss* why it is you hired me and what your grand plan really was."

I pull out one of the chairs and sit down with a sudden unexpected burst of confidence.

Valerie looks to Melanie for advice.

"Oh come on, Melanie, please tell me. I can't believe you're so desperate that you would resort to something so ridiculous—but wait, that's your style, right? Didn't I hear that you even fabricated some photos to break up Alexander and Helena?"

If looks could kill, I'm sure I would be dead and buried right now.

"I don't have any idea what you're talking about. It sounds like you're listening to that awful Helena again. I guess it's true—you know, that saying about a women scorned." She shakes her head. "Helena blames me for their marriage breaking up, but the truth is she only has herself to blame."

It's my turn to glare at her.

"Really? But it worked in your favor. With Helena out of the picture you had Alexander all to yourself." I stop and give her my most sweet and innocent smile. "That is until I came along."

Valerie's looking back and forth between us—I wouldn't be surprised if she made a bag of popcorn to go along with the show she's getting.

Melanie starts laughing. "Yes, you came along—a quick replacement for that self-absorbed, cold bitch he was married to. The funny thing is I'm still here, too. I was there when he and Helena broke up, and I will be here when you two break up."

It takes all my strength not to lose my cool. I want more than anything to tell her that's never going to happen, but I don't know that. Instead, I ignore her and look at Valerie.

"Well, I'm assuming this means our partnership is over. Although, it wasn't really a partnership, was it? The complaints about gray paint colors and finding the perfect wall mirror were all part of this ridiculous idea. I give you credit, though, you had me completely fooled."

She shrugs, not able to look me in the eye. I have a feeling she does feel some kind of remorse despite being besties with Melanie.

"I will tear up the contracts and considering the um . . . situation . . ."—I give Melanie a side-glance—"I won't take legal action because I'd rather be done with all of this nonsense."

I grab my bag and make my way toward the door. I stop and turn around.

"I'll be sure to let Alexander know how unfortunate it is that we're no longer working together."

I leave before Melanie can twist the knife any further in my back. The fact is she's absolutely right about her being in Alexander's life and there isn't a damn thing I can do about it. Unfortunately, I just have to wait for him to finally make his choice.

∼

"When are you coming back? You are coming back, aren't you?" Helena asks, raising her voice slightly. I'm not sure why she's so concerned with me leaving because getting in touch with her on most days has proven to be an act of congress. This may go down in history as one of the longest projects ever.

"Of course I'm coming back. I just need a few days away."

I'm standing in front of my closet, looking at the many items hanging in front of me and still wondering why I have nothing to pack.

"Is Xander going along on this holiday?"

I cringe.

"No, he's not. His work is keeping him busy." That's the easiest answer. I'd rather not discuss my relationship issues with my boyfriend's ex-wife. Seriously, I feel like I'm living on a trashy talk show.

"Yes. It always does. You might as well get used to it."

"Mmmhmm. Anyway, I just wanted to let you know. I will touch base with you again when I return."

After we hang up I continue to look through my clothes, mainly because I need to pack but also because I need a distraction. Angie says it's too hot to function right now, so I decide on a few dresses, swimsuits, and some shorts. I neatly roll my clothes and place them strategically in my carry-on suitcase.

As I look around my apartment, it occurs to me that it was almost a year ago I was packing for my beach trip with Jake. I remember being so excited to spend that time with him; of course, I had no idea what was about to happen. I remember I had just finished redecorating his boss's summerhouse and I was on top of the world. Everything was perfect and just like that—poof—eighteen months was gone in an instant. I suppose I should have expected something to happen; nothing in life is ever that perfect.

This is different, though. The way I love Alexander, these feelings are so much deeper than what I felt for Jake. When we're together, it feels like all the puzzle pieces in my life fit perfectly. Which makes this time apart even harder. "Ugh. Snap out of it, Summer," I scold. I refuse to second-guess myself anymore. I deserve to be number one in his life, and if he can't make me that—well, then perhaps the puzzle doesn't fit as perfectly as I thought.

Chapter Eleven

Finally. I've never been more ready for a vacation in my life. I'm just about to walk out the door to my awaiting cab when Mrs. Rothera appears at my doorway. Not even she can ruin my good mood. She looks down at my suitcase and back up to my wide-brimmed straw hat.

"Where are you off to?"

Shouldn't she already know the answer, you know, being a psychic and all?

"I'm going to see Angie."

Relief washes over her face. Maybe she thought I was trying to sneak out. Honestly, the thought has crossed my mind.

"That will be nice. Please give her my best."

"Sure," I say nonchalantly.

She clears her throat. "I'm glad I saw you before you left. I've been trying to catch up with you but . . ."

"I've been busy," I interrupt. I look in my bag to make sure I have everything.

"My cab is waiting, so if you'll excuse me."

I double-check the lock and rush out toward the cab. Mrs. Rothera follows me, practically running alongside me.

"I wanted to tell you something . . . and I think you may be happy about it."

The cab driver puts my suitcase in the trunk.

"You know what," I snap. "I don't need anyone to tell me what's going to make me happy. I've decided that I can make my own happiness, whether that includes Alexander or not."

I climb into the cab.

"But it's about your move."

"Good-bye, Mrs. Rothera." I close the car door, not giving her a chance to tell me what she wanted.

I lean my head against the seat as we make our way toward the airport. I'm not going to lie, I'm curious about what she wanted to tell me. But, I also don't want anything to ruin my trip. I don't want to talk about my move or Melanie or even Alexander. I just want to relax on a beach far away from my life and all the stress that goes along with it.

∼

"You've lost weight," Angie yells as soon as she sees me. "Are you eating, because it doesn't look like you've had a good bowl of pasta since I left."

I notice several people looking at us in the middle of the airport terminal.

"Ha-ha. Of course I'm eating."

She gives me a skeptical look.

"I'm so happy you're here," she shouts, engulfing me in a huge hug.

We both squeal like a couple of teenagers.

Angie is talking a mile a minute as she rushes out of the airport. I'm breaking a sweat trying to keep up with her. As soon as we exit, the humidity hits me. Holy crap. Don't get me wrong, it can get humid in Connecticut, but it's like a sauna out here.

"Wow. You weren't kidding about the heat."

She laughs.

"It's summertime in Florida, what else were you expecting?"

I can't believe I'm here. I look out the window at the blue skies and the palm trees. Maybe I could live here? It's hot as hell outside, but the idea of no more brutal winters is promising.

The plan is to stay at Angie's house in Orlando tonight, and then head to the beach tomorrow. Honestly, I don't care what we do. I'm just so happy to be here.

∽

I haven't laughed this hard in months. It's been so awesome just catching up and reminiscing with Angie. I really miss this.

"Too bad Gina isn't here," Angie says, dragging me out of my thoughts. "She'd have plenty of stories to share."

I laugh. "Yeah. She told me she wanted to come, but I don't think she could be away from Vinny that long. To tell you the truth, I was a little worried that she was going to bring him. I really didn't want to be stuck with two happy couples all weekend."

She shakes her head. "No need to worry about that. This is a girls only weekend, which is why I banished Brett from the house tonight."

I give her a grateful smile, which quickly turns to a frown.

"Oh, Ang, did I mess everything up with Alexander? Deep down, I know it was time to stand up for myself, but I haven't given Alexander a chance to explain since it all went down. Maybe I should . . ."

"Don't," she interrupts. "You did the right thing and Alexander will realize that."

The familiar feeling of dread has returned. I was hoping to keep this feeling away from invading my trip but no such luck.

"Enough about that," Angie yells. "We probably should turn in. We have to be up early in the morning for our massages."

"Massages?"

She smiles.

"Yep. My treat."

I don't know what I did to get such an awesome friend, but I couldn't be more thankful for her than I am right now.

∽

I need to move to the beach. I feel like a completely different person than I did yesterday. It could be the amazing massage I had this morning, or it could be the fact that I'm sitting on a balcony of our hotel room listening to the waves. I've only been here a few hours, but I'm beginning to feel like my old self. The confident happy woman I used to be before I let other people affect me. Angie rented us a two-bedroom suite and it's completely amazing. I offered to split the bill with her but she went completely ballistic on me. I'm just glad I won't be around when she gets her credit card statement next month.

Angie decided she needed to take a nap, which is funny because we haven't done anything other than lie around all morning. I take this opportunity to catch up on some emails. I know I'm not supposed to be working, but I can't unplug completely when I have my own business.

The first email I see is from Chantel, another referral from Alexander. She's ready to meet to discuss my upcoming project decorating her home. This is a huge relief, especially after the whole Valerie disaster, and since I'm obviously down one client I will need the business. And I'm sure Helena's apartment is going to drag out until the end of time.

The second email is from Gina's friend, confirming our meeting to look at her house. I reply immediately with a "Yes, definitely." I manage to stop myself from responding in all caps, not wanting to look completely desperate (which I am).

"What are you doing?" Angie yells, startling me.

"Crap. You scared me," I shout. "I thought you were taking a nap."

She furrows her brow. "And you're supposed to be on vacation. That means no emails and no work."

I quickly close my laptop. "I am, but I had to check in—I'm done."

She sits down. "I have a surprise for you."

I give her a worried look. "Another one? I appreciate it, Ang, but you're going into major debt from this weekend. Please let me pay for something."

She laughs. "I'm not spending any money on this surprise. Someone is on their way to crash our weekend."

I can feel my pulse pick up and for a second all I can think about is Alexander.

"He's coming," I exclaim.

She looks confused.

"He? No. It's Gina. She just called to find out where we are. She and Vinny flew in this morning, but don't worry, he's staying with Brett. No boys are allowed here."

I can feel my heart sink, but I do my best to recover and hide my disappointment. Having Gina here will be awesome.

"Did you think Alexander was coming?"

I shrug and turn back to face the ocean.

"Summer?"

"For a second I did." I swallow hard to try to get rid of the lump that's returned in my throat. "Or I was hoping at least. I guess I'm feeling guilty because I haven't returned any of his calls. I didn't even tell him I was coming here."

"Maybe you *should* call him or at least text him," she says.

I turn back to face her.

"What do I say?"

She puts her arm around my shoulder.

"Just tell him you came to visit me and you're willing to talk when you get back. You don't have to say anything else."

She's right.

I reach for my phone and make my way to my room. I start to type a text but erase it about ten times before sending.

> *Thanks for your messages. I'm in Florida with Angie. Let's talk when I return.*

Ugh. I sound so formal.

I'm about to send another text when he texts me back.

> *There's nothing more to say. I'm tired of trying. It's over.*

I stare blankly at my phone, suddenly feeling dizzy. I sit down on the bed before I pass out.

I'm too late. He's tried contacting me several times and I've ignored him, not even giving him a chance to explain. Giving him an ultimatum wasn't enough; I've pushed him further away and quite possibly into Melanie's waiting arms.

"Gina should be here in about an hour. How about we . . ." Angie stops and stares at me. "What happened?"

I can't even speak, so I hand her my phone.

"It's over," I say, my voice barely over a whisper.

Those are the only words I can say before collapsing into the ugly cry. Maybe this is a sign I should avoid the beach in the summertime. Heartbreak two years in a row is more than enough.

Chapter Twelve

The sunlight is pouring into my bedroom, it's so bright that I cover my eyes with my arm. I can totally hear Gina and Angie talking in the living room. It's not like Angie could ever whisper anyway. After Gina arrived with Chinese takeout last night, I told my friends I wanted to be alone. Alexander never texted me again, and I certainly didn't respond after he made it clear that there's nothing else to say. So, that means in two days I will return to Connecticut and make a fresh start—again. I wish I never sent that text. Actually, I take that back. I wish I had responded when Alexander was trying desperately to reach out to me.

Gina wanted to call Uncle Dominic for back up to take care of Alexander. Thankfully, Angie stopped her from making that call as she already had the phone in her hand. Angie's convinced that things will get work out when I get home. I'm not that optimistic.

Ugh. This is so pathetic. I need to pull myself together.

I drag myself out of bed, brush my teeth, and put some clothes on.

"Good morning," I say, joining my friends in the living room. I'm trying to sound as cheerful as I possibly can.

They're both wearing running clothes. Holy crap, did they already go running? What time is it?

"Good morning, we were just getting ready to grab some breakfast."

Hmm . . . I am pretty hungry. "That sounds good. I just want to take a quick walk on the beach," I say. I put a hat and sunglasses on to hide my bed head and my swollen eyes.

"That's a great idea. We'll come with you," Gina says, jumping off the couch.

I hold my hand up to stop her. "I just need a few minutes. I've decided I'm going to have one last good cry. Then, I'm coming back here and we're going to have an awesome day. I refuse to let another man ruin another vacation."

"Good for you," Angie yells. She's takes a long sip of her coffee.

"We'll grab breakfast when you get back."

I give her a grateful smile.

I walk down the path toward the sand. It's already hot outside, but there's a nice breeze off the ocean. I know I told Angie and Gina that I would have one last cry, but for some reason there are no tears falling. Maybe I knew deep down that this was going to happen. As amazing as my time with Alexander was, I was always looking over my shoulder waiting for something to go wrong. There could be some deeper meaning here—like I was meant to meet Alexander to help me get over what happened with Jake. Or maybe we were meant to meet to help grow my business.

I stand at the water's edge with the waves crashing against my feet. I close my eyes and give myself a little pep talk once again. I know I'm going to be okay no matter what happens. For now, I'm going to enjoy the rest of this weekend with my wonderful friends and try not to worry about my life back home.

My stomach growls reminding me that it's time for breakfast. I begin to head back to our suite when something catches my eye . . . actually, someone.

I must be hallucinating because it looks like . . . Alexander, or maybe it's his long-lost twin. Either way, this gorgeous man is walking toward me.

Despite the rising temperatures, I'm completely frozen. When he approaches, my mouth drops open.

He looks exhausted, and he's dripping in sweat.

"Summer."

I open my mouth to speak but no words come out for a few seconds.

"What are you doing here? Your text . . ."

He hangs his head. "I didn't send that text."

I'm so confused.

"Melanie sent it. We were at a meeting, and she had access to my phone when your text came through."

I shake my head and start laughing. "Of course she did. I should've known."

He stands there still looking down at the stand.

"I fired her."

I stop laughing. What?

"Summer, I'm so sorry. I should have listened to you. I was so scared of how it would affect my work if I let her go that I almost lost you."

I wonder if this is what shock feels like. I woke up this morning ready to move on with my life without Alexander in it and here he is, right in front of me.

"I wanted to see you in person to tell you I was going to let her go. I've been in touch with some business associates in search of a new assistant. And then, Mrs. Rothera contacted me. She told me everything—what happened with Valerie and that you had left town. In the meantime, I caught Melanie with my phone and it all . . . well, let's say it wasn't pretty."

My head is spinning right now.

"Finding you here was even harder. Your friends are tough."

I give a half smile and nod my head. "It's supposed to be no boys allowed."

He gives a nervous laugh, and then reaches for my hand. I let him take it.

"Please tell me I'm not too late. I know I don't deserve you after everything, but I came all this way to tell you that I choose you. From the moment you walked into my office with the bare walls I knew . . . I fell in love with you that first day."

I know with all my heart that he's being completely honest with me. I can't believe the nightmare is finally over. Well, I guess I was right when I told my friends I would have another good cry, because slowly the tears start to fall down my cheeks. Last summer, my heart was broken at the beach. This summer, it's completely mended.

"You're not too late," I say softly.

Before I can say anything else, he engulfs me in his arms and lifts me up off the sand.

"I love you, Summer," he says between his overpowering kisses. "And I refuse to let anything or anyone else come between us ever again."

"I love you, too."

He places me gently down on the sand and takes my hand. As we walk along the beach, my hand in his, I place my head on his shoulder. My love of this season is restored, and after the wild year I've had, I'm overjoyed to feel like myself again and return to Summer.

Epilogue

Thankfully, Angie and Gina got over the whole "no boys allowed" rule for our beach weekend. They even invited Brett and Vinny to join us after Alexander crashed our party. I know Gina was beyond excited to break this rule. Her relationship is still way too new to be away from her man for that long. I completely understand how she feels, and since Melanie has been removed from the picture, it's like Alexander and I are starting over once again. It really is amazing what a difference a year can make.

The exciting news is that I'm finally moving out of my apartment this weekend, and I'm not moving in with Alexander. As tempting as it is to become the lady of my dream house, it didn't feel right just yet. Things are really good just the way they are.

Speaking of my move, Mrs. Rothera and I had a long talk when I returned from Florida. I've come to realize that her intentions are always good; she just needs to learn not to cross any boundaries. I made a promise to her that I would come visit her often and even let her give me advice from time to time.

I finally ordered the last of the furniture Helena requested for her apartment makeover, so I will soon be free of most of Alexander's past. And Helena just broke the news that she and Jacques are engaged. I couldn't be more thrilled for her and even more thrilled that Caroline (her best friend) was wrong about Helena and Alexander being soul mates.

Gina told me that she heard Jake was dating someone, and her name also happens to be Summer. What are the chances? Anyway, that seems kind of strange to me, but I wish him well.

Angie and Brett finally set a date for their wedding, and of course it's none other than Halloween of *next* year. We did make a life-long promise that we would spend every Halloween together for the rest of our lives—this year we're spending it at some big Halloween party at Disney World. I certainly don't mind. I still miss her a lot, and I get to take another trip to Florida.

Alexander hired a new assistant and he says she's doing a great job. She seems really nice, and best of all, she's happily married.

Summer Interiors is doing okay, unfortunately business has slowed down, but I'm hopeful that it will pick up again in the fall, just like this past year.

This year has been such a whirlwind, but looking back I wouldn't change a thing. Each season brings a new adventure, and I'm ready to move forward onto the next adventure, with Alexander right by my side.

THE END

Dear Reader

I hope you enjoyed the stories in the Seasons of Summer Novella series. Please take a few minutes to leave a review on Amazon and don't forget to visit my website for updates. Stay tuned for my next book coming soon.

Authormelissabaldwin.com

About the Author

Melissa Baldwin is an avid runner, planner obsessed, and has always had a love for writing. She is a wife, mother, and avid journal keeper who took her creativity to the next level by fulfilling her dream with her debut novel, An Event to Remember...or Forget. Melissa writes about charming, ambitious, and real women and is now a published author of ten Romantic Comedy novels and novellas.

When she isn't deep in the writing zone, this multi-tasking master organizer is busy spending time with her family, chauffeuring her daughter, traveling, running, indulging in fitness, and taking a Disney Cruise every now and then.

Connect with Melissa
authormelissabaldwin.com

Made in the USA
Columbia, SC
17 January 2018